# The Scene Was Horrific

All four members of the Phoenix Pack stared aghast first at the carnage, but then at the creature they saw.

Vaguely crinos in shape, it stood at least twenty feet tall. The flesh of its chest was ripped open to reveal the bone beneath. Mammoth legs the size of tree trunks rooted it to the ground. Enormous, flailing arms windmilled in mad motions. And the tongue. It whirled and lashed as if possessing a life of its own.

Around it were Sarah and Oliver. They danced like angry ants. Cartwheeling in and out of the monster's guard. Changing shape faster than any Pack member could follow. Bleeding from dozens of wounds.

The beast threw back its head and roared a maniacal laugh, though it was barely heard above the insane wind. Then it showed that it had been toying with its prey. In one swift motion, it raised a foot and struck, clubbing Oliver in the head. The blow sent him spinning and he collapsed too close to the beast. As the creature pounded down on the prone form of the Stargazer and then heaved him airborne with the kick of a clawed foot, the Phoenix Pack attacked.

# THE WORLD OF DARKNESS

## WEREWOLF
Wyrm Wolf
Conspicuous Consumption

## VAMPIRE
Dark Prince
Netherworld

## MAGE
Such Pain

## WRAITH
Sins of the Fathers*

*coming soon

# THE WORLD OF DARKNESS
## WEREWOLF

# CONSPICUOUS CONSUMPTION

Based on
WEREWOLF:
THE APOCALYPSE

**Stewart von Allmen**

HarperPrism
*An Imprint of* HarperPaperbacks

This is a work of fiction. The characters, incidents, and dialogues are products of the author's imagination and are not to be construed as real. Any resemblance to actual events or persons, living or dead, is entirely coincidental.

HarperPaperbacks    *A Division of* HarperCollins*Publishers*
10 East 53rd Street, New York, N.Y. 10022

Cover illustration by John Cobb

First printing: August 1995

Printed in the United States of America

HarperPrism is an imprint of HarperPaperbacks. HarperPaperbacks, HarperPrism, and colophon are trademarks of HarperCollins*Publishers.*

❖ 10 9 8 7 6 5 4 3 2 1

For Gretchen,
because my three-month deadline
was the eve of our wedding,
and for fasting instead of consuming.

# CONSPICUOUS CONSUMPTION

# EARLIER . . .

Guides-to-Truth realized the darkness and cramped-ness of the emptied walk-in closet, but that was inconsequential to his current predicament. The gloom and restraint of the closet behind the copper-tubbed bathroom of the kindly Stargazers did not register in the mind of the Garou, because the blackening prison of his spirit was what truly tethered him beyond his people, the ones he'd so recently championed.

In the very dim, and fading, point of light yet apparent to Guides-to-Truth, he imagined himself before. He saw the sparkle, now muted, in the eyes of the youths lit by the mystery of ancient lore he imparted. He saw the flashes, now dulled, in the minds of the elders ignited by the wisdom he implored.

So much hope. Why despair? The battle is not lost as long as one Garou at least hopes.

But in the twilight all around that pinprick point, Guides-to-Truth saw that from which he could no longer hide. A chill rippled over his flesh as he

1

confronted the darkest secrets of the world, the Umbra, the entire Tellurian sphere. He saw the rotten and perverse core of the Wyrm, and unfortunately survived.

Was this the real truth?

The weight was too great. The battle too hopeless. The enlightenment too unlikely. The shadow too encompassing.

And so, the one who'd inspired so many himself sank into a dream from which he doubted he'd return. Lids sank and entombed his glistening eyes. A light once burning bright looked to be reborn.

# CONVERSATION

"You must be patient, Sarah. We who stand waiting for the stars to arc from one corner of the sky to the other must now calmly await the resolution of our careful planning."

"Our planning was careful, wasn't it?"

"Well, yes. Because of our diligent performance of the Rites, Luna's glowing countenance illuminated this path."

"So, planning as meticulous and flawless as ours has every hope of success, yes?"

"Certainly, dearest, but no guarantee. We expect to see the moon every night, but it is no guarantee."

"Hush! I won't hear talk like that. It most certainly is guaranteed! Guaranteed by the life and blood and will of every Garou who runs over Gaia protecting her and the other Celestines such as Luna."

"Guaranteed by those like our charge?"

"Weasel!"

"But now my point becomes clearer. We can indeed

expect success because all our visions see us favored, but perhaps this task is beyond our accounting."

"We've spoken about this before."

"You seem so impatient. I wonder if you've forgotten."

"No. Only I sit and watch Alexander for hours. The sky is still your beacon, Oliver, but his face has become mine."

"Has another Garou found favor over me?"

"I would lay down my life, Oliver, to spare you the sights this one must have seen. It's marked on his face. The stars that are his eyes and mouth. His forehead and jaw. They are my stars. I look there for answers to my hopes. A wrinkle that has set harder, or better, relaxed. A questioning in the corner of the eye. Any sign that he sees what we show him and hide from the others."

"Do not hope. Just continue to expect, and it will come in its time. All the lines will relent and his spirit will revive, and the nightmare visions inflicted on his senses will disperse. Just as Luna's face will show clearer in coming nights when the haze of the night air clears."

"Because the events are out of your control. As we sit tucked away in our caern, our hope does nothing to see that the sun rises each morning. We are doing nothing to directly ensure that it does. We can only expect that it will. We are waging our own battles."

"If others even knew he was here, do you think that they expect that we will heal him?"

"No, but I'm certain they hope."

# 1

# ASHES

Perhaps the new metal bleachers below, inaugurated for this final home game, were more comfortable, but Simon disdained them in favor of the solid if worn wooden seats higher up the slope. Besides, Simon, for that's what he was called in his human guise, needed the advantage of height so he could clearly see the playing field and all the areas adjacent to it, like the backfield where the pep rally was winding to a close. It wasn't a desire for a perfect view of the action of the game that encouraged Simon to such heights, but rather a need to monitor one of the participants in the coming game as he wandered from pep rally to the field house and finally to the playing field where he hoped to orchestrate an upset over a school about ten times the size of Little River High.

Simon preferred to stay in one place lest he and his withered right arm be warily eyed, so he needed a single seat with a view of everything. He wished most not to even be here, but the quarterback, Tucker Statton, was his friend, and even more importantly, his packmate. Simon knew the impending game was of great importance to Tuck, though the urgency of the game currently seemed little on Tuck's mind. Watching the pack leader's face during the ceremony, Simon concluded that Tuck was very distracted. Perhaps the game wasn't so important to him after all.

Regardless, Simon required himself to be present and watch his pack leader in the event something critical happened to him tonight. Who could predict when a momentous event in Tuck's life would take place? Simon intended to tell the story of Tucker Statton many times in the coming years, so he dare not miss a moment. How would the young Philodox deal with the glory or misfortune of the evening? When life among the Garou, the society of werewolves to which they all belonged, teetered so precariously between acclaim and infamy, one or the other was likely.

Tuck was worth watching, Simon reminded himself. He sensed something, well, heroic about the young man. Simon had been learning, telling, and interpreting stories of great events and great Garou for much of his life (it was his passion and, as it turned out, his destiny), so he had developed a sense for powerful moments. Or the beings that made those moments possible. Tuck Statton smelled important to Simon. No, more than important. Symbolic.

That was the best he could describe it when thinking aloud in human words with human thoughts. Born a metis, an outcast and sterile offspring of two Garou who dared disobey the very first tenet of the

Litany forbidding such intercourse, Simon was nevertheless among the most knowledgeable of the ways of the Garou. Too many humans and wolves (Simon refused to call them apes or ferals, respectively) developed outside the embrace of Gaia. Even as cold and scant as his own embraces were, Simon thought more like a Garou and instinctively understood more of the symbolism than many of his purer cousins.

It was in the symbolic language of the Garou that Simon most understood Tucker Statton. And it was Simon's grasp of this symbolic language that made him wish to share his thoughts through stories. Such stories required eventual revelation, or at least illumination, of the symbolism, but that was for later. After Simon himself understood the complexities of the Tuck metaphor, then he would be ready to share the tale.

Even while the Drayton Ducks' papier-mâché effigy burned, Tuck sensed the Wyrm. His football teammates were relying on him to remain sharp for this last regional playoff game at Little River High, though, so Tuck relied on his packmates to remain alert for trouble.

If Tuck trusted his senses, then the game be damned, and he would prowl the ends of the county for the source of blight. The jaggling responsible for teaching Tuck the gift that allowed him to sense the Wyrm's supernatural presence taught no degrees of gray in a black-and-white presence or absence of the Wyrm. The Wyrm was the greatest enemy of the caern protected by Tuck's adoptive parents, but the subtle itching that roused a sense of the harbinger of darkness and decay in Tuck was probably just pregame jitters—knots in the stomach that made him tense now but that would help him relax and play better later.

The stench of smoke and the tribalistic ceremony taking place before him, involving young people dancing and chanting as the mock-up of their enemy was slowly seared by flames, reminded Tuck of the moots and gathering of his new people, the Garou. The garishly painted faces of the students, though matted with the school colors of silver, blue, and black instead of the red of blood, only reinforced Tuck's sense that he was with his people and should be on guard for the enemies that threatened them.

At the same time, though, it made this seem like a trial run. It made him think the Wyrm-scent he detected cloying the ether and the air was just a facsimile summoned as a reminder of how his life was changing.

The sense he had was very faint and did not shift, so the dreamlike quality was even further enhanced. His decision to let it ride for now and rely on his packmates was affirmed when a huge hand slapped Tuck on the right arm, his throwing arm, and massaged the passing muscles there briefly. "Wake up, Tuck, we've got to win this one."

Over the cheers of the gathered student body—and almost all the students showed up for the rally and game, so there were almost two hundred of them—Tuck heard the words but couldn't recognize the voice. It was certainly one of his offensive linemen. The guards and tackles orbited around Tuck during the rallies like Secret Service agents and surrounded him in the huddle like fortified walls. They were more protective of their quarterback than his packmates were of their leader, but Tuck was slowly winning the respect of the other werewolves.

It was the respect of his teammates that was on the line tonight, though, and he directed his attention away from the bonfire yet again. Besides, the hand of the offensive lineman was now directing Tuck's attention toward the cheerleaders who were forming a circle around the bonfire. The pretty faces helped Tuck recall his school spirit and concentrate again on the kinds of pass plays that would beat the Ducks' tough secondary. There wouldn't be a second chance to win a place in the regional championship game one week from tonight.

Because of the falling darkness and the play of shadows engineered by the roaring bonfire, and no doubt with a hint of disbelief, the two hundred or so students of Little River High assembled for the outdoors pep rally thought the wolf at the side of the Kachina twins was a husky. It was good school spirit to bring the school's mascot to the last scheduled pep rally of the season. School spirit was not uncommon in either Ally or Tom Kachina, both athletes extraordinaire transferred from California the previous school year.

Any admiration the students had for Ally and Tom paled to the esteem the twins felt for Verse, the Garou masquerading as a wolf masquerading as a husky. Only recently retired from life in the northern forests as a wolf without knowledge of his heritage, Verse was suffering repeated petting and grappling from an assortment of beings all belonging to the only species ever to cause him fear.

Tom noted, though, that Verse was not so much enduring the attention as he was completely unaware

of it, so intent was his attention on the looming bonfire. Verse seemed entranced by the bonfire constructed by the pep club earlier in the day. When
Tom bent closer, he could see that Verse's eyes
seemed to follow the flickers of the flame.

Maybe the fire seems magical to him, Tom
thought to himself. The only times he would have
seen it before recently was after a lightning strike on
a dry tree. But Tom brushed the thought aside. He
recognized it as the sort of homocentric thought that
ferals often found distasteful. Similar to being called
upon to be a football team's mascot.

For a time Tom lost track of Verse's fascination with
the bonfire and realized his own appreciation for the
scene. He stood with his sister and Verse on the back
field of Little River High. A break in the chain-link fence
behind Tom and to his left led back to the main football
field and the uneven track that surrounded it. As ever
when they passed that area of the track to reach the
backfield, Ally would bob her head in chagrin at the
ripple turned rut on the track that had sent her sprawling in a race last track season. The fall cost her a
twenty-seventh straight 200-meter victory, an unbro-
ken string dating back to the twin's life in California.

Their normal life in California. Before, like Verse,
they were unaware of their heritage. Already proud of
the Native American blood in their veins, the twins
were introduced to a society even more strongly
attuned to their traditions and way of life. The variety
of the human blood flowing through their veins set
them apart even in Garou culture and made them
members by default, if they accepted such status, of
the Wendigo tribe, the fiercely independent tribe made
of Garou descended from Native American stock.

Strangely, the move to the Midwest took Tom and

his sister closer to the roots their Wendigo birthright, for it returned them to a harsher, colder environment, the realm of the wind and winter spirits honored most by the tribe. For the time, though, both Tom and Ally gave their service to the new pack led—though not without Ally's dispute and contest—by Tucker Statton and formed by Sarah and Oliver, the two elderly Stargazers, kindly and timely enough to spare the twins from much confusion. Tom recognized the wisdom his adoptive aunt and uncle possessed and determined that he would learn from them before moving on to pursue the goals of his blood.

Tom turned to watch Tuck where he stood among his football teammates. The spitting and sparkling bonfire partially intervened, but Tom looked hopefully at Tuck. The boy was a leader, all right. Tom readily admitted that. It was evident in the way his teammates stood beside him and in how they shifted and moved when he spoke in order to allow themselves to hear instead of Tuck moving to make himself heard. Or when in a noisy huddled mass, how others sometimes glanced sidelong at Tuck when they spoke in order to be sure the idea or opinion they espoused was not contrary to what Tuck felt. The slightest rebuke or questioning from Tuck inevitably led to a joking withdrawal of the remark.

Since there was no real reason to lead the pack himself, Tom eventually conceded the battle for leadership to Tuck and Ally. It was hard to be reasonable, though, when it came to earning respect and recognition, but for now Tom controlled his counting-coup urges.

A gust of cold wind reminded Tom how cool it would be if not for the large fire. The chill seemed to quiet everyone a bit now that the organized cheers were over. The cheerleaders themselves pressed their pleated skirts down to their sides to provide maximum, if still skimpy, cover for their goose-bumped legs. But the moment passed and the bonfire sprayed to life again with a crack and whoosh that sent a burned and smoky odor rolling past Tom.

Apparently that was to be the end of it. Tom saw his sister suddenly conferring with the firemen who were at hand with the county's brand-new red fire engine just in case the fire raged out of control. That last crack of the fire apparently signaled to the firemen that the pillar of wood and flame was loosing its stability. A strong-willed girl herself, Ally was competently dealing with the firemen. Tom kept himself from marveling at his sister's good looks too often because it was egotistical, but ever since he and his sister's First Change shortly before their Rite of Passage with Oliver, Tom was unable to put aside an ethnocentric appreciation for her dark-haired beauty and athletic structure. It was no wonder she ruled the social scene at Little River High, though it had earned her the enmity of the prior heiresses.

Sensing the demise of their fiery rallying totem pole, Tuck gathered his teammates around him and led them in a chant that surely no one could understand. A wild cheering and raucous yelling issued from the mass of bench-pressed muscles and padded uniforms as the gathering split and spilled around Tuck in a sprint barreling toward the field house at the opposite end of the playing field.

Tuck jogged at the center of the mass.

Tom watched the group briefly and held his ground through the charging departures of rallying students who ran behind the throng of players. He glanced to see that Verse safely survived that exodus as well, and that's when he found the wolf still staring intently at the diminishing flames.

As he studied Verse, Tom wondered if that chill breeze earlier was meant as a communication or omen from his Wendigo spirit father.

Water rumbled down the length of the hose and sprayed a fine, strong mist over the fire, which succumbed shortly and vanished in a pyrotechnic display of embers and smoke. Walter and Denim, the two firemen, hosed the collapsing wood frame one more time to make sure the fire was out and no other would ignite.

Both wore their protective gear sloppily, obviously not expecting major trouble, but perhaps too as a sign of how in control of the blaze and situation they felt. Ally laughed to herself. Didn't they know that high school kids had already outgrown any fascination with the duties of firemen? The firemen were too young to forget that.

She hoped they weren't simply trying to impress her and her friends. Denim had introduced himself with a bit of self-importance, as if his different name alone was reason to pay him more attention. Then they began to pack, including rolling the hose, and Ally refused to spend any more time dreaming motives into how the firemen talked or acted. She turned her attention to her pep-club clique.

Ally could see that she was about to be abandoned by the other girls. Apparently assured their duties here were done, they all hustled to claim seats for the coming game. A couple of them had boyfriends who would save them seats, but the others were involved with football players, so they sought their usual seats where they would be an easily spotted beacon of support and encouragement. The rush back must have been instigated by Monica McClure, the previously reigning queen of Little River High, who was taking any chance possible to exert control over the others to the detriment of Ally.

It didn't bother Ally, though. Now she'd just have an excuse for the next slightly cruel and unthinking thing she did to each one. The girls would be hurt but would fall back into line even though the latest deed would be at their expense. It actually helped keep them in line.

Ally did vaguely wonder at this behavior of hers. Why did she care? But she put it aside as she waved off the firemen. "Thanks for your help."

"No problem, miss, I'm just glad to be heading home," Walter said. "I hope the rally helps the team. After tonight one of these teams will qualify for the regionals. Hope it's our Huskies."

"It will be," Ally assured him. "My friend, Tuck Statton, is the quarterback. He'll crack that defense."

Then Denim insisted on saying, "Don't think so. My second cousin's a linebacker for the Ducks. He'll sack your friend once and then twice for good measure."

Ally, who had turned to walk toward Verse and her brother after her friendly and supposedly conversation-ending comment, wheeled to face the ruddy-complexioned Denim. Her feet were set wide and her hands locked over hips as she glared at the foolish firemen. As a Garou, especially one born under a full moon, Ally had means Monica McClure couldn't dream of to police those who crossed her.

The fact that Denim laughed at her insolent posture only made her fire burn brighter. And that fire burned in her eyes as her glare lengthened. Denim made the mistake of locking eyes with her. With a shudder that sent him stumbling, Denim's will and spine turned to rubber, and he floundered away from the wet and smoking fire.

"Bullshit!" Ally shouted after him.

Confused, Walter extended a hand to Denim, but Ally watched no more as she whirled about again and moved to rejoin her packmates. She didn't give another thought to the linebacker's cousin, who slowly regained his balance, if not his composure, behind her.

She found Verse keenly eyeing the areas of the bonfire extinguished last. The areas that still spouted rippling velvet smoke stacks. She wondered if Verse was perplexed at the disappearance of the fire, but surely he'd seen rainstorms douse lightning fires during his two years in the forest. Then again, maybe not.

Either way, as soon as the smiling pep-club kids had left, Ally pulled near Verse. The wolf growled softly, almost musically.

"What'd he say, Tom?" Ally asked as she drew to her brother.

Tom said, "I don't know, Ally. The rustle of the wind becomes words to me, but the speech of the wolves is still unclear."

Ally paused a second to chuckle. "Is Oliver teaching you to talk like that?"

Verse was looking at them both and Ally shrugged her shoulders questioningly. It was body language the wolf didn't yet understand instinctively as any other human would. So she tried holding empty hands toward Verse and just shaking her head no.

That seemed to do it, because strange images began to fill her head, and from the look of his expression, Tom's too.

———

The glow of the fire was different. That was the first thing Verse noted when the bonfire was burning. At least that's what he thought he detected. He and the red flower had rarely crossed paths before, but the scarlet glow was too luminous, too spiritual. Just in spots, though. That was the part that confused him the most, so he studied the fire with all his attention and all his gifts.

He was in his natural form, that of the wolf, so his senses were naturally heightened beyond those of humans, but his senses unnaturally surpassed even that. Of course, Verse never really considered this additional amplification of his detective abilities to be unnatural, though it did explain why, when he was but a pup of less than a year, he was the only one of his pack to waken and run the duration of the night with the strange wolf who invaded the pack's territory. As he ran that night, it had seemed to Verse that the breadth of the earth was being laid bare before him. What he reasoned in his wolflike way to be a carrying wind bringing scents from afar had actually been his connection with the spirits and most of all the earth mother Gaia who made possible a connection no physical reality could explain.

It was not until the morning after the run with the brown wolf, who smelled of soils both wet and dry and vegetation both evergreen and deciduous, that Verse realized he also heard sounds from afar and smelled odors against the rush of the wind. Then he knew it must have been a spiritual visitation, for the wolves did speak of such things among themselves, but later he wondered where his strength had gone when he was fatigued after a mere ten-mile jaunt that morning.

With his new understanding as a Garou, Verse would argue that even these enhanced senses were therefore not unnatural. For what created by Gaia could be anything but completely at home with the natural world?

So, whether natural or not, whether descended from his Garou nature or not, the senses Verse possessed beyond those of the humans around him detected several of these luminous areas. He watched as they danced and whirled in the flames of the fire. In that frenetic spinning was Verse's clue that they were more than just the fire. Though the motions made these spots seem to be the fire itself, they also at times fought against its crackling currents. So while at one moment several of the resplendent points surged along the length of an arcing arm of the bonfire that gouged upward, at the next the same points would hang in the air, suspending the draft of the fire an instant longer than it should have held. The swirling movement made Verse dizzy.

When the firemen prepared to douse the fire, Verse half expected them to be in for a surprise. Would the fire relinquish its fiery hold on the charred wood? Would it succumb as easily as they presumably anticipated it would?

Verse put aside an instinctive dislike of the men with the water hose. The natural fear of mankind he still felt pulse in his wolf blood was piqued by these two. He calmed himself and watched them go to work.

The water spraying from the end of the hose had the flat odor of captivity. Verse smelled a slight tinge of metal from the holding tank on the nearby shiny red engine. The force of the gushing water also eroded much of its natural fragrance. Verse was used to all his senses mingling to create an impression of beautiful, flowing streams. This flood of water overwhelmed the musical tinkling. The metal grappled with the fresh perfume. The way the water pummeled the blazing wood removed any hope of a velvety wash. Verse refused to let his ignorance of the human color his perceptions, but where the bonfire danced with vitality, the water extinguishing it exuded a sense of corrosion and infection.

But as water inevitably does to fire, it put it down. Verse felt defeated. Misaligned. Smoke poured from the blaze and the flames struggled for life, but each lick was suffocated. The two men tugged hard on the hose, and more of its length snaked from the engine as they repositioned themselves for a better shot each time.

Once this process was well under way, the crowds of children swarmed around Verse again as they began a migration away from the execution back to the sports field. Verse steeled himself against the dozens of pats and brushes he endured again. This time it was more difficult, though. His dreams of bringing his wolf music to the world of the humans suffered a severe setback, but his generally calm nature allowed him to remain in check.

Finally, the wave passed him. Trying to keep his mind off the lingering human scent on his fur, and trying to get the twins' minds off the sport game with a cryptic comment, Verse ambled forward. Cryptic because it was wolf speech, and he was certain he'd spoken too quickly for either Tom or Ally—neither yet understood the lupus tongue with 100 percent effectiveness. At least to the middle stage of crinos, the battle form of human shape but wolf-headed, preferred by the twins. He could loose a howl that would make them understand, but the matter of the fiery glows within the flames was still too subtle, too much an unknown, for a warrior's response.

That's exactly how the Ahroun Auspice of the

twins would prompt them to react. Despite the frequency of his own howls sung at the silver sphere, songs consistent with and said to grow from his own gibbous moon nature, Verse still couldn't completely believe how much the moon's placement in the sky could possibly affect his life and the lives of the rest of his packmates. But instinctively he knew it was true, so he held back from alerting the instincts of his packmates before the time was right.

He spoke to them then by means taught him by a chimerling in an incident of his youth that he knew for certain was a dream. In the minds of the twins he drew a picture of how the bonfire had appeared to him moments before. He removed his own sense of ennui and any hints of danger or fear, but simply let them see it that they might draw their own conclusions or at least be aware that something untoward may have taken place. Or be taking place.

Then the twins began to shape the communal vision. Tom, wondering what Verse thought of the luminous spots, approached the bonfire that still burned bright in the dream and drew Verse's attention to them.

The spiritual conversation abruptly ended, though, when the charred remnants of wood suddenly burst aflame again.

Simon allowed his attention to wander among the dozens of children in the bleachers around him when he happened to look back out at Verse just in time to see the bonfire spring to life.

Verse stood very near the edge of the burned wood, though he was turned away from it and facing Tom and Ally. The board nearest the wolf suddenly burst aflame and shot a small, fiery arc at the wolf.

Because Sarah and Oliver so strongly stressed how the human mind did not easily deal with that which it could not explain, Simon's first instinct was to look around and see if anyone else oversaw the bizarre event. Apparently none had. Everyone's attention was directed to midfield, where some ritual of the football game was taking place.

Simon ripped his gaze back out to Verse and saw that the wolf was both quickly dancing away from the bonfire and wisely not crying out. Simon knew immediately that something unusual was happening. This wasn't simply a pile of hot embers that Verse had accidentally uncovered. This was a powerful moment.

Both Ally and Tom had dropped into a steady ready stance and were closely watching the bonfire. Simon was impressed by the twins and how they seemed to be prepared for trouble from the fire.

The fire died away again.

Verse circled back to join the warriors and seemed to attempt communication. Perhaps Verse has a clue as to what's going on, Simon thought. Simon and his three packmates on the spot all quickly looked up when a spot of flame reappeared on a board that had fallen several feet away from the main pile. It was a palm-sized flame that burned steadily and without fluctuation of either color or size. It must be a spirit of the flame, Simon reasoned. It seemed to be revealing itself to Verse and the twins.

Then, with a speed that strained Simon's eyes to keep up, several more flames sprouted to life. They were spread out all over the mostly burnt boards that had once fueled the bonfire. From his vantage point high in the bleachers, Simon saw that their seemingly random points of combustion actually drew a sort of enigmatic pattern.

Verse continued to hang back and sniff at the air, but both Tom and Ally began to take careful steps toward the fires. Ally neared one before Tom; it was the first one, the flame burning on a board that had fallen away from the fire pit. Simon watched as Ally glanced back at Verse and then knelt beside the flame.

It shot a lick of yellow at her. The small fireball sailed at her face, but Ally deftly dodged it and hopped away from the board. She carefully crawled back toward the board, but this time toward the end that was not burning. She suddenly grasped the board and hefted it into the air. The flame shot off the board in a flash of smoke, its fiery form spinning toward the fire pit, where it landed on another board and resumed burning with the same steady intensity.

As if in response to that, all of the other spouts of flame—there were perhaps two dozen in all—winked out of existence only to reappear one by one instants later in new positions. Simon wondered at it.

Simon also realized his craning and gawking were drawing the attention of a few others. He risked missing something important, but he settled back into his seat. A few people continued to glance over their shoulders in his direction, though, so he resorted to an ugly technique. As part of appearing to reposition himself in his seat, Simon revealed his misshapen right arm. Bent backward at the elbow like a wolf's leg is from a human's perspective, the arm tapered to a slender end about halfway down the forearm. Two rough digits curled from that tip.

Simon knew that people would be too embarrassed to look anymore, so after the split second it took for them to stare and turn away, Simon returned to his vigil.

He found Tom roaming the edge of the fire pit,

carefully keeping his distance from any one of the flames so that it wouldn't hurl a yellow fireball at him too. Ally was hesitating to join Tom, but finally she did, and so it went for several more moments.

Though the speaker system was far removed from the center of his thoughts, Simon heard it reciting yardage and jersey numbers and commentating on the events that commanded everyone's attention. The game was apparently under way, but Simon continued to watch the twins inspect the fire instead of turning his own attention to Tuck's activity on the football field.

So much time just staring at the scene from his overhead perspective burned the pattern of the small flames on the boards into Simon's mind. The steady flames eventually seemed to waver as the sight became mesmerizing. The intense and prolonged stare eventually caused the flames to blur completely, and that's when Simon cracked the puzzle of the shape.

The flames were organized into a defensive position.

It was a conclusion a mind unattuned to the subtleties and nuances of the patterns of life and the spirit world would be incapable of rendering. And it was one impossible to describe. His mind honed through countless conversations with the spirits themselves, Simon suddenly realized that these were elemental spirits of fire, probably all of them that existed in this region, and they were organized in a defense of their existence in the realm of matter.

Simon wanted to join his packmates at the site, but he was learning too much from this vantage that would otherwise have been unknown. He didn't dare risk missing any of it. So he waited and watched, only infrequently allowing the ball game to intrude on his thoughts.

———

The Ducks deserved their spot in this regional playoff game. They were from a larger school and thus had better equipment and no doubt better practice facilities, maybe even more than just a free-weight bench press. Like the Huskies, the Ducks had lost one regular-season game, but as the two teams never played one another during that time, the tiebreaker for home-field advantage went to the Huskies because the Ducks lost to a team the Huskies had defeated. But that team had a strong running game, and the Ducks were best suited to stifling a passing attack.

Tuck reclined in the field-house locker room and considered how thoroughly his team was being beaten. Three fumbles, one on the opening kickoff return that led to the only touchdown of the first half, effectively kept Tuck's offense off the field. Tuck had attempted only four pass plays. The one reception resulted in the second fumble. The others were two incompletions and a sack when the pocket collapsed around him.

The Ducks' secondary was good enough to play man defense on any receiver, and that allowed the linebackers to blitz. Good coverage plus allowing very little time to throw meant a very good pass defense.

And it meant the Huskies were down 10–0.

Tuck blamed himself. He didn't feel his concentration was perfect. He couldn't get the sense of the Wyrm out of his thoughts. Was he doing the right thing to ignore that foreboding? What if his packmates were not aware of it? He owed a debt of honor to his football team. All of them worked so hard and long to win this opportunity, but his packmates were his destiny. He felt a kinship for them that his easy friendships with the other players could not begin to match.

In the end, it was his reliance on that bond, the stronger bond, that allowed him to refocus on the game. He would send word to Simon, who he knew sat high in the bleachers. Simon shared his sensitivity to the Wyrm. He spoke of it once. Of all his packmates, Simon was therefore the most suited to be on the lookout, because of both his position and his attuned senses.

Tuck called one of the freshmen water boys to his side. Convincing him to leave the locker room with such a message would be difficult, but Tuck had his ways. A conversation with an ancestor spirit who imparted many secrets the night after Tuck's Rite of Passage left Tuck with the capability to be extremely convincing.

It was a moment after Tuck's mesmerized messenger completed his charge that Simon recognized the indisputable stench of the Wyrm. Too lulled by the elemental spirits and the puzzle of their pattern, Simon overlooked the creeping presence of the Wyrm.

That was part of its might, he recalled. The destruction and corruption it wrought was insidious. More an infection that festered unseen until the damage was irreversible, the Wyrm once held a defined place in the cosmology of the Garou, but some time ago something happened to the Triat that defined and created the Tellurian—all that seemed real to the sense. The Weaver, Wyld, and Wyrm, once in careful balance, were tipped, and all of reality has ever after been out of control.

All of these teachings, all of the imploring from elders to be on the lookout, and all it took was the puzzle of fire to distract Simon.

That's what the elementals had assembled themselves to battle!

Simon pressed his spiritual senses to tell him more of the Wyrm. Nothing. Or everything. There was just nothing to pinpoint. It was if the entire area was under the shadow of the Wyrm. It was a spirit, though, and not some inhuman agent of the Wyrm, like a Fomori, a misshappen human gutted by the infernal influence of the Wyrm. That would be safer for the spectators, but probably more dangerous for the Garou. Simon accepted that risk, and felt the others would as well.

He had to get word to the others. They were in the face of the fire elementals, so their attention was undoubtedly more directed than his own had been. They were more apt to be blindsided by the Wyrm.

He had no means, however, to do so.

Unless . . .

But Simon hesitated. It would put him at greater risk, but at the same time it might do something to help defend the elementals.

Simon looked around for a safe place, and found it. He stood and went higher yet, to the very top of the bleachers. Here were a few old giant billboard signs advertising decades-old Little River stores. Simon slipped behind one of the signs; it read, LENNY'S: A BREAK FOR THE WHOLE FAMILY. He wouldn't be able to watch the progress of the game, and the second half was under way with the Huskies kicking off to the leading Ducks, but that would have to wait.

From his new position, Simon could still see his three packmates below. Tom and Ally stood poised for action. Their pacing had ceased many minutes ago. Verse was moving, though. The wolf poked his nose toward one of the steady flames. When it didn't fling sparks at him, he pressed closer until he almost touched it. The heat, not the antagonism of the elemental, held him back now.

Simon withdrew his withered arm again. He looked upon it with familiarity and disgust. It was the reason he sought a new pack, and now that one accepted him he would not fail to stand with them. Even if it meant a risk like this. Even if it meant drawing the Wyrm's attention from the elementals it presumably sought.

The sign hiding Simon from the Huskies fans was still very sturdy despite the discoloring designs on the front side. The floods illuminating the field were blotted out back here, but Simon could clearly see once he transformed his eyes toward those of a wolf. With that night vision, Simon found a scrap piece of wood wedged between the sign's supporting beams. It was ragged, so Simon withdrew it carefully to avoid splinters.

Holding on to the wooden slats on the back of the Lenny's sign with his good hand, Simon crookedly extended his blighted hand out and upward. The two fingers on that hand clenched the wood fragment and brandished it like a weapon.

Concentrating with a flash of intensity, Simon caused the fragment to ignite. The flame flickered to life and then sputtered to strength. Simon continued to hold it aloft, not really certain what would happen, but fearful of what might.

Just as a great cheer rang out from the fans now obscured from Simon's sight, one of the spheres of elemental fire quivered and then vibrated until like a rocket it blasted upward toward Simon's torch. Simon averted his eyes toward the end zone, but the light seared through his tight lids.

When he looked again, the elemental had achieved the same evenly burning state possessed by the others still below. Simon brought it closer to his face, but the heat of the elemental was scalding. Good thing the ruined nerves of his malformed hand and arm couldn't feel the tremendous heat beating upon them.

Simon spared a glance down and saw he had certainly succeeded in gaining the attention of his packmates. Verse, Tom, and Ally were all turned to look at him. The smoky trail of the elemental rocket was dispersing. Watching them as they were, the others neglected to note that all the other elementals once again shifted their positions on the wooden remains.

Redirecting his attention to the nearby spirit, Simon began to speak to it, but the presence of the Wyrm suddenly became overpowering. The steady fire that was the incarnation of an elemental perhaps as old as the mountains quivered.

"Tuck!" the lineman shouted. "We're still down, but we'll score again. Cheer up, man, we just scored. We're on the board!"

Tuck nodded, but he felt cold. Isolated. He should be with his pack. Especially now that the shadow of the Wyrm blotted the entire field. This time Tuck was certain. This was no mistake of jittery nerves. This was the ancient enemy, or an agent of it, before him.

"Thank my ancestors I sent Darryl to say something to Simon," he muttered to himself.

Just as quickly as the Wyrm appeared, though, it was gone. Tuck didn't see Simon in the stands, and he hoped his friends were the cause of the Wyrm's retreat or demise.

———

Tom and Ally stood gaping at the sight above them. One of the elementals was now a torch in Passer's hand. It was an awesome sight. As tortured as the body of the metis was, Passer (for they had to think of him now by his Garou name) personified the ideal his Silent Strider kinsmen sought. Both of the twins sought renown in the community of the Garou, and this vision—Passer with his wolf eyes reflecting the light of elemental fire—would remain with them for a time as a reminder of the heroic status they might attain.

Then Passer became mortal again. When the elemental on his torch became agitated, Passer too lost his composure. Tom and Ally soon understood why. A sickening, invading feeling overcame them and they knew the Wyrm was near. They reassumed battle stances. A gentle breeze began to swirl around them as they both called upon their Wendigo heritage to confront this venomous enemy. Tom's claws shone with a razor's sharpness.

A slapping, flickering sound from behind caused them both—and Verse, who was nearby—to turn. All of the flames bent now. Suddenly they flared in what must have been defiance.

Ally stepped forward. Her fist pounding the air, she shouted to join the fire. "Me too, Defiler. We all stand ready."

But she was left in silence and without confrontation when the flames dissolved. Puffs of smoke caught by her Wendigo breeze swirled for a moment and then they too dispersed.

# CONVERSATION

"But what if his enemies pursue him here? What's our role then?"

"Then we rely on the Phoenix Pack to defend us all."

"Are they capable of it? They are all so young, so powerless."

"Isn't that the heart of our plan, dearest?"

"Of course, but what if the caern itself is threatened? What if any vengeance against Alexander includes the caern?"

"Isn't that the risk we took?"

"Would you please quit reminding me of all the decisions we've made. I'm worried."

"Didn't we know we would worry?"

"You're so frustrating."

"Well, then, seriously, doesn't our plan require that the Phoenix Pack be tested? Presented with a challenge greater than they could reasonably hope to overcome."

"Yes, but isn't this a bit transparent? Will Alexander be so gullible?"

"Yes, I think he will be. It's transparent, yes, but it is unrehearsed and honest. Perhaps our plan will fail and we will join him in Harano."

"I guess we considered that as well, didn't we?"

"Yes, but we can teach the pups much, and even if we fail in this task, at least we will have guaranteed protectors for the caern. Tuck will bring them together. He's a very capable leader. In fact, perhaps an excellent one. The twins are able, intelligent warriors. Their Wendigo blood makes them fierce, but they have thankfully grown outside that one-sided environment. Simon will be an excellent Theurge. You will personally make certain of that, dearest. And Verse, among his obvious talents, provides the wolf element necessary to create a balanced pack. This is a classical Garou pack. The kind formed in older times. That we found these Lost Cubs is surely a credit to the fates that bind and guide us."

"Do you think Alexander watches them? He never seems to move. Aren't our efforts in vain if they go unrecognized?"

"Who knows the roads the heavy spirit of Guides-to-Truth travels?"

"Don't speak his name!"

"It is already done."

# 2

# FEEDING FRENZY

Tuck's pack couldn't explain anything to him until they managed to pull him aside at Mr. Italy's Pizza, the only fun place to hang out in Little River, after the victory party had taken over the place. Tom worked hard to push his way to the side of the winning quarterback, whose late-game heroics, including a scramble for a first down on fourth-and-six and an undesigned rollout pass play for the game-winning touchdown, saved the day and earned a 14–13 comeback.

The small place was packed, and since winter was approaching and the evenings were cool, the outside seating was closed. That meant packed in here was every student who wanted to celebrate Little River High's first berth in the regional final in thirty years, when some fullback who went on to be the last one cut from the Chicago Bears, led the team into the regional final. All of the red vinyl-covered booths were piled with kids. The old-fashioned checkered tablecloths bore the brunt not just of spilled food but the overspill of students too, for many made seats by nestling precariously on table edges.

Tom liked this place, though he preferred it less crowded. It seemed to him one of the hearts of the little town that was his new home. Crudely framed pictures lined the wall, as well as more carefully framed newspaper clippings of important events from the last twenty-five years.

Despite its age and the obvious lack of modern amenities or remodeling, the place was spotless. Samuel Harper, Mr. Italy's very un-Italian proprietor, took great pride in his hand-carved high-backed wooden chairs, roughhewn tavernlike booth benches, hand-printed menus, and friendly service. The latter, despite the crowd, was being well doled. In a sign of good faith for the Huskies and the need for a celebration party, Sam operated at full capacity this evening. The full-time waitress, Susan, was present, but both of the part-timers, Rhonda and Emily, were here as well. They efficiently took care of all the orders, including the ones shouted across the room by a tableful of football players ready for their third all-pepperoni, as well the ones placed by more timid voices who would otherwise have been lost in the chaos.

Tom saw Tuck in a booth near the front window of the restaurant. That meant Tom would have to fight his way over the entire length of the place, because he and the remainder of the pack had arrived early to improve their odds of speaking to Tuck, but the hero was detained and arrived late. A prominent booth was waiting for him, though.

Skirting kids who were throwing olives into the air and catching them in their open mouths, Tom pushed near Tuck but had to face the mightiest challenge yet to reach the quarterback's side. Every cheerleader in the school fought tooth and nail with Tom, but he finally made it.

Tuck's booth was crowded at the edges, but the seating was relatively spacious. Melissa Frankel, one of Tuck's more vocal constituents—though Tom doubted that made her any more successful with the often taciturn prize of the school—was seated next to Tuck. On the other side were Bobby Gunther and Sharon Turner, a couple that was as good as set in stone. If this were anywhere but Little River, Tom would have mocked the faith people put in how those two would stay together, but in Little River a commitment was a commitment. The wedding vows were as good as made.

Tom caught Tuck's eye. The full-moon warrior plainly saw on Tuck's face that the pack leader knew something monumental had happened. But where Tom was elated from the flush of battle, though it had never been met, Tuck seemed long in the face, as if something tragic had occurred. Certainly, finding the Wyrm in your backyard was not the happiest Friday-night discovery, but it meant the pack's battle against the Wyrm had been met. Besides, what could be the extent of the danger when a mere shouted challenge from his sister scared the enemy away?

Actually, Tuck seemed even more down than Tom thought at first. The pack leader's face, when it turned to the Ahroun, barely hid a shamefully apologetic look. There was also a hint of hope of salvation, which Tom understood as a plea for extrication from the social climate surrounding the victorious quarterback. Garou were intensely social animals—after all, both blood branches of the Dying Race, wolf and human, were unrelentingly social creatures—but Tuck was obviously trapped. A caged wolf.

Heedless of who was talking or what was being said, Tom interrupted. "Tuck, your family wants a moment alone with the conquering hero."

Everyone knew who formed the family, though they could scarcely imagine the forms the family members could take. Tuck, Ally, Tom, and Simon were more than Lost Cubs saved from a cruel fate; they were also the legally adopted children of Sarah and Oliver.

The pack once discussed how their Stargazer mentors possibly managed these adoptions. The pack ultimately concluded that gifts, tricks taught by various spirits to one or the other "parent," were responsible. On the other hand, Oliver could argue very persuasively if he desired; his logic was usually infallible and therefore indisputable. He may well have convinced the various human-resource officials that the adoptions were in everyone's best interest.

Silence settled over the booth. Tuck glanced from side to side, apparently surprised no one complained about this departure. So, he shuffled as if to rise and follow. Melissa, who was seated on the outside of the bench, stood so Tuck could slip out.

"Hurry back," was all she said. She made to hug Tuck, but he either didn't see her or pretended not to see the attempt and took quick steps behind Tom along the path that opened through the ranks.


Tuck found something oddly evocative about gathering with the rest of the Phoenix Pack behind Mr. Italy's. It was something in the sight of the proud Garou around him—how they waited patiently, but warily and ready. Something in the scent of sausage and tomatoes. Something in the denlike comfort of an alleyway lined with a brick drive and buildings with stone chimneys.

It must have been the brush with the Wyrm, Tuck reasoned, that lent this sudden coziness with the others a special nostalgia. The something was something being lost. Tuck couldn't put his finger on it, but he guessed it might simply be that tonight ended any privately muttered or half-spoken questions about the veracity of the claims and demands made of the Garou people.

Bad things were out there, and humans obviously didn't recognize them as ought but the vile and venom and viciousness that man spread among itself. But it was separate from man. It could be stopped. It was the Wyrm.

Tuck wanted badly to remove these thoughts from pure conceptualization and put them in words for the pack, but he was too embarrassed. His embarrassment was also important, and fortunately easy, to express. "I'm sorry I wasn't with you all when this happened. I felt it, I still feel it, but I felt obligated to play out the football game."

Passer chimed in immediately, "You got word to me about the Wyrm. That was enough."

Verse flopped to the ground near the wall of a building opposite the back entrance to Mr. Italy's. He curled up, but his ears remained perked and alert. Apparently he felt no need to discuss the matter.

Tuck looked mostly at the twins, especially Ally, who had already challenged him for the leadership of the pack when it first formed. Tuck worried about more than another challenge based on his failure. He worried about losing her respect as her leader.

Full reverberations of big metal pots sounded from the kitchen behind the pack and filled the moment of silence. Tom was tense as well and edged back a half step to remove himself from the corner of his sister's eye.

Simon began to speak, but Tuck glanced his way and cut him off. When he looked back, Ally was smiling.

"It's a good thing you played too. We wouldn't be at the regional final without you, and all my pep-club efforts would have gone to waste."

Tuck began to relax, but Ally's smile didn't naturally fade. It stayed a bit too long, and she didn't mind that he noticed. Everything was fine, but just for now.

Ally took the initiative again and explained as accurately yet succinctly as possible what had happened at the bonfire. How the blaze had been put out by the firemen, but then reignited itself and seemed to dance in patterns and even flash out to attack Verse. And finally how the flames had just as mysteriously vanished again when she challenged the Wyrm.

Tuck mulled over the story when Simon offered a detail. Unfortunately, Sam was still in the kitchen, and the banging of pots and pans rang louder than Simon's soft voice.

Tuck said, "Say again, Simon?"

Simon waited through another episode of rattling cookware until he heard an oven door snap shut and silence ruled again. "Each fire was a spirit, perhaps more than one, and the positions they took on the bonfire formed a pattern. I'm certain the pattern was a defensive posture of some kind. The elemental spirits of fire were defending themselves against a threat."

"Pattern?" came an amused shout from the kitchen window, where Sam's head thrust into the alley. "You still talking about football back here, Tuck? From what I've heard, it wasn't so much the patterns Greg and Marty were running, but the perfect spirals you threw to them."

The shoulders of everyone in the pack slumped as if they had been caught doing something seditious, but Tuck put on his happy I'm-going-to-the-regional-finals attitude again and said, "You've heard the wrong stories, Sam. A good pass is as much the receiver as the quarterback. Besides, they're the ones that have to take the hit at the end of the play."

Sam was smiling. "You're too modest, I think, Tuck, but still, what are you doing out there? All the pretty girls are inside, and I'm sure your pizza's getting cold."

Ally put on airs of being insulted, and Sam noticed. "Sorry, Ally. I meant no offense. It's just that cousins aren't supposed to look pretty."

When no one immediately continued the game of verbal tag, Sam pulled back into the kitchen, where pans started knocking together again.

"We'll take this up later," Tuck said. "There's going to be no peace at least for Tom, Ally, and me until this evening is over."

And then he added, "But no one go snooping around. This could be extremely dangerous, and from here we go as a unit."

They all returned to the celebration.


The celebration continued for some time. Tuck tried to push thoughts of the fire spirits aside for the mean-time. That discussion could be resumed after this night. Tuck knew they should all forgo the revelry and begin an investigation immediately, or at least talk to Sarah and Oliver, but on another level he didn't feel quite so apologetic. Making the regional finals was a great victory of its own, and memories of this feat would probably make as much of a difference to many of the students of the school as a victory over the Wyrm. Perhaps it would even mean more to them. Passer's stories often reminded Tuck of the power of myth and legend.

Tuck hoped this wasn't simple rationalization.

"You sure look out of it, Tuck," Bob said as Tuck completed the unconscious walk back to his booth. "That family celebration choked you up, huh?"

Tuck snapped to and realized it wasn't so much the Wyrm that worried him as it was his decisions. He was beginning to realize just how much the discovery that he was a werewolf was impacting his life. Like the others, Tuck had thought it was just an additional responsibility. It was turning into *the* responsibility. He would simply have to trust his instincts. If that made him a good leader who made the right decisions, then so be it. If not, then perhaps Ally was the best one for the job.

Tuck said, "Sorry guys, just kind of tired after the game, I guess."

"Not too tired for some fun down at the lake, I hope," said Bob.

"No. Definitely not."

"Good, because a couple of the fellas are already on their way to Lenny's to get some beer. A whole bunch of us are going to the lake to get a little bit rowdy."

Tucker laughed. "Lenny isn't going to sell beer to any of us. And there's no way anyone's going to sneak it out past him. And they better not try! If someone is suspended from the final game because they tried to steal beer . . . Oh, boy, they'll be talking to me!"

Bob smiled and said, "Well, I've heard that Lenny sold his place the other day, and the new owner doesn't have a problem selling beer to you if you have the cash."

Tuck was surprised. "Who'd he sell it to?"

"I don't know, and what does it matter?"

"I guess it doesn't," Tuck said, but he didn't like the idea of Lenny not running his place anymore. The place would lose a lot of its charm. "Is the new owner still going to call it Lenny's?"

"Who cares. We can get beer now." Bob smiled at Tuck and then kissed Sharon.


Tom and Ally also decided to stay for pizza and celebration. They sat with a couple of Ally's friends. One of the girls, Susan, obviously had a crush on Tom. She was cute, but Tom had learned years before at his old school in California, after their father suddenly returned to the Arizona reservation one night, that it was bad news to date one of your sister's friends, so he kept his distance.

The three girls were chatting when Sam came by to see if they needed anything more. Tom took a refill of Mountain Dew and didn't interrupt the gabbing until he heard Susan say something about the trouble the firemen had putting out the fire. Tom and Ally exchanged worried glances. Did Susan see the elemental fires?

Susan continued, "You and Tom even had to help them. At least that's how it looked from the bleachers."

"You should have been watching the game," Tom said, trying to change the subject. "I heard we fumbled the opening kickoff."

Susan hesitated. "Well, I was waiting for Ally and you because I saved seats, and I saw you both still down by the bonfire."

Ally put the issue to rest. "Yeah, that's all it was. The fireman said that big fires like that don't always stay out the first time, so after they'd dowsed it really good, Tom and I volunteered to stay and kick out any little flames that might reignite."

Ally gave a worried look to Tom, though Tom wasn't really sure what the danger was. What could possibly happen? Surely Susan wouldn't come to the conclusion that the bonfire had become a dance floor for a couple dozen spirits of elemental fire.

Sam returned with Tom's refill just as a lot of the kids were starting to get up to the cry of, "To the lake!"

"Are we going?" Tom asked his twin.

Ally looked at her friends and then nodded to Tom.

Tom called after Sam, "We'll take the check, Sam."

"I'll check you out at the counter, Tom. You can see my brand-new register." Sam then hurried to take care of the kids waiting in line, who evidently already knew there was a change in the checkout procedure at Mr. Italy's.

Tom volunteered to pay the bill, since he had eaten most of the pizza, so he got into line as his sister and friends went outside to wait. Tom noted that as soon as Ally stepped outside, Verse trotted right over to her. He played the role of a loyal dog very well. That would be worth a couple of jokes at the Moondancer's expense.

It was a long wait in line, and by the time Tom made it to the counter, he wasn't in the mood to talk with Sam about his new cash register. Tom saw that Sam wasn't in the mood either.

Sam was writing the bills and doing the arithmetic

by hand. "It just stopped," he complained, hitting the back of his hand against the computerized device. "I wish I still had the old one. I kind of miss the way the ten-dollar key always stuck."

Tom paid and made it outside just in time to jump in the back of Todd Wellington's truck.

It was a long walk home, but Passer figured that he needed the time. Besides, it was more time to savor the wild and strange events of the evening. He should be following Tuck for the rest of the night as well, but he was merely an observer, not a video recorder. Passer already had too much to contemplate.

The chilly autumn air extracted all the fragrances from the northern forest. It was a night so full of itself that the wind carried countless perfumes, but none of them obscured the mysterious odor of the wind itself—that ephemeral aroma, invisible, but constructed through countless memories until it conveyed a nostalgia, a not quite definable familiarity and peace.

At home in the forest, and acquainted with the lay of the land in these woods, Passer found more meaning in his name. He distributed stories, but he also moved soundlessly over the colorful, fallen, yet not quite desiccated, leaves.

The dark shadow. It had destroyed spirits. That's what ruled Passer's thoughts. After many hours of wandering, Passer gave up, refusing to be the only one pondering the enigma this night. While the humans frolicked at the lake and while some of the night still remained, Passer would change and run as a wolf.

He slipped down into the woods and began to change and escape the bonds of the human culture completely.

Passer had no conception of what sex was like because he was a metis, the sterile offspring of two werewolves, though he had certainly seen both wolves and humans copulate. He didn't need that experience to draw what seemed an obvious conclusion: The act of reproduction, or even the seemingly pleasurable imitations of the act, could scarcely compare to the loving oneness with Gaia Passer felt when he changed.

It was his one secret vice, the one way he could receive physical pleasure in this world. So he concentrated to deliberately make the change progress gradually, though of all Garou, metis were able to transform quickest, or at least that's what Passer assumed, since he was significantly faster than any other Garou. With training and repetition, a werewolf could change from full wolf to full human within a fraction of a minute. The various forms of half man in between could be assumed in an even shorter amount of time. The change for Passer consumed him and fifteen minutes.

He lowered himself to his knees and elbows with his good hand clutching his hair. He began to shiver. His back itched at first, but then Passer felt a warmth as it flushed with blood. An unpredictable spasm shook his body. Passer's hands dropped and dug into the earth. But already his fingers were stiffening and becoming incapable of independent action.

Then the cracking started. His spine began to buckle, but the ribs were the most dramatic. Popping, they rounded out, slimming Passer's torso. His chest pushed toward the earth. All over, his body electrified as hair pushed out from below. Each such escape was like a quick jab of a pin, and the process seemed to ripple over his body like leisurely waves, each time receding with a little more hair in place and then returning to thrust out more.

His body was thrown flat and he rolled onto his side. The joints at his knees and elbows hardened so that he couldn't bend his limbs. The immobilization was maddening, but then the release came. Slowly. The joints sizzled with intense heat and reversed themselves. He soon found the use of those limbs and gingerly gained his footing, though now on four legs.

Meanwhile, his nose and mouth quivered, and the jawbone seemed ready to literally explode with energy, but Passer held the energy in check, so he was actually able to watch the lower part of his face stretch forward. He kept his head low, so his mouth ground into the earth and his ever heightening sense of smell pulled in the hearty odor of the earth and hardwood trees.

In an instant, that sense of smell was all he had. His ears melted away and his skull closed the aural cavities. With his eyes clenched tight too, he couldn't see or hear. Slowly, his skin began to stretch upward on top of his head and harden into cartilage at the base. His skull opened again, and the gentle rush of the wind carried a thousand more sounds to him than before. The fluttering of birds, wings in the trees above tantalized him for sensations of more.

Then an abrupt pain shot through his body. The change was almost over, and this last part was one that he couldn't slow. His spine punched out of his body and snaked its way into the air as Passer thrust his behind skyward. For the barest instant the nerves that formed on the tail were bare, and even the slight wind seemed to pummel them with uncountable excitement.

Then a final, soft wave rippled down the extremity, leaving tufts of brownish fur in its wake.

Passer stood, breathed a wolf-lungful of air, and sprinted into the hardwood forest, his crippled right paw apparently causing him little trouble. It was a long way home, and Passer intended to use no shortcuts.

The truck had filled quickly at Mr. Italy's, and Bob and Sharon were separated from Tuck and Melissa. Tuck did his best to entertain Melissa on the twenty-minute drive to the lake. The easiest way was to fall into the dumb-jock role and talk about the game, though he knew it bored them both to death. He wasn't sure what exactly he felt about Melissa. Or maybe it was simply confidence that he lacked.

He smiled at that. Imagine, a Garou pack leader unsure of himself because of a woman. The grin became a grimace when he realized that Passer could probably tell dozens of stories full of just such irony. Tuck didn't doubt that in many cases that small indecision was what brought the champions of the stories to their knees.

Melissa was intelligent, playful, and awfully cute, but whether he still didn't feel attracted to her or whether he was but didn't know how to begin with her was a mystery to him. Tonight, fortunately, he had an excuse. A very real one: the Wyrm. It did dominate Tuck's mind, so it wasn't a complete ratio-nalization.

Tuck's mind wandered for a moment as the rattle of the truck washed the thoughts from his mind. He snapped to when he realized he was staring at Melissa's breasts. He looked up at her in embarrass-ment, but she was staring ahead of the truck where the headlights broke the darkness.

Tuck was about to say something more when Lake Waganta shimmered into view and the paralyzed conversation ended. Tuck was at once relieved and anxious when the ride was over. Mostly anxious, because now he must find new ways to pass the time and avoid facing the awkward situation with Melissa.

Everyone piled out of the truck, and many hit the ground running. The reveling kids lapped down onto the sand and rock beach just as the cold waters of the Waganta rippled their way up the beach. The easy quiet that Tuck always felt here was somehow disturbed. Never before did it seem like the motions of humanity and the water could be so at odds. He pushed the thought away, once again blaming an overactive mind still bent on the mystery of the fire spirits and the Wyrm.

Some of the kids pulled their pant legs up and started wading into the chill water. Piles of shoes and socks were forming, and Melissa looped her arm through Tuck's to lead him over there. "Come on," she said.

The pair stripped their feet bare and rolled up the legs of their pants, too. Tuck dropped all the footwear near the pile. Then they waded into the water. It was colder than Melissa had expected, so she jumped onto Tuck's back. Tuck was strong enough to hold her up, but he almost slipped on the slick bottom of the Waganta. Melissa's laughter rang out and carried across the broken mirror of the water.

All around Tuck the other kids were splashing, shouting, and, now that the beer arrived, drinking. Down the shore toward the bridge, Tuck saw that Bob hadn't been quite as stable as his quarterback. Both Sharon and Bob were completely soaked and were running out of the water. A little later they might be drunk enough to go back in, Tuck thought. That's when they catch a chill and really get sick.

When Tuck glanced in the other direction along the Waganta, he saw a pair of people he didn't recognize. It was a couple, and the way they were dressed they definitely hadn't just come from Mr. Italy's. They wore turtleneck shirts and pants made of some crinkly water- and windproof material. Then Tuck noticed backpacks reclined against a tree, and he knew that they must be campers, or maybe hitchhikers. And they didn't seem to like the idea of their quiet hideaway being invaded by a high school party.

No one else seemed to notice them yet. Tuck wanted to go talk with them, but Melissa was clinging to his back and shouting joyfully.


Quarters were cramped, but the trip was finally over. All the kids in the back of the pickup were anxious to join the fun when the truck pulled into the gravel lot near the beach. Many others were already on the beach and obviously having fun. Tom jumped out and then helped Ally and her friends down. Verse leapt out, landing far from the truck. Tom watched Verse wander off absently following a scent trail.

Ally and her friends hurried down to the water. By the time Tom made it to the shore, the girls were already barefoot and wading. When he saw Tuck walking toward him, Tom looked for Melissa. She had joined Ally and the others.

Tuck asked, "Can you help me with something, Tom?"

"Sure," Tom replied, a bit on guard.

"Can you entertain Melissa, or at least keep her occupied with Ally and the other girls for a while?"

"I suppose. Why?"

Tuck glanced over his shoulder and down the beach. "See that couple down there? I just want to talk to them for a minute and Melissa won't give me a chance to breathe."

"Sounds like the responsibility of leadership is dragging you down, Tuck. If I remember right, you were the one hunting for Melissa when we all first started at school. Now you could finally have her and . . ."

Tom trailed off teasingly, but Tuck really did look like he carried a weight. Tom continued reassuringly, "If you're worried about that stuff earlier tonight, then just forget it for a while. You just won the big game. Every victory's worth celebrating for a while."

His voice heavy, Tuck said, "It just doesn't seem like there's time anymore to celebrate. And it's not just the bonfire. Things don't feel right everywhere. Something else on this beach doesn't feel right, and I'm going to go talk to that couple down there to see if they have anything to do with it."

Tom glanced down the beach. "You better hurry, then, because it looks like they're packing up."

Tuck looked too and then immediately started toward the hitchhikers. Then he stopped and spun to look back at Tom and say something, but Tom spoke first. "Don't worry, I'll cover Melissa for you. Besides, we're on a beach, that's my place."

Tuck nodded and turned again.

To Tom, of course, this beach was nothing compared to the places back in California where he and Ally used to play. She'd swim and he'd play volleyball. Picking up girls with the crashing of waves nearby was second nature to Tom. Besides, if Tuck didn't want the spoils of his win tonight even after suggesting that everyone take it easy for one more night, then that was his problem. Melissa was a cute girl, and she was not a close friend of Ally's.

"Excuse me a minute," Tuck shouted to the couple.

The man and woman both stopped buckling their almost cinched backpacks and waited as Tuck drew near. They also waited for him to speak again.

"Sorry to scare you folks away, but our school just won a spot in the regional football finals tonight so we're here celebrating."

Within speaking distance, Tuck could more plainly see the hitchhikers. They appeared to be an at least moderately well-off married couple. They carried the highest quality equipment, the kind of backpack and supplies Tuck wished he owned, though he guessed that since he could turn into a wolf now it was a rather moot point. The equipment was also very new, so he guessed they were not very experienced campers—all the more reason to find out about them, since the Wyrm might still be in the county.

One thing was also for certain. They weren't hitchhikers, as he'd assumed. They were young professionals, perhaps from Chicago, on an outdoors vacation. Little River was not a tourist stop, and that made Tuck wonder about the pair.

The man stood up and stepped toward Tuck. He said, "That's the way it goes, guy. We were here first, but you're the locals and you've got numbers." He seemed comfortably dressed in jeans and a fresh flannel shirt. The bright yellow portion of the shirt's checkered pattern almost glowed in the faint moonlight reflecting off the surface of the Waganta.

Tuck also saw a slim smile wrinkle the man's mouth as he spoke. Good to know he was just playing and not really looking to start trouble.

Tuck decided to play back and hopefully disarm any potential trouble. He said, "Thing is, in nature, numbers only work when there's cooperation, like among wolves." Tuck waved his hand back at his classmates and continued. "Nobody, not even our football coach, could get that group organized now."

The woman laughed, and the hood of her rain slicker fell back to reveal bobbed red hair. The man dropped back a step, evidently no longer worried about Tuck.

Tuck spoke again. "Where are you folks hitching to?"

"Hitching?" asked the man.

"Yeah," grinned Tuck. "Nobody comes to Little River on purpose."

The woman found her voice and stopped tying rolled-up blankets to her backpack. "Well, we did. It sounded so nice."

"You're not hitchhiking?" asked Tuck, though he knew for certain the woman was telling the truth. The last time he'd been fooled was by the mischievous falcon spirit who'd taught him how to be wary of lies in the future.

The man said, "Not at all. Our car's parked on that side of the lake." The man pointed. "We're hiking out to camp until the food we bought runs out. We thought we would stay here tonight by the water and then move on, but we didn't come to Little River to be a part of the crowd, so I think we'll just be moving on."

Tuck was still surprised that anyone would come out to Little River to hike or camp. Sure, the town was surrounded by pristine nature, thanks to the Steins and the vigil they held over their small caern, but it seemed nobody really knew about the little town. Whenever Tuck and the pack went to big cities like Chicago or Milwaukee and talked about their home, nobody had heard of it. Of course, they didn't wander into such haunts of the leeching vampires any longer.

Then he knew. "You must have grown up around here."

"No." The man paused and then said, "Listen, is there something wrong with being here? The book said that the lake was public property and that there were no rules against camping in the forest. Is that wrong?"

"The book?" was all Tuck could manage.

The man said, "Sure, don't you know about it? Little River's featured very prominently too."

Then the woman proudly said, "You'll have all sorts of tourist business now." She seemed genuinely excited for Tuck and Little River, but the prospect only added another brick of dread to Tuck's growing wall.

"It's right in here," the woman said. She opened a side pouch on her backpack and wedged her hand inside. After the fumbling went on for more than a moment, Tuck spoke to the man so he wouldn't rudely stand waiting on the woman.

"If you want to move on, I suggest heading that way." Tuck indicated a direction behind the couple. "There's a trail over there that leads to a little clearing after about a hundred yards. You shouldn't have any trouble finding it."

"Thanks," said the man.

"Here it is." The woman thrust a book toward Tuck, who took the well-thumbed volume.

Tuck looked at the book. The title read *Wandering the Northern Midwest*. Then he looked inside at a couple of pages and flipped to the index. The woman quietly watched Tuck, beaming with pride as if by virtue of the book it was she who knew these woods the best. The man looked at a pocket map and then in the direction of the trail Tuck noted. The woods became denser that way.

In the index, Tuck found the listing—*Little River pgs. 238–258*. He turned quickly toward page 238. How could there possibly be twenty pages of material on Little River?

The first page he saw was page 245, and the words there terrified Tuck. "I don't suppose I could keep this book?" asked Tuck without even removing his eyes from the pages.

"Sorry, guy," the man said, "but we really need it to keep track of where we are."

"But none of this stuff is here," Tuck said numbly.

The woman smiled. "Oh, we know that. We just wanted to see the area before it was."

Still moving swiftly through the forest in the hours before midnight after almost a day of travel, the Garou was acutely aware he was wandering in the territory of another pack. His instincts itched against such a trespass, but the drive for revenge, and also an instinctual confidence in his ability to force his way through even if delayed or challenged, carried him on. Few could withstand the assault of Sower of Thunder.

Like all Red Talons, Thunder preferred his birth form of the wolf and despised the puny, hairless human shape. With his rage full upon him, though, Thunder barreled through the forest as a crinos. An impressive wolf that could become a six-foot-plus human, Thunder stood almost ten feet high in this form. His massive arms hung too long, almost ape-like, but that allowed him to run on all fours even in this middle form that was suitable for bipedal motion as well. It was Thunder's enormous paws and claws, though, that gave him his name even at an early age, for a blow from him resounded like the clap of a terrible storm.

Finally nearing his destination, Thunder slowed and considered his likely opposition. There was once only a lonely pair of Garou here, probably Wyrm-tainted and parents of a dozen or more deformed mule pups, but Thunder smelled the traces of others too. Perhaps the others were the pups. Now grown and full of the Wyrm. Full of treachery. Perhaps the small caern here was now home to a pack of Black Spiral Dancers.

The fury and irrational hatred Thunder felt pounded in his mighty chest. Except now the killing and hate wouldn't be irrational, or done simply for the sake of destroying. Now a half-dozen more wolves of the dwindling population were gone. Destroyed north of this territory but just within the boundary of the human-created state lines.

The solo wanderings that took the bulk of his time had a mere day ago resulted in the discovery he both sought and hoped never to find. That's what put this rage in his heart.

He smelled it from miles away and pursued the scent in an enraged gallop to find the three mutilated wolves. Two young females and a cub. All gutted. Scarred. Decimated. Obscenely contaminated.

There was the stink of death and corruption, but the stink of the perpetrators clung to the grisly site as well. Such carelessness could only mean the Wyrm-tainted

Garou who'd performed the villainous deed were not familiar with Sower of Thunder, the ronin who followed the urgings of his wolverine totem and who proclaimed himself the sole and ablest avenger of the wolves of North America. The killers would learn of Thunder just before he annihilated them.

There was one odor in particular that drove him into a frenzy, and the enemy responsible for it would pay most dearly of all. It was the soft, sweet scent that Thunder knew only because he had spent a short amount of time among apes. It was chocolate, a treat for sunny afternoons of play or during festive occasions. Thunder shivered at the memory and his entire gigantic frame shuddered. It was repulsive. Did the killer attend his mission in a mood of celebration? Delight?

Only a wolverine could perform such wholesale destruction with such thoughtlessness. So it was mockery, Thunder decided. They mock the powerful Wolverine.

Certainly, there was a joy in killing, in conquering a foe. But the wolves had been killed without a hunger. Thunder did not lack cause. He hungered for the death of all who dwelt in the steel and plastic scabs on the land. But even worse were the Garou who dwelt among the humans and performed the same heinous deeds.

Then he smelled it. Not the ice cream. That would have sent him into a frenzy. It was the odor of one of the Garou pups. It was familiar. The so-called Stargazers had indeed spawned a litter of corruption. Each of Thunder's exhalations was jagged with rage. Suddenly, he lost control and pounded hard through the forest.

———

Still in troubled awe of what he read in the book, Tuck sat in the darkness at the very edge of the beach. Partying went on all around him and would continue now that another truckload of beer had arrived. A few people were already collapsing into unconsciousness, and couples were spreading out over the beach to seek momentary pleasures. Plenty of others were still drinking and splashing and swimming.

He wanted to be alone, to think, but he also wanted company. Scanning through the darkness, Tuck found only one of his packmates—Verse. The wolf was sniffing around the edges of the beach, but as that area became populated with copulaters, the Garou hung his head and slowly walked toward a truck and folded himself on the ground near a rear tire.

Then Tuck found himself looking for Melissa. Now wasn't the time to think of her, though, and for once he was able to push her from his thoughts. Since he had a hard time speaking to her under other circumstances, then now, when even if he did speak she would be unable to comprehend, was not the time to try again.

He wondered why he felt such a strange sense of dread about the campers. The book, he supposed. Do not blame the messenger for the message, he counseled himself. They were indeed only innocently investigating the area because of the misinformation provided in the travel book.

Tomorrow Tuck would have to find that book, even if it meant a trip to Chicago. He would check back with the campers first. Maybe they would sell the book to him. Anyway, it provided a good excuse to find out more about them.

Tuck settled back against a tree.

———

Like her brother, Ally didn't drink, so she just played in the water for her fun. Tom had wandered away with Melissa, though Ally was a little confused, since Melissa supposedly had this major thing for Tuck. Well, she was a little drunk and maybe just trying to make Tuck jealous.

The evening air was growing cold, and that made the water seem chilly even for her, so Ally knew it was time to get out and join the fun on the beach. She started to wade out, but found that she was heading for trouble.

On the shore, about thirty feet in front of her, two boys argued, and they were drawing a crowd.

"I found it," shouted one.

The other shot right back, "Only because I pointed it out to you."

Ally could see that neither of them held their alcohol very well. One boy was Frank, a poor, strapping farm boy who didn't do much other than go through the motions of school. The other boy was Jesse Turner, one of Tuck's offensive linemen. Ally remembered Tuck saying that the best running plays were those they ran behind Jesse Turner. This would be a major-league brawl if it got out of hand.

For now, it was still at the argument level.

Frank said, "Well, I've got it, so just back off."

Then Jesse landed some heavy blows. "Need something to play on the farm, Frank? Shoveling manure just isn't good enough for you anymore?"

"You should talk, you stupid jock."

"Give it to me now," Jesse warned.

"Hell, no. I don't know who would leave a Gameboy at the beach, but I'll be damned if I let you take it from me."

"You won't let me, I'll make you." Jesse started forward.

It was so convenient, though Thunder didn't need it to be convenient. He was prepared to wander the entire night before finding human victims to satisfy his bloody designs, but the two he detected would suit perfectly. The Litany forbade such activity, but in light of the threat of these Wyrm-spawn the Litany could be damned.

They were sleeping in a small clearing to the side of the trail Thunder followed. They were still a little tense, Thunder sensed, so they hadn't been asleep for long. They could have been wide-awake and armed to the teeth with guns and explosives and still they would be no match for the raging Garou.

Thunder slipped off the trail and into the forest to circle around the edge of the clearing. His pitch black frame disappeared among the dark outlines of the moonlit tree trucks. He moved with careful, quiet precision.

He slowly, almost casually, slipped from the woods to stand over the sleeping campers. He crouched low over them, savoring the thought of the coming storm, confident that they would not wake on account of him until he wanted them to. His fingers flexed a few times as the dark ebony tips of his claws began to gleam. The edges of the claws glistened. They were perfectly sharp now, so Thunder struck.

The woman was first. She was sleeping on her stomach, so Thunder grabbed her hair and hefted her torso into the air in a quick motion that left only her knees and lower legs on the ground. Thunder whipped his right arm toward her, extending but one finger. The sharpened talon peeled through her skin as if it were melting the flesh. Her artery and vocal chords were severed in an instant, but the eyes told Thunder that she was still with him. Her body reflexively tried to twist away, but Thunder didn't let it budge. His mouth drew open and despite an insistent weight pulling back on the girl, he shoved half her head, her entire face, into his mouth and snapped down. Blood squirted into his mouth.

Terrified, the man was now awake and he tried to save his companion. Thunder's eyes locked on the man's and they exchanged messages. Thunder told the man he was dead, and the man knew it.

Still holding the gaze of the man, Thunder opened his mouth slowly so that the remains of the woman's head dripped from his mouth in saliva-coated chunks. He smacked audibly on a piece that did not fall and then swallowed it. Thunder was livid with anger and need, but he didn't feel the need to even touch the man. The power of a vicious gift would entertain Thunder most.

The man readied a scream of his own, but only blood erupted from his throat. Still crouched over the remains of the woman, Thunder visualized himself killing the man in the same way. It was tiring to use this gift, but Thunder needed to see the man die horribly. Already the man's throat was ripped out, but next Thunder was able to see the punishing effect of his jaws on the man's head without actually surrounding and tasting the weak flesh. An invisible maw as tremendously large as Thunder's crunched the man's skull. Horribly mauled and bloodied, the man collapsed.

Rage was still upon Thunder, but he was able to clear his head for a moment and realize what his anger caused him to do. He felt no remorse for the killing. It was not murder. Not like what had been done to the wolves. This was war. He was sorrowful only because neither of the dead was a Wyrm-tainted pup. But a demonic smile pushed at the corners of his dark and bloody mouth. The campers would be found, and more humans would overrun the secluded woods where the Black Spirals sought to hide. But revenge could not wait that long. Perhaps another target would be just as convenient. When enraged, Thunder found it easy to rationalize more killing.

When he smelled beer down the trail toward a large body of water, Thunder loped off immediately. Convenience.

Something was upsetting Tuck. Verse could smell the worry in Tuck's sweat, and the wolf padded away from the woods to lay beside a truck where he could easily see the pack leader. The last time Verse smelled this on his pack leader was just after Tuck's battle with Ally for control of the pack. The fight hadn't given Tuck any pause, but when the sudden weight of leadership was upon him, Tuck panicked for a moment. That hesitation, the recognition of responsibility and how it humbled Tuck, is what won Verse's heart and made him part of the pack. The fight with Ally had determined who would lead, but it didn't control who would follow.

The same hesitation was on Tuck now. Something important was at hand and forcing this dramatic thought process. Verse didn't leave Tuck's side. Who knew how long it would take?

Try as he might, though, Verse's attention to Tuck was drawn away by violence on the beach. A large crowd was gathering around a pair of big boys apparently prepared to pummel each other senseless.

Verse's inclination was to not get involved. Years of running with the wolves had desensitized him to constant displays of superiority and position.

Then Verse saw Ally striding out of the water toward the conflict. It's like her to be in the thick of it, Verse thought. She seemed concerned, though, so Verse intervened. Besides, the commotion might disturb Tuck.

He sang.

The song was slow to gain volume as it began very softly. A sudden, loud song might still work, but the humans might get a sense of the unworldliness of it split seconds before the power of the song took them. Verse remembered too well the first time he had encountered a human while displaying his Garou heritage. The insanity that completely overwhelmed the human was shocking to Verse.

No, it was better to first make it an indistinguishable part of the background. Melt with the delicate rolling of the waves. Harmonize with the soothing wisps of wind. Blend with the sharp clatter of the crickets. Sing Gaia.

As he was not in the center of the action and did not have to fear for his personal safety, Verse was able to give himself completely to the music. He also lost sight of the progress of the humans' battle, but knew that it had gone to a punching stage before his voice began to become an element apart from Gaia.

The spectators were the first ones affected, of course. The song initially calmed the most composed. Soon the spectators were losing interest in the fight. Then they were trying to stop it, but only by interceding—it would have been unthinkable to them to get physically involved to break up the fight. By the time the magical song had reached the ears of the combatants, the spectators were outraged by the display of violence. The crowd broke into dozens of stumbling individuals all looking for a quiet place to sit and compose themselves.

Then the fight stopped. An object dropped to the ground between the combatants as they slowly walked away from each other.

Verse's nose twitched of its own accord and caught a slim hint of a foreign scent. Too calm himself to be excited by it, Verse forgot anything unusual had even been detected.

Thunder hurtled through the forest. The smell of beer had excited him, but the odor of sweat and sex caused the Garou's eye to momentarily roll back into his head. His need for vengeance was intense and insatiable.

But then the planet spoke to him. Gaia refreshed him with the water, wind, and crickets. And the rage was gone.

Thunder stopped and slipped back the way he had come, confident now that the campers would now be enough. He could smell their scent on the path. Surely the kids had scared the campers away. At least a few of the human snots would be sober enough to remember the pair when they didn't show up again.

Regardless, Thunder knew a crazed maniac would cause more fear than an attack of wild beasts. He would hide the bodies. That's something wild animals wouldn't do.

And then he would stay out of sight for a time. He needed to learn the lay of the land. He needed to know the terrain just as well as the Wyrm pack. Thanks to special gifts the spirits who favored him had taught, they would never detect his invading scent.

# CONVERSATION

"It has begun. I can sense it now, even as we stand and watch the clouds sail past the stormy light of the moon. Our enemy is among us."

"You mean his enemy."

"Yes. It is his enemy too."

"You're purposefully misunderstanding me. I mean, it's his enemy who has come."

"The Wyrm is our enemy too."

"Of course, you weasel, but this aspect hunts us now because of him."

"Yes, the spirit of the Wyrm has come to finish its work with Alexander. Yes, we stand in its way."

"What of the caern?"

"I suspect the Wyrm has few thoughts of our small caern. Alexander is a repository of far more energy than any but the greatest caerns of old, and it is he who is sought. The Wyrm must act quickly to destroy our charge before he has regained his cause."

"You mean before he can bring himself to even face the Wyrm again."

"Do not question—"

"I know."

"Do not qu—"

"I know! . . . All right, say it. . . ."

"Do not question Alexander's will, for who are we, who is anyone, to believe themselves more capable of even facing what he has faced down?"

"I sense it now too. A dark shadow across the land."

"Yes. It blots out the moon, or will."

"I see it too. Tall buildings that will starve the ground for sunlight. Arrays of artificial light that will glow and wash out the delicate radiance of distant suns. Oh, Oliver! How shall we see the stars? How shall we ever hereafter be able to dance beneath a sky open to the horizon?"

"We must hope that the light that burns bright now will burn brighter with rebirth. Our battle now must ever be two steps forward and one step back."

"But all the world, all the Garou, are faltering. We fall two steps back for every stride we attempt."

"We must keep trying. Do not despair. Who is truth, you or the Wyrm?"

"I am."

"Who is life? You or the Wyrm?"

"I am life."

"Yes."

# 3

# LITTLE RIVER

"Smells like you were running last night," Ally said without a hint of innuendo or conspiracy as she greeted Passer in the kitchen. She knew that Passer liked to roam the woods at night. They all did, of course, but the humans did it for the strange, exhilarating freedom it provided, while ferals ran to return to their natural state much as humans had to return to civilization. Small Town, USA—Little River, Illinois—didn't fill the latter need for Ally. Mules, though, found peace or release in the belly of Gaia. Ally was sure Passer found both.

Oliver and Sarah Stein's home, which was now also home to five teenagers, was typical of century-old midwestern houses: two stories, fewer but bigger rooms, large and winding staircase in the foyer, smaller and cramped staircase up from the kitchen, and an old staircase down there too. Down to a musty, earthen and stone cellar. There was a brass tub in the master bathroom, and bunk beds in the two rooms where Ally and her packmates slept. She shared a room with Tom again for the first time since they were younger than ten. She couldn't recall exactly when she first got her own room. Tuck, Passer, and Verse shared the other room. What a sight that was in the morning when all three still slept. Passer in the bunk over Verse, and Tuck curled into a too-small bed in a too-crowded corner of the room.

The kitchen seemed very fifties to Ally, or at least it fit her impression of that time. The pastel yellow countertop. The deep, unadorned sink and plain, long faucet. Ungrounded wall outlets that made a number of modern appliances unusable without appropriate extension cords. A grate in the ceiling that was a heating vent but also aligned with a similar grate in the floor of the Steins' bedroom. This allowed communication back and forth but forbade late-night rustling in the kitchen. It was also a problem for early risers like Ally, but the Steins were usually rousing by the time she returned from her morning run.

She noticed all this again as she regarded Passer. The Garou was now in his human form, and he wore the same long brown robe he always took outside with him when he intended to change into lupus or hispo, the near-wolf, forms. The long, wide sleeves helped cover the genetic damage done to his arm, though Ally's glances usually glossed over the folded flesh of that arm anyway. That concerned her as little as his solitary forest pleasures. It was part of him, so she looked over it much as one does the black hair of a friend seen daily. You come to not notice it.

Ally didn't need reminders, though, to place Passer on the lowest rung of the pack's hierarchy. He was a mule.

He looked a bit sheepish, though, and Ally didn't

understand why. She greeted him under similar circumstances a few weeks ago, and that occasion passed without insulting or mocking comments from Ally. She kept them to herself.

Ally had been in wolf form and out for her morning run when she greeted Passer's return from a late-night rendezvous with Gaia. Ally had smelled the unmistakable tang of sex on Passer, an odor now too fleeting and fading to catch with a human nose, but she didn't say anything to him about it partially because he had made no attempt to hide it and partially because she didn't trust her senses. Mules, by their nature and their name, were sterile. And deformed, like Passer. Sterile apparently didn't mean completely incapable, but that's the point at which she didn't want to pursue the question further.

Passer had cringed a bit then as now. A human would have been embarrassed to be caught wandering smelling of semen, and while Passer possessed a silent, mysterious nature, he didn't make a secret of how he found relief in a physical pleasure largely denied him by his birthright, but mostly, perhaps, by Garou society.

A disgusting thought Ally entertained, tried to dismiss, but couldn't stop from entertaining, was Passer's possible intention to attract her. She imagined being overwhelmed by his male pheromones on the heels of his sex with Gaia, but it was laughable. She didn't say anything, though, because as the future leader of the Phoenix Pack, Ally didn't want to ostracize a potential ally. Besides, she may be Garou, but she doubted she could ever love anything but a human.

She asked, "Find anything?"

"No. But I didn't look." He sat across from Ally at the round oak table in the large kitchen. His fingers rubbed along the lines of deep grooves in the wood, and she knew he was looking at her. She wondered again if the mule found her attractive. All the boys at school certainly did. She'd been the runaway victorious homecoming queen a month and a half ago.

No one could overlook her long black hair. Her full, yet athletic figure. Her smooth skin, with a hint of a darker hue that cast her as perpetually tanned but was actually her Native American heritage.

Ally took another bite of her breakfast cereal. It was oatmeal with almonds, and tasted good.

Passer asked, seemingly troubled and definitely recognizing his place below Ally in the pack hierarchy, "Should I have looked? I thought last night was to be a potential last night of freedom before we face up to the immensity of possible peril."

"It was," Ally managed between bites. "I just thought you might have noticed something." She liked this wolf and Garou way of dominance. Among humans you had to work so hard to attain it, and then work doubly hard to maintain it. Among the Garou, if you earned it, then it was naturally so unless something dramatic happened. It seldom did, though nowadays Ally supposed it happened more often. Especially among certain tribes, or so the Steins said. Turnover among the Red Talon leaders probably weakened, not strengthened, that tribe.

Some turnover can be good, Ally reminded herself. It just had to be at the right time. A peacemaker during peace. A warrior during war. It was how it should be. And if war was coming soon, Ally would be prepared to assume the mantle.

The pair sat in silence for a time before Passer asked, "Everything okay at the lake last night?"

"Except for a fight between a couple of stupid

boys. Verse settled it down, though, with one of his songs."

"Was it beautiful?" Passer asked, excited, his fingers now tracing the outlines of stains in the oak.

Annoyed by the question, Ally answered, "I suppose. It stopped a stupid fight, so it worked."

"Oh."

Unsteadily, yet quietly, padding into the kitchen, also on only two legs, came Verse. In human form because it was required by the Steins whenever a Garou was in their home, Verse felt ill at ease. Not only because of his clothing, like the blue jeans and sweatshirt he currently wore, but also because there was so much he could see about him that he knew he should be able to sense more deeply. The aroma of the hot breakfast cereal Ally ate. Or the earthy taste of the same when he fed on it too. The texture of the floor covering beneath his paws. *Feet* was the word, he unconsciously reminded himself as he tried thinking to himself in English. And the sound of the weather outdoors.

Outdoors. Where he could run as a wolf.

Or the lack of fur. It seemed strange to have so much skin directly exposed to the environment. Even after several months, Verse still felt he looked odd—a feeling confirmed when saw himself briefly in the window over the kitchen sink as he did every morning.

His plain brown hair was rough-cut and unkempt. His face looked so rounded because of a wide nose and thick, high cheekbones. Not at all like the sharp outline of a wolf's head.

Verse thought that as a human he must look very ordinary, though he had little means of judging. Appearance mattered little to him, especially in light of the difficulty he was having—adapting to being so near females who were sexually active once a month instead of once a season. And sexually willing every day. That was a hard instinct to overcome.

He sighed, and it caught the attention of Ally and Simon.

"Good sunrise," he managed as he walked to the stove and scooped a ladle of oatmeal into a bowl retrieved from a nearby stack. Man-form wasn't entirely lacking assets, Verse admitted as he carefully watched the as yet untrained movement of his hands.

Verse walked to the table, where he placed his bowl of cereal and with practiced grace took a seat. Ally was on his left and Passer on his right. Reading human body language and facial expressions was still difficult for Verse, but it seemed to him that Passer looked a bit off balance. Squeamish perhaps. No, he looked like he'd been interrupted.

Verse glanced at Ally, but read nothing but her confidence. She ate resolutely and without a look at either himself or Passer now that she'd pulled a magazine to the side of her bowl. Verse smiled crookedly at Passer, a gesture that seemed threatening to Verse, but he knew humans read it differently. To Verse it seemed like a snarl because he showed his teeth.

"Ally said you stopped a fight last night," Passer said warmly.

Verse briefly paused to translate in his mind, but then answered, "A song to calm the boys."

Passer continued, "Why were they fighting?"

Verse looked to Ally to answer because she had been closer to the near brawl, but she concentrated on the magazine, or what Verse now saw must be a clothing catalog. Looking back to Passer, he replied, "Something found on the beach. They both wanted it."

"Stupid."

"Yes," said Verse. "They also bothered Tucker, who was thinking after talking to the hunters."

Ally looked up. "Hunters? What hunters?"

"A male and a female at the lake. Tuck spoke to them."

Ally pressed. "Hunters? Or campers?"

Verse didn't hesitate to admit his language mistake. "Campers."

Ally rolled her eyes and returned to her catalog.

Tuck walked into the kitchen behind Verse and placed his hands on the lupus's shoulders. He sighed deeply and said, "Don't dismiss it that casually, Ally. It's bad news, especially on top of the Wyrm we detected."

Verse said haltingly, "I knew something was important."

"Let's wait a moment for Tom, though, before I say more."

A voice cried out from the base of the stairs two rooms away, "I'm here." Soon, Tom, still pulling the final sleeve of his red-and-black sweater up one long arm, hustled into the kitchen.


Tuck declined to take any food or a seat at the table, but he looked comfortable and relatively at ease standing in the center of the kitchen. Partially this at-easeness was an illusion perpetuated by his clothing—loose-fitting, baggy pants and too-large flannel shirts over a T-shirt—but it was also his demeanor. Usually solemn, there was rarely wasted movement on his part. His blue eyes registered everything without darting. His callused hands looked strong and ready, but did not twitch. His stance was light and graceful, but his foot did not tap. His short blond hair was not parted. A slight curl held it in shape.

When a wry grin wrinkled his face, and it didn't now, this stoic was transformed to an affable, approachable young man. Athletic and handsome, he was the picture of all-American health and vitality.

Tuck looked at the assembled pack. They were all are sitting and regarded him attentively. Simon overeager to hear it. Tom ready to face the news. Ally ready to face down the news. Verse ready to roll with it.

He felt, and knew the others did as well, the oneness that came over them all when the pack was united. It was a powerfully maturing feeling. Like when Tuck traveled to England a few years ago. That country felt old compared even to the seemingly eternal and infinite cornfields of his midwestern home. The history of the island nation was a palpable weight, and so too did the culture of the Garou manifest when the pack was together.

Tuck knew Oliver and Sarah would overhear everything he said through the grate in the corner of the kitchen. Tuck wouldn't have asked them to be late for breakfast if he thought they wouldn't hear the news anyway. What he discovered last night really concerned the Steins more than the pack—after all, this was the site of Sarah and Oliver's caern—but Tuck wanted an opportunity for the pack to coalesce by rallying as one against the magnitude of the threat.

"Well, what is it, Tuck?" Ally asked impatiently. An Ahroun always ready for battle, Ally was prepared to discuss a battle against the Wyrm, but a conflict more intricate than that concerned her. And there appeared to be more to the problem. She could see Tuck preparing himself to drop a bomb of news on them all.

Tuck took a deep breath and opened the hatch. "According to a book I looked at last night, Little River will soon be the resort destination of a million or so people each year." He paused briefly. No questions yet, just questioning faces.

"An area of about twenty thousand acres with downtown Little River at its approximate center, and stretching as far east as the lake, as far north as past the high school all the way to Landerson Bridge, far enough south to gobble the Henderickson and Oitcliff farms, and"—another pause—"far enough west to encompass the caern, will be covered with water and amusement parks, shopping malls, and . . . well, you name it, but most of all lots and lots of people."

Ally joked, sounding keenly interested, "Shopping malls?"

Tom cast her a dark look. "Ally, that's not funny. This sounds awful." A picture of steel and plastic and concrete and smog covering this small town and its wilderness flashed into his mind. "Just awful," he whispered again, looking back at Tuck.

Ally shook her head. "Be serious, Tom. You too, Tuck. How is that possible? Who the hell would want to build that stuff in Little River?"

Tuck shrugged his shoulders in resignation, "I don't know, but Little River commanded a section of about twenty pages in a book titled *Wandering the Northern Midwest,* written by a lady named Janice Severnson."

Verse spoke with certainty. "No more roads in Little River. No more buildings. No more cars. No more people. Not allowed."

Everyone nodded, but Tuck said, "That's what we hope, Verse, but it may not be easy. People have a way of going where they want, and all the power, all the intentions, and all the will of the Garou have never stopped them."

Simon was baffled. It didn't make sense. Though he was trapped between two worlds, he knew a lot of each. Books had always provided an easy and accessible means of exploring the human world from the human perspective. How could such a book be published when it apparently discussed things yet undone? He raised his voice to be heard. "Assuming the book wasn't fiction . . ." He paused and looked at Tuck who slowly shook his head. "Then it must be discussing long-range plans for a major development operation in the area. We'll rally against it. I can't imagine the Hendericksons or Oitcliffs selling their land for any amount of money. This should be easy to stop."

Tuck wasn't happy. "Come on, guys. This isn't something that can be so easily dismissed. Besides, the book was really strange. The few sections I read, including one short one I memorized that talked about how Little River was becoming so popular that there were plans of expansion, including a new roller coaster at the amusement park and a division of the Museum of Science and Industry from Chicago. They were not written in the future tense. They book read as if these things were already built and operating!"

"That's ridiculous," Ally blurted. She was getting angry and couldn't help but direct that anger at Tuck.

"Of course it is," Tuck admitted, "but there was the book."

"Where's the book now?" asked Tom.

"It belongs to the couple I talked to last night at the lake."

Verse, always stating the obvious, but always the first to do so, or at least the one willing to do so, said, "We should look in the book. Read more information."

Ally had no patience for the obvious, so she glared at Verse but managed to keep silent.

Simon said, "We certainly must. Who published the book? It must have been a small press. I can't imagine a large press printing what sounds to be a travel book that contains information about features that don't even exist yet. I mean, the kinds of things you're talking about will take years to construct. Any journal would be out of date by then. They rewrite those kinds of things every year as it is!"

"No, Simon, it seemed like a real book," Tuck said calmly and evenly, trying to balance Simon and Ally's slowly slipping control. "I mean, it had one of those bar codes on it and everything. I think it was from one of those big New York publishing companies."

Tom said, "Let's find these people then. They can't have gone far, and no matter how far they've gone we can find them if they stayed on foot."

Tuck said, "The man mentioned they had just loaded with supplies and would stay in the woods until they ran out of food, so I'm certain they'll be out and around for a time."

"You should have just taken the book," Ally spat. "I mean really, Tuck, something that is this odd . . . You have to take extreme measures."

"Wrong," Tuck insisted. "First, I assumed we could find the book ourselves, and second I tried not to make any impression on the couple so they wouldn't think the difference between reality and what the book said was so vast. They thought the information in the book must have just been an advance look at what's coming, and I want them to continue thinking that. Something this big to such a little place means that everyone here must know about it, or so they would think. Better to play along than have them alerting everyone in town about something that I think is connected to the encounter with the Wyrm yesterday."

"All right, already." Ally rolled her eyes, but she hadn't considered that the book might have something to do with the Wyrm. That changed things completely because it suggested the coming confrontation could be more than a simple outright battle. And that meant there might be cause not to challenge Tuck for leadership.

"Do you really think so?" Tom obviously didn't like the idea that the events were connected either.

"I don't think it makes sense," Simon muttered.

Tuck heard and asked, "Why, Simon? Surely these events happened too close together to be pure coincidence? It seems obvious to me that they're connected. Besides, I feel in my gut that they are."

Simon explained. "Civilization, with its amusement parks and shopping malls, smacks of another of our revered Triat—the Weaver. In days of old, the Wyld created boundlessly, purposelessfully. It vomited with abandon anything that could be created. The Weaver grasped particular pieces of this endless creation and wove into being that which we behold. The dreaded Wyrm kept them both in check. Neither chaos nor order would advance too far ahead of the other, and the Wyrm guaranteed this with its entropic might. But now the Weaver and Wyrm are perhaps mad. The Wyrm destroying all things, and the Weaver attempting to subjugate all that the Wyld creates into forms that are unchangeable and unmalleable. Either way, of course, the Wyld, which is the source of our hope in our battle against the Apocalypse when all creation is gone or soured into unalterable shape, is pushed back. The Wyrm would snuff the spirits of elemental fire, but it's the Weaver that brings the ways of modern life."

"Take a breath," Tom chuckled, but he shook his head in confusion. As did Ally and Verse. Only Tuck nodded in understanding.

Simon relaxed. If Tuck followed it, then he would explain it to the others not as familiar with Garou cosmology. It was actually very simple when broken down into English, or any human language, Simon supposed, but perhaps others without the aptitude or the "benefit" of metis birth would never fully comprehend such stories as the heart of the Garou culture. The stories were more appropriate, somehow more believable or real, in the language of the Garou, where subtle shadings could be used to avoid the rigorous exactness, the language demands of the Weaver, of humans.

"It doesn't feel right, Simon, but what you say sounds right. The Wyld is raw matter, the Weaver assembles the matter into patterns, and the Wyrm, once an indispensable player in Garou cosmology, destroys the excess of either. I'll think it through some more and let you all know what I come up with."

"Thinking and talking won't stop the Wyrm," Ally said hostilely. "Let's track the abominable spirit and destroy it."

Verse said, "Hard to do. Hard to find."

"Surely Sarah or Oliver could point the way," Tom suggested.

"Perhaps," said Tuck, "but they have important duties at the caern itself. We should be as independent as possible to end this threat. Besides, we need practice and knowledge. Both are gained best through trial and error. We can turn to our elders for guidance if we can't succeed on our own, but I think we can, and I think we should try."

Ally asked, "So, then, what's to be the next step?" She wanted to put Tuck on the spot.

But Tuck knew what he wanted. "We look for the book," he said. "Maybe it will have some clues as to what happens next."

Tuck didn't know if it was a wise decision to split the pack like this, but time might be of the essence, so it seemed a necessity. Still, with so many unexplained events, Tuck felt for the first time not completely safe in this hideaway of Little River.

This town and the area around it really seemed a part of America out of time. Tuck's hometown, a smallish town well south of Little River where the Steins discovered him about a year ago, lacked many of the amenities of cities like Chicago that seemed like a different world entirely, but Little River was truly diminutive.

It was the kind of semimythological municipality where crime is unknown, friendship is easily given, and the next generation is under no compulsion to leave. There was an old air-raid siren that still went off at seven every morning in time to make certain all the farmers were up and in their fields. There was a main street still called Main Street, and the center of town was where the county road crossed Main Street. It was here that the town's small collection of retail establishments did business.

Mr. Italy's, so recently overrun by the postgame party, was here. As was HandyMan, a family-owned and so-called hardware store. Actually, it was mostly a wholesale business that sold to the area farmers, but hammers, nails, other tools and such were available as well.

The Citizen's Bank was on the corner, and Tuck regarded it as he and Simon approached on foot. Its now familiar black-and-orange sign proudly proclaimed that it had been operating since 1954. All the savings accounts of the county were held in this bank. Oliver and Sarah had a sizable account here. Tuck recalled seeing a withdrawal ticket once that indicated the amount of money remaining in the savings account, and it was something over one hundred thousand. Something with six digits before the decimal, anyway. Tuck didn't make out the first digit.

Only a few other stores operated in Little River. The economy here was not so vast, Tuck supposed, to support many more. Only Lenny's, which wasn't really Lenny's any longer, was not in this small downtown area because when it was built some years ago, it was apparently considered imprudent to sell alcohol in the center of the town. Well, that wasn't entirely true. Tuck knew that a handful of businesses operated out of people's homes, but those didn't really count. That was a holdover of the old bartering days, days that Tuck admitted still went on here, so maybe he couldn't dismiss them.

And there was the Shell station down the county road, but that was on the other side of the county line, about eight miles away from Main Street, so that didn't count either. It was, however, the nearest chain store, so it was worthy of note. No one seemed to miss such businesses within the town. There was no McDonald's. No Nike shoes for sale. No place to buy lottery tickets. In fact, almost all the commercials that Tuck could barely pick up on the Steins' radio had no bearing on the residents of the town.

The other shops here were few. There was Ideal Home that sold mattresses, furniture, and some clothing.

Frank Putnam operated a small, nameless barber shop with two chairs. Frank's uncle—Tuck didn't know his name—had died a few years ago, so one of the chairs never saw any use because Frank said no one could replace his uncle. There wasn't really any reason for there to be two barbers anyway. Though since Frank also ran the post office from his barber shop, you sometimes had to wait to get your mail or buy a stamp until he finished a buzz that needed to be just so.

Patty's was a small grocery store still frequented by everyone near the town despite the recent scandal of only a month ago when Patty changed the name of the store from John's. John was her husband, whom she divorced and won the store from with the help of an out-of-town attorney. John sold the land his family had owned for four generations and left Little River.

Patty's stood on the left just past Citizen's Bank on the roughly north-south-running Main Street. Tuck and Simon would pass it on their way to their destination—the library. Tuck wondered if Patty would still operate the small ice cream parlor at the back of the store. It used to be open from May 1 until the end of the football season, and since the Huskies won last night, the season was not yet completed.

Tuck was burning with curiosity about the Severnson book, and that's why he and Simon were on their way to the library, but a brief detour was permissible. The other pack members were tracking down the campers. It would have been better, Tuck knew, to find the campers himself, since he had spoken with them the night before and he knew about the book, but Ally was intent on the need to have the book and might try harder than he would, so he sent her with Tom and Verse. Besides, Tuck felt for no good reason that there was a better chance of running into trouble in the woods, and while he was not hiding from the danger by taking the less dangerous assignment of walking to town, the Ahroun twins and the lupus were certainly more capable of handling confrontations than he and Simon.

"Simon," Tuck said, "let's stop briefly in Patty's for ice cream. All that talking this morning made my throat sore. It could use a little relief."

Simon said, "Sure."

There was not a lot of conversation during the walk to town. Tuck figured Simon was batting ideas and thoughts around in his own head. The events of the past day were very mysterious, and if anyone in the pack was going to crack the puzzle, then it would be he or Simon. A good reason for the two of them to go on this mission, Tuck thought.

Leadership was difficult. There was so much to consider. But that was the same old topic, and Tuck didn't have time for it again now.

He did have time for the ice cream, though, and pushed open the glass door at the storefront. Tuck was wearing the same clothing as this morning, though the flannel shirt was tucked in and covered by a goose-down-lined vest. It was later in the morning now, about ten o'clock, but the wind was still chilly. It would warm up later in the day.

Simon no longer wore his large robe. That wouldn't have been very appropriate for the library, so he'd slipped on a pair of khaki pants and a sweatshirt of Tom's. It wasn't enough to keep him warm, but metis were particularly adept at transforming only portions of their bodies, so everywhere under Simon's clothing Tuck was certain there was a layer of short fur.

Tuck went in first and immediately realized that the place had changed. The once dim lighting was brighter. The old handwritten price signs were replaced by printed signs with the names of food companies and pictures of their food packages on them. The same old shopping carts were lined up, but now there was also a pile of plastic baskets in a stand with the words QuickTrip Shopping written above them.

"Patty must have gotten some money from John too," Simon whispered. It sounded like he was going to make further suppositions, but Tuck caught a glimpse of Patty walking toward them and waved Simon to silence.

A man in coveralls followed Patty around the corner, though, and she chittered away at him, so there was little chance of her overhearing.

In fact, after just a moment of standing in the store, it became apparent that Patty was dealing with a number of different coveralled men. Tuck recognized one of them, Willford Stems, whose son played linebacker for the Huskies. Tuck walked toward him. Simon slipped off to make his own way around the store.

"Good morning, Coach Stems," Tuck greeted him. Willford Stems was kneeling on the floor amidst an array of tools more obscure than was available in HandyMan. At his back, against one of the grocery's sidewalls, leaned a number of pieces of wood. There were cuts of all different sizes.

Stems fidgeted with a pile of nails strewn on the floor before looking up. "Ye . . . oh, Tucker. What a sight. Congratulations, young man, on your great playing last night. You did some job on that over-rated pass defense of the Ducks."

Tuck smiled, "Thanks, Coach Stems. It's a team effort, though. I know Brad made several crucial plays. He pulled their big fullback down for a loss on that third-and-short play. He must have had four or five tackles."

"Four it was, Tucker. He should've knocked the ball loose on that third-down play, though."

"Whatever he did was just enough," Tuck laughed. He liked Willford Stems. The man had a pleasant manner, an easy laugh, and apparently felt no shame in revealing his passions. Tuck recalled meeting him before and wished he'd lived in Little River during earlier school years so he could have played for Stems, who coached the elementary school team.

That was in his spare autumn time. The rest of the day in that season, and presumably full-time the rest of the year, Willford Stems was a carpenter.

"There seems to be a lot of work going on here, Coach." Like every other person who's ever played sports, Tuck was in the habit of calling anyone who was, or who had ever been, a coach by that honorific.

"I think Mrs. Fr . . . uh, Ms. Yeager—her name's changed now, you know—has a mind to make a lot of changes," Stems said, whispering the buried remark so only Tuck could hear it.

"Just so she keeps the ice cream parlor, she can make all the changes she'd like." Tuck laughed again.

Stems smiled too, but then he said, "Good luck, because I think someone else is back there working on that parlor."

"Uh . . . thanks. Sorry to delay you from the work. Say hello to Brad."

"You bet. See you a week from now in Headway for the battle for the region."

Tuck nodded his head and shook Coach Stems's hand as a farewell. Tuck walked away gravely, though, because he suddenly had to wonder about the football game. He wasn't going to be able to play if this mess with the Wyrm wasn't cleared by then. It was one thing to play in a game locally even when he detected the Wyrm, but it was another entirely to travel one hundred miles to play a football game against the powerhouse of the state, and defending state champions, when he knew the Wyrm's influence was focusing on Little River and there was possible danger from other directions as well.

Also food for later thought, he decided, and he filed the issue away with that of leadership for some time when he had a spare moment for such rumination. Tuck picked up his step to join Simon at the ice cream counter.

And Tuck ran right into Melissa Frankel. She was standing just out of sight around a corner near the head of an aisle in front of the canned vegetables, a plastic shopping basket looped around her arm, and Tuck smacked directly into her. The basket slipped off and hit the floor as she threw her arms wide to catch herself from the imminent fall. A small collection of cans jumped out of the basket.

Tuck, though, reacted well and managed to both regain his balance and catch the falling girl. Barely. He was stooped over at the waist, and Melissa was limp in his arms a mere two or three feet above the floor. Tuck had no clue until then who it was he had barreled into. When he saw it was Melissa, he panicked and almost drop her.

"Don't knock me down again, Tuck," she laughed

as Tuck recovered from this second shock and helped Melissa regain her footing.

"Uh . . . sorry," Tuck muttered as he bent to hide his embarrassment and retrieve the cans he'd sent flying. When next he stood with about a half-dozen cans clutched between his arms and chest, Melissa was looking admiringly at him with the plastic basket outstretched. Tuck slowly dropped them in.

"I guess that's one problem with these new baskets," she said. "They spill easier than a big cart."

"Right," Tuck said, trying to salvage some sort of composure. A battle he knew was lost even if he hadn't just about bowled Melissa over.

She smile a soft smile that warmed Tuck's heart. "Don't worry about it, Tuck. There are things piled everywhere in here because of all the moving around and changes Patty is making. I'm sure I'm not the first person to be knocked over in a grocery store, even in conditions better than these adverse ones."

Tuck said, "I was just in a hurry and wasn't thinking."

"Well," Melissa grinned, "at least you caught me. For that, I owe you a kiss." Before Tuck's addled mind could filter the meaning of the words, Melissa's hands were locked behind his head and she leaned into him. His lips were hard, yet they yielded when Melissa pressed hers to his.

Then it was over.

So brief.

And Tuck was in more shock than a moment before. Melissa's grin was even wider, and one of her eyelids twinkled at Tuck.

Torn between so many conflicting emotions—duty and love topped the list at the moment—Tuck didn't quite know how to react. He closed his eyes and exhaled hard to clear his head and relax, mindless of how Melissa would interpret it.

"Like that, huh?" she asked.

Tuck opened his eyes. Melissa's beautiful smile was lavished upon him. He looked at her clearly again, realizing how gorgeous she was, and wondering how much his continually blossoming desire for her was coloring his impression of her, but suspecting that it didn't change it much.

He remembered seeing her the first day at his new school in Little River. A knot of girls were clogging the hallway, and Tuck was pushing his way through them, trying to ignore the thousands of questions they were asking, when he caught sight of her skirting the edge of the same group but going the other direction down the hallway. She'd glanced in his direction and turned away instantly. Tuck recalled having the impression that she'd seen him already and was simply being shy, an impression confirmed in the following weeks when he heard that she'd noticed him almost immediately and started asking questions.

That second of sight was freeze-framed in his mind's eye. Her shoulder-length black hair. Wide open, wondering, and intelligent eyes. Delicate face, with cheeks rounded from lots of smiling, that narrowed little chin that was the perfect partner for her button nose. She'd been wearing a tan turtleneck shirt partially covered by a green-and-gold vest and black pants.

He realized she was wearing the same vest now. He caught a glimpse of it beneath the multicolored windbreaker she wore with blue jeans. He wanted to say something, but thought better of it. Her hair looked different, though.

Completely missing her question through the haze of his daydream, he asked, "Did you do something to your hair?" It looked shorter and a bit curled at the ends, too.

"Yes," she said, flipping it with her free hand. "My mother cut it this morning before I came here. Like it?"

"Yes. It's very pretty."

"Thanks." She smiled.

"I was going to get some ice cream," he told her. "Would you like some too?"

A questioning look flashed on her face. "This early? I thought athletes were supposed to have good diets?"

"I usually eat well," Tuck insisted. "I just wanted another cone before Ms. . . . uh . . . Yeager closed the parlor for the year."

"Don't worry about that," Melissa said. "She's putting in some new freezers and will be serving ice cream and frozen yogurt year-round. I saw the machines while I was back looking at the cereal."

"Cereal? I didn't see . . ." Tuck was scanning the ground to find where the box had flown when he'd run into Melissa. He didn't see it.

"Oh, don't look. They were out of the kind I wanted. In fact, she's pretty much out of all her cereal."

"So, you don't want an ice cream?"

"Thanks, but not now, Tuck. I have some things I have to get here, then I have to check on a furniture order, then get home to make lunch for my sister."

"Okay," Tuck said, suddenly nervous again. How was he going to say good-bye? He dropped the thought from his mind, steeled himself, and leaned into Melissa. He kissed her full on the mouth, and she accommodated him before pulling away.

"Just think if you hadn't wandered off at the lake last night," she whispered mysteriously as she grabbed a can of corn and slipped around the corner and out of sight.

Tuck savored the taste of her on his lips for a moment, but then walked away to join Simon at the ice cream counter.

It was going to be a long walk through the woods to Lake Waganta for Tom, Ally, and Verse. Thankfully, it would be in wolf form, so it wouldn't take that long after all. They had the option of using the Steins' pickup truck, but Ally insisted they go on foot in case they could learn even more by seeing the forest. Besides, she convinced Tom—Verse didn't need any persuading—he and she needed practice in lupus form.

The decision suited Verse just fine. He was ready to stretch his legs on a lengthy run. The only difficulty would be on the other end, when they would need human form again in order to adequately communicate with the campers without completely frightening them. Fortunately, there was a solution—a second brown robe that was the mate to the one Passer often wore.

These robes belonged to the Steins, though they were now primarily used by the pack. They were talismans previously enchanted by the Ritual of Dedication. Verse believed the rite to be a simple ceremony, assuming you knew you were adept in such matters, but that was only if the object was dedicated to yourself only. Once the pack was assembled, Oliver performed additional ceremonies that attuned the robes to the entire Phoenix Pack.

Once dedicated, objects such as the robes—Verse was certain both Oliver and Sarah had one or two other items that operated in the same manner—

mutated in order to suit the new form the Garou chose. So from the human-shaped homid through glabro to the dreaded crinos, and on through hispo to lupus, the dedicated item will either shift to an appropriate form or magically blend physically into the very being of the Garou.

Such was the case with the robes. They remained robes when the wearer was either in homid or glabro forms, but once the transformation was made to crinos or beyond, the fabric of the robe became one with the shifting body and swept away in a sudden ripple to join the fur sprouting in waves across the body.

Ally, Tom, and Verse all walked about a quarter mile into the woods where they shed their clothing. Verse did this readily as nakedness held no social stigma to him, and Tom did it easily as well. Ally, even, showed little reluctance, though Verse thought she might, based on what he knew of humans from watching the black-and-white television Sarah sometimes turned on. Verse supposed this lack of embarrassment might be because the other two present were only her twin brother and a wolf.

Verse and Tom began their transformations while Ally slipped on the robe talisman in preparation for her own change.

As the lupus form was his natural form, Verse had little trouble slipping back into it. It was a completely delicious sensation. A combination of the satisfaction of returning home after a long journey and quenching a thirst too long unslaked.

Being able to change forms was an interesting ability and one with countless uses in a world so poised to crush and scatter the Garou, but the sensation of regaining his original form is what made Verse feel most natural of all. The Garou as a race worshipped Gaia, the Mother Goddess, she who is all things, who is the greatest of the Celestines and who knew great pain as the Wyrm rampaged out of control and destroyed and warped all the creations that were a part of her. The wind. Trees. Water. All the natural world and the counterparts of these that existed in another realm, the Umbra, with which Verse was largely unacquainted.

Verse certainly had great familiarity and almost by default great passion for nature, but the Umbra was a mystery to him. The Umbra was the spirit realm that lay just beyond but paralleled this one of matter. That Verse had been born beneath the gibbous moon did not help his understanding of the realm that he felt was more accessible for those born human anyway. Though the idea of the Umbra stank of the philosophic concepts of humans, Verse felt a deeper communion with it, and suspected his misgivings sprang at least in part from the manner in which the Steins first described it to him. Though they were mystics, they were still human and perhaps analyzed the spirit realm a bit too much.

A Garou born under a different Auspice, like the crescent-mooned Theurges or the half-moon Philodoxes, such as Simon and Tuck respectively, had a greater natural inclination to such matters. Seers such as Simon were the most adept in dealing with all things spiritual.

As far as Verse could tell, Auspices were faultless in what they said about an individual. He recognized and admitted all that the waxing of the moon toward full told of him. It said that he was a Moondancer, a Galliard whose duty it was to remind the others of the pack—or sept or tribe, depending on his status and conviction—of the beauty of that for which they fought. The wind, trees, and water. But more too. A respect for the past and the inherent appreciation of making a better future that respect for the past demanded.

Gaia extended love and appreciation for all life. It was this love that Verse tried to communicate in the songs he sang. His voice rang out to Gaia to remind her there were warriors fighting for her survival, and it rang out to the Garou who were the warriors to remind them of their charge.

It was widely believed among the Garou that Gaia's existence was threatened. The impending, and possibly inevitable, Apocalypse that the Garou at once attempted to fend off and prepare for would mark the end of her. And with her would go all creation. Everything that was real in the sense Verse understood would be gone. There would be no scents to be carried by the wind. No wind at all. And nowhere for it to blow if it had not gone too.

That is why his voice was so true that he earned the name Verse, even among the wolves, before he learned of his Garou heritage. His howl was always the loudest and longest. The one that did not crack or waver. And it was no wonder. He sang from the heart of Gaia to communicate her need.

The same energy he felt when he sang was what he felt he regained when returning to his natural lupus form.

So it was a great relief to see—more than that, feel and smell!—the fur across his entire body. He was an average-sized gray, or timber, wolf, so he stood about three feet high at his shoulders and ranged about four feet long. His fur was whiter than most other wolves from the climate in southern

Canada that was his home, but there was enough gray mixed with black and brown to mark him unmistakably as a timber wolf.

Still standing despite the rapidity and intensity of the change of form, Verse delighted most in his long neck, which instinctively craned skyward. He resisted the urge to howl, though, as he did not wish to draw attention to wolves when he was still so near the Stein home.

He also felt the tireless muscles of his legs knit together. The leg of the human might have more leverage and allow bipedal motion that freed the front limbs for manipulative efforts, but the wolf leg was a marvel too. On these, Verse knew, he could run for hours and at a swift pace. Long and fast enough to determinedly catch the most ephemeral prey.

He then turned his attention to Ally and Tom, who were still in the middle of their transformations. Twins by birth, their resemblance persisted even in wolf form. Their black hair and reddish skin also remained in the coloration of the timber wolves they now resembled. They were much larger than the average timber wolf, though, so they also loomed over Verse, who walked between them as their changes completed.

They were mostly a reddish brown with lots of gray and patches of black. They stood a good head over Verse and their jaws were bit shorter, but they looked stronger. Perhaps due to their Auspice, Verse reasoned. They were full-moon, Ahroun warriors. Their size and obvious power made their birthright evident as well.

They were twins, but Verse had no trouble noting which one was Ally. His senses perked in her direction. She seemed to regain her senses, though, and after also regaining her footing she initiated a swift pace eastward. They would have to skirt Little River to the north or south while maintaining the generally easterly direction in order to return to the area of Lake Waganta.

Also, although the two were twins, it seemed to Verse that Ally was by far more adroit in this form than Tom. In fact, she seemed to him the more brazen of the two, period. Perhaps Tom was the runt of what was a rare human litter. This didn't affect Verse's opinion of Tom one bit. The boy had a good spirit, and certainly a fighting, competitive spirit, and was probably better balanced than his sister.

Verse still worried over the trouble Ally might cause in the pack. She was bound to challenge Tuck's leadership another time, and perhaps another time soon considering the coming stress and danger. Verse would follow either of them, but he doubted he could put his trust as much in Ally in times other than those of war. Such times might be coming, but the more levelheaded Tuck still had Verse's vote.

Voting didn't count for much among the Garou, at least in situations like this. The Litany, the ancient code of ethics, rule, and law the Garou were supposed to honor, did count. The Litany sounded awfully complicated, and Verse knew only a few portions of it. Philodoxes like Tuck apparently feel compelled to know it backwards and forwards, because the young pack leader was trying to learn more than the few basic tenets that the Steins insisted be observed.

The Litany was a simple and straightforward code. Combat the Wyrm wherever it is found, don't eat the flesh of humans, and submit to those of a higher station were some of the basics, but only the basics for some tribes that apparently did such things as sing the Litany as a song that lasted for hours. Verse couldn't imagine most Garou, or Garou culture in general, tolerating such a thing too amicably.

One of the codes of the Litany as presented and upheld by the Steins stated that the leader of the pack could be challenged at any time during peace but was beyond challenge during a time of war. One problem was where exactly the line between peace and war was drawn. Had that line already been crossed now that the enemy had been noted, or only when the enemy and its plans were identified? Or met?

Also, there was an unspoken subclause to this portion of the Litany that claimed a leader could be challenged during a time of war if there was one more fit to lead in war.

On the march, Ally continued to set the pace, but she motioned Verse into the lead. For all her gumption in this form and natural affinity for it, Ally was probably still unfamiliar with the idea of leading herself by her senses alone. Verse knew that humans of modern times were too used to being lead by the roads they drove. Though the concrete and tar paths might wander and turn in awkward and wasteful ways, if followed they would eventually deliver the humans traveling them to the destinations of choice. The complete freedom to go in any direction was a little much for most humans, Ally included.

So Verse hastened his pace long enough to gain the lead before settling back into the gait Ally set when she first jumped into motion. The trip wouldn't take long now.

———

All the odors of the earth, and of mankind, assaulted Ally's nose.

The long run to Lake Waganta concluded more quickly than Ally thought would be possible, even when considering that she was running with another Ahroun and a Garou natural to the lupus form. She and Tom now scuttled about the vicinity in search of the scent of the campers. Of course, Verse knew right where they could pick up the trail, but Ally asked him not to interfere so she and Tom could practice using their new senses.

The search for the scent became a bit of a contest between the two Ahroun, each racing madly about with nose hovering just over the surface of the ground. Ally wished she at least had an idea in her mind of what the odor would be like so she might realize when she smelled it. What would give the odor away? There were plenty of noteworthy scents, but none that she could imagine being that of anyone other than one of the reveling students of Little River High.

Ally smelled the musky odor of the earth. The penetratingly clean wash of the lake. The tang of the forest and its trees was largely lost on her after miles of running, so it neither hindered nor entranced her.

Neither did she heed a whole host of scents beyond her normal range of detection. She smelled decay in the heart of a tree that still seemed to live. She smelled the crisscrossing paths and spoor of what she thought must be rabbits and squirrels. She also smelled the remanents of last night's man-children. The alcohol. Sex. And drugs. For a moment she thought that was the giveaway scent of the campers, since it was a new scent, from wolf form at least, to Ally. Intellectually she knew that drugs pervaded the United States and its grade and high schools, but somehow she never imagined anyone in Little River submitting to their enticements. Small-minded of her, she supposed. The use of the marijuana was seemingly limited to a small handful of students, since the pungent, sweet-smoky odor of the weed was limited to a small area.

Then she caught it. A whiff of a combination of odors that said to Ally that these must be the tracks of the campers. It was insect spray. Certainly none of her classmates would be so forward-thinking as to actually have brought such a thing to the game last night with hopes of its being of use hours later at a victory celebration that probably no one really expected anyway.

She barked a short series of words to Tom and Verse. "I have it. Let's go." She turned away from them both to face the direction the tracks led, went slowly to make sure she had the scent firmly set in her mind, and then she accelerated to a run, carefully aware of any hint that the scent was becoming too fresh. She didn't want to startle the campers.

It was difficult to determine how fresh the scent actually was. After all, Ally could smell it so much more deeply than even the most fragrant odor tickling her human nose. She sought for more discrimination in her discernment, and concluded the scent was from the previous night because it was somehow covered by the hint of the morning's dew and the touch of midday's sunlight.

Such subtleties were for others, though, like Tuck, who had the inclination to ponder them. Ally just wanted to roll. But she came to a sudden stop when she smelled the blood. Verse and Tom came to a stop at her flanks. Glancing at them, she knew from Verse's chagrined expression that he smelled it too. Tom was confused for a moment, but Ally watched as his nose went to work, working hard to glean the odors from the wind. His nose wrinkled and he winced.

Verse let out a low whimper.

Ally went to her other senses. She heard nothing but the wind and the scampering of a squirrel. Saw nothing but the forest. So she moved in.

After a few strides when the clearing at the side of the trail became visible, Ally worried, for she knew the blood she smelled was that of the campers.

Verse hung back at the edge of the small clearing, but Tom advanced with her to the place where the bodies were buried. They were not covered well, so a moment of quick digging revealed enough mutilated flesh and torn clothing for Ally to get a mouthful of waterproof jacket and tug the woman's body free.

It was headless.

Ally felt no cruelty or shame in grinning. This was the kind of enemy she wanted to face. The kind of malevolent killer that would do this. No flesh, except for the incidental amounts pulled free at the sites of attack, was eaten. This kill satiated needs other than hunger. It was the kind of irrational monster that Tuck would be unable to predict. Only another warrior, who thought with muscle as well as mind, would be capable of handling the monster. Ally reasoned that only she was capable.

She didn't realize for several moments, though—and then only after she watched Verse puzzlingly sniff around—that there was no scent other than the remains of the campers. There was no hint of the killer.

Ally shivered. But it passed. Calmly, she rooted through the pile of dirt and gore and tugged free all the bags and backpacks. The book would be inside one of them.

Verse maintained a good distance, but Tom came forward and helped Ally sort through the blood-drenched belongings.


"It's a good thing you were able to find the book, though I obviously wish the conditions were different, because the book wasn't in the library, of course," said Tuck. The entire pack was sitting in the cozy den in the Steins' home. It was an odd-shaped room wedged on its sides by rooms and stairs that received the most consideration when the house was built. Outlandishly designed and outfitted by the Steins, the room had every sort of decoration: old English-cavalry swords from the Napoleonic era; a large Mexican-woven rug with the emblem of an eagle; Caribbean idols suspended from the ceiling; and paintings by Rousseau, Rembrandt, and Parish among many other quirky items.

The group had convened here a short time before Tuck and Simon returned. The others, with their bloody cargo, arrived earlier and were reading portions of *Wandering the Northern Midwest* when the two entered.

Tuck and Simon took the news of the mutilated campers with long, shocked faces. Both also refused to handle the bloodstained book and wondered at Ally, who flipped through it without regard for the red smudges she spread across its pages and her fingers. Tuck sensed a slight change in Ally, too. He suspected this was the first time she saw the results of the kind of destructive power she too could unleash. The first time she saw dead people, even. The smell of blood and the sight of the carnage might have flipped a switch hard-coded by instinct in her brain.

That was moments ago, and Tuck was informing the others about what they found on the depressing trip to Little River. He continued, "When we asked about the book, Ms. McMurtry looked in something called *Books in Print,* but she didn't find it or even any other listing for the author Severnson."

Ally asked, "What about future books? Even if the book isn't supposed to exist, it might be scheduled to exist sometime soon."

"No," said Tuck, "Ms. McMurtry also has listings of upcoming books for the next several months and it wasn't anywhere to be seen."

Tom said, "Darn, we'd hoped you'd found something at the library, because there's not much in the book by way of clues. We figured the only leads we might have would be from when the book was published or something."

Simon said, "The only possibility is to follow up with the author. Perhaps we can find out where she lives or what she's writing now?"

"That might take a long time," Tuck said. "We'd probably have to call or write the publisher, and if the book's not scheduled they might not even know anything about her either."

Ally said, "I think we should just wait to see what happens next and then act. Act quickly!"

Then, trying again to catch Tuck without a plan, Ally turned to the pack leader and posed, "So, what now?"

Tuck gave a small shrug of his shoulders and took a sip of soda before answering. "It's time for a moot," he said. "It's time to reattune ourselves to the land."

# CONVERSATION

"What do you make of this odd book Tuck discussed?"

"It's hard to know with such sparse information."

"Well, go out on a limb for once, weasel. You might consider this to be a time in the course of all our plans that will not allow for careful selecting, intricate plotting, and long, lazy hours of considering."

"Finally a time more to your personal liking, I take it."

"Yes."

"Immediate results, eh? It's your Galliard nature, dearest. Passion shall win the day, and as passion can be fleeting the day must be won quickly."

"A bit unfair and you know it. Not all passion is fleeting. Take ours for each other, or Gaia's for all creation. Is that passion not the point of our entire battle, our struggle against the Apocalypse?"

"But passion must be tempered with reason and forethought. Passion can provide the impulse to move, but care is required for the movement to be best and appropriate."

"Is it? Is it not best to be truest to your nature and act as your spirit calls upon you to do so?"

"We do not have time for such debates today, dearest. We have the book, and the Wyrm, to consider."

"More considering? You're changing the subject only because I'm winning."

"A weak moment for me, Sarah. I'm concerned about this recent development."

"Yes."

"Can one man be worth what may be wrought upon our entire region?"

"Don't question our decisions, Oliver. This is the reassurance you should have from acting with forethought. Haven't we already weighed all these possibilities? Isn't that how you allay my fears? Passion can know sudden moments of terror because plans made under their influence can be faulty. Trust our wisdom, though, and don't let Harano grab you too."

"You're arguing against yourself now."

"I thought we were done debating."

"We are."

"So stop keeping score. Alexander is worth our efforts. You know that. Gaia is but one thing, and we are willing to risk everything for her. Is not one Garou, especially one who has done so much, worth a risk as well? What's the point of fighting if it's not to provide peace for Garou like him?"

"Harano is a difficult thing."

"Yes."

# THE MOOT

"I know your moots are usually uncomplicated affairs," Tuck said to Oliver and Sarah, "but I believe the Caern at Little Rock is threatened by powerful forces of the Wyrm." He then extended his attention and addressed his pack as well as the pair of elders. "Such danger calls for a potent renewal of our energy and our dedication to the land here."

Tuck continued his speech, trying to sound inspirational. "We must renew our mark here, and make certain the Wyrm knows the Garou still protect their land and will not roll over, tail between our legs, no matter the enormity of the threat posed."

Tuck rolled on, thinking of nothing but the unrehearsed words flowing easily from his soul. "There have already been deaths. Perhaps because the campers carried words that warned us of the Wyrm's mission, but surely because they were caught behind the lines of war, these two innocents became casualties. But even before halting death, our foremost mission is to preserve life.

"We do battle as much to defeat the Wyrm as we fight to preserve Gaia. Nothing must stand in the way of that goal. The Wyrm, Weaver, or even Wyld itself may have to bow to the safeguarding of this most holy intellect.

"Oliver-rhya, will you honor this pack, the Phoenix Pack, the sons and daughters of your sept, the Sept of Little Rock, by leading us in a moment of silence to help us see our mission?"

The seven Garou were assembled in a crescent arcing around one side of Little Rock, the center of the caern guarded so zealously by Oliver and Sarah for many years. They were all in the forms of their birth. The two elders, Tuck, Tom, and Ally all held homid form. Passer was the only crinos and Verse the lone lupus. They all wore the same ceremonial colors. Verse alone was not dressed in robes of the dark blue of twilight, the time when stars first become visible to the naked eye in countless numbers, as were the others, but he wore a harness of the flimsy cloth that looped his neck and middle and was connected by lengths along his spine and the center of his chest.

Little Rock itself was a barren boulder of granite. It was a boulder that stood higher than even Tuck's or Tom's heads, so Verse still did not understand how it could be called Little Rock, and he always assumed it was a joke related to the name of the town. Tom once tried to assure Verse that there were larger stones of the same sort, including one called Stone Mountain that stood far to the south, so comparatively it was small. Compared to a mountain, Little Rock was small, Verse conceded, but it was the largest piece of lifeless rock he had ever seen.

Lifeless until exposed in the Umbrascape. In the Umbra, Little Rock literally seethed with creation and life taking shape. The caern was not very power-ful, and was even a dead-end route among the moonbridges that arced in every direction across the globe of Earth and served as a means of instanta-neous travel from one point to another, but it was still a source of the Wyld, so it oozed the potential to create. Also, the Stargazers had dedicated the caern to the totem of their tribe, Chimera. Called the Ever-Changing, Chimera only contributed to the dynamic nature of the life on the rock.

Vines sprouted and twisted and writhed across the surface. They flowered and seeded the stone so more would spontaneously generate, or they died away, wrinkling and browning as quickly as they achieved the lush green of maturity.

Tom, like Verse, was always mesmerized by this display. The cycle of life and death represented on the face of the stone was hardly complicated to grasp, but it was poignant, and that ephemeral importance made it worthy of contemplation.

There was only one feature of the vines that stood out to Ally, and that was how the tips seemed to poke her in the face because they grew against the grain of the march around the granite that allowed unthinking egress in the Umbra. It was a means of entrance available only to Garou. Those who com-pleted three counterclockwise circles around the perimeter of the stone and ended this cycle facing the largest piece of reflective quartz embedded in the granite shifted into the Umbra at that moment.

The shift into the Umbra this evening brought sur-prises for the only Theurge in the sept, Passer. He was still watching the vines intently, but their growth didn't seem as uncontrolled and unimaginably bizarre as they normally did. Maybe he was looking too hard for hidden meanings, or perhaps his brain was finding pattern where there was none because of the order he'd discerned in the arrangement of the fire elementals the evening before, but some of the vines seemed to grow in repeating patterns. As he watched for them again he decided they must have been an illusion.

Tuck and Sarah sat with their eyes closed, struggling for answers to questions they couldn't quite put into words.

Oliver drew his gaze back down from the stars above and said, "Praise Gaia," and unbeknownst to the assembled Garou, the moment of silence they did not perceive as ever beginning came to an end. "And praise our Lady of Mirrors, Chimera, who shows us many forms and many ways and gives us many clues, but who leaves it to the wisdom of her children to divine the true path."

Looking upward at the heavens as he spoke, Oliver seemed to the Phoenix Pack the embodiment of Chimera's wisdom. Darkly complected, Oliver was a man of average height. His face had the quality of tuning into that which absorbed his attention. His brown eyes focused slowly as if taking in the details, and his nostrils flared and his lips flattened when he truly began to observe. He stood composed and with purpose, but seemed at the same time very relaxed. It was the searching posture common not only to Stargazers but to masters of martial arts. Oliver was both, for he pursued the art of Kailindo.

He continued. "We seek your guidance, Chimera, in untangling the enigmas before us as we sit beneath the stars. But we ask that you first hear our voices." He paused, then looked to Verse. "Master of the Howl, please begin."

So Verse, the Master of the Howl of the Caern at Little Rock, began the Moot Rite. His mouth open and his nose stretched to the Umbral sky, Verse sang. At first, the sound was soft, less than a whisper, and seemed to come just from Verse's lips. Then the song grew suddenly stronger and fuller as the source moved further down the wolf's throat. When Verse reached the pitch and volume he desired, his voice held without wavering. It was one continuous note to underpin the others that would join it.

Suddenly, two voices joined. In unison, the twin voices of Ally and Tom rang out. They seemed to first fold together with complementing tones and notes before rushing skyward to merge with Verse's song, though theirs was weaker coming from human lungs. Because Ally and Tom so completely harmonized each other, the song still largely consisted of one solid tone.

Sarah was next. Her voice was lovely, and even though human lungs were her source too, it was powerful. Her song ranged up and down the scales in a random but strikingly lyrical way. Sarah was a slim, aging woman who nevertheless had an ageless quality about her. The kind of woman, it seemed to the members of the pack, who was made to be a mother because of her patience and a wisdom that was accessible and loving.

Next was Simon. His song was truly like the howl of a wolf. His voice stuttered in short gasps before ringing for a longer time. His was the deepest voice, though, as it came from the ranging, if crippled, body of a crinos Garou.

Tuck was the last of the Phoenix pack to join. He was not a very talented singer and had no real force to his howl. His eyes were clenched tightly shut, and he as much yelled skyward as he sang or howled.

The cry gave a passionate undertone to the whole of the sept's song.

The song carried on thus for a moment. Verse still held the same long breath and the same true note. The others had the advantage of replenishing their oxygen with a grasp before continuing their songs again. As Master of the Howl, at least the Master of the Howl of the Caern at Little Rock, Verse was both the beginning and end of the Moot Rite. He had to hold until all the voices of the sept were one.

And he didn't know why Oliver was holding back. What was the elder Garou trying to communicate by being so long joining? Verse worried that he was doing something wrong.

Tuck, too, worried and cast a furtive glance at Oliver.

Then Oliver joined. He cupped his hands to his mouth and released his howl. It was the same hollow and unearthly cry he always gave. With a hint of melancholy, but also, somehow, with a touch of hope. It was the hope that cleared his throat when Verse's voice gave out, and by the magic of the Moot Rite all voices were silenced when the Master's exhausted.

Everyone was breathing heavily and attempting to catch their breaths, but Oliver, who exerted less than the others, spoke. "The power of the caern has been replenished. Our homage to the Ever-Changing is complete. Usually we have business to discuss now, or Sarah, Verse, or Passer have a tale to share, but there has been much talking of late. So much talking that I suspect I am the only one not bored by it. So while you are still gasping, prepare to run the night and not recover your breath until morning."

He paused, then said, "Begin your Revel, Phoenix Pack. Run the land as wolves, and spread your spoor to mark it as our own."

Already in crinos form, Passer shot from the caern, and hence from the Umbra near Little Rock, to the realm of matter surrounding it. He was the physically weakest member of the pack, and so felt no shame in hurrying away as the others shifted form. There was no question that he would be overtaken in the nightlong run, but he intended to delay that moment as long as possible. And by means fair or foul.

At least as long as he could clearly think to even make plans. Revels, meant to mark the territory of the Garou and frighten away interlopers, were notoriously ferocious affairs. Garou sometimes lost their heads a bit, and the rampage became a bit more severe than perhaps would be wise.

He wanted to be out of earshot by the time the first of the others emerged. It would probably be Verse, as the change from lupus to crinos seemed to involve less than the change from homid to crinos. But Ally and Tom would be champing at the bit to complete the change and might be able to force theirs faster. Tuck, Passer figured, could well be the last one out, but he wondered if Tuck might not last the longest. He was an athlete, after all, even if he wasn't Ahroun. And he would probably keep his head longer than either of the full-moons, and that might help in the end.

Passer crashed through the forest. He tried to maneuver around the obstacles, at least, so he didn't clear too great a space to make the route more traversible for those who followed. The forest was thick here, though, but that's why he choose this direction. Running alone, without jostling for position with others who might be beside and around him, Passer could concentrate more on the terrain.

The going would be harder for a small group of four battling for position. He hoped it would help maintain his lead longer.

The pack had decided before the moot that the Revel would be a chase. Those behind must follow the path of the leader. The one in front had the responsibility of choosing a route, which needed to crisscross the county in every conceivable direction. The winner would be the one in front at dawn, or more likely, the one still running at dawn, or most likely, the one who was ahead last, as they would probably all collapse prior to sunrise.

Normally, any of them could run all night, and Simon had considered trying to pace himself to win by dint of sheer perseverance, but there was no way, he knew, to keep the rage away. A Revel was more a measure of determination and will than endurance.

Passer cursed, because he heard the first bark of pursuit sooner than he'd hoped. It was Verse, which Passer realized worked in his own disfavor, as Verse would be better able to sniff his path out immediately and give chase sooner. The others, less experienced with their noses, would be able to follow the sound of Verse, who would not be so far ahead as to be out of earshot. At least, thought Passer with a trace of pride, I'll be in the lead for a time. Some of the others may not be able to make that claim.

He ran hard.

In the battling crinos form Verse looked powerful. His gray, black, and brown pelt was a bit more matted than a wolf's and was thicker. In some of the areas he found that fur remained, even when he was in homid form.

Verse was surprised at the route Passer chose, but he crashed into the thick forest without pause. He was at a slight disadvantage in this race because it was a two-legged one. The first few obstacles he leapt did prove to be a bit of a problem. He shifted his weight a little inappropriately and almost fell forward onto his face. But he stumbled on and regained his balance after a few additional steps.

Verse felt he had the advantage of woodland familiarity. He knew how the land would rise and fall, where the ground might be damp and slick because of the kinds of plants that grew, and where to step higher and surer because some trees tended to have above-ground roots. The one outdoor advantage he did not have was familiarity with the region. Fortunately, no one in real contention for the race possessed that either, because only Passer did. That would make the beginning of the race difficult and frustrating, though, as he and the others raced to overtake the metis.

A growl sounded behind him from many paces back at the spot where he returned to the realm of matter. Another Garou was coming. From the sound of it, Tom was currently running third, and he seemed to be moving quickly.

A thunderous howl resounded from Little Rock.

Verse tried not to concentrate on the Ahroun and instead stayed focused on winning the front position from Passer. The course Passer was taking struck dead eastward, a good ploy because the nearly full moon was then behind the runners and threw shadows in front of them, making safe footing more difficult, which of course made it more so for Verse most of all.

So Verse needed to be tricky too. He also needed to gain time on those following him. The Galliard wanted to bait the Ahroun by throwing him off the track a bit, by veering from the path he knew Passer had taken and looking for a means to double back, but such was not how the Revel was to be run. It was purely a run. Trickery, evidently, was a possibility only for the one who led.

Even more reason to run harder and gain the lead from Simon while he was still out of the sight of the others.

Very audible farther behind him, Verse heard the snarl of a wild bitch—Ally. She was the one to beat. She was the one Verse needed to fend off to attain the lead spot.

Verse ran hard.


When Tom burst into the forest he knew that Verse was only a few moments ahead of him. Heedless of the brush and tree limbs, Tom charged at a furious pace. He knew he was clearing a path for his twin sister to follow, but this was a Revel, and worrying about that was thinking too much. Even as his short fur snagged on the brush and he smacked his shoulders into limbs and even trunks, Tom felt his thoughts slipping away.

He let out a great howl. He felt prehistoric. The power of the crinos form surged through him and carried him closer.

A wild snarl sounded close behind him, though, and he knew Ally was charging hard. She was quick, and years of soccer helped her build incredible endurance.

Then there was a long, unmelodic howl. Tuck. But silence followed, and Tom knew when he listened so closely that he should be able to hear the crashing of the woods as Tuck took up the chase. Passer was too far away, but Tom could hear both

Verse, distantly, and Ally. The confidence of pausing unnerved Tom a bit.

He ran faster.

Leap the fallen tree.

Sprint the clearing.

Scale a small cliff of stones.

Splash through the wide stream.

All while keeping the Garou ahead and behind him in his senses. He didn't hear himself growl and howl, but he knew it was his own voice echoing through the woodlands. Blood streaked his coat, but the wounds were inconsequential. They would be healed instantly, and even greater wounds could and would have been ignored.

He smelled the one running ahead of him.

After a time, the Ahroun realized there were two Garou running furiously in front of him, even as he sensed the one pursuing him was closer than ever.

Just then the Ahroun smelled a large, open field. His prey were near the boundary of the bawn, the area under his protection, and were finally forced by virtue of geography to abandon the forests for a time.

The enormously muscled legs of the Ahroun flexed and prepared to stretch in a hard sprint.


After his single howl and the eventual clatter of wood and brush that signaled Tuck, Ally did not hear Tuck behind her. Well into the Revel when her rational mind began to play tricks on her and she forgot she could not hear him, she panicked and thought she had perhaps been overtaken and was running last. But he had not passed her. She was relatively sure of that.

Victory was the only thing that rang in Ally's mind. No one behind her would catch her. She just had to overtake the weaklings running ahead of her. The path was not hard. The pace not severe. She ran with a wild ferocity and irrepressible determination.

She smelled the open field as well, and she knew everything could change in the course of that space. All five Garou had an opportunity to claim the lead by the time the forests came again two miles north. Ally, though, knew that only she belonged in the lead.

When she burst from the woods and saw three others sprinting across the open space, a predatory instinct leapt strongly to her mind. Her long legs, sturdily muscled from organized athletics, found not just one but two extra gears of speed, and Ally shot across the landscape in a blur.

Ahead she saw that Verse now ran in the lead. Simon was second but was traveling far more slowly than Tom, who was gaining rapidly. Verse veered to the left to skirt a farmhouse. As Tom caught and overtook Simon, who now seemed to struggle through the land rather than glide over it as Ally sensed the others did, Ally realized that Verse's run was designed to take them right by the farmhouse.

Simon glanced over his shoulder at her, and with a look he challenged her to the farmhouse. He sought a little victory, but she must have all those for herself. Ally dug in, searching deeper for speed, but found none. She shrieked insanely and managed only to maintain her phenomenal speed.

Neither of them faltered, but it was Simon who had needed to find something more. Ally gained on him at a rate that would win her the farmhouse. At the edge of the chicken coop, with Tom running fifty yards ahead and Verse still leading one hundred yards away, already past the globes of illumination created by the farmhouse lights, Ally overtook

Simon. At the same time, a middle-aged but healthy-looking man and his dog stepped from the farm-house onto the front porch.

Ally leapt into the air as she neared him, and she saw fear bubble out of his mouth as a vomitous gruel. The Delirium took the man and he collapsed, but the dog dashed at Ally and collided with her upon landing. The dog yowled, pummeled by a kick of those mighty Garou legs, but Ally still fell back into fourth when Simon hobbled by her.

She got up and ran hard again.


Tuck wondered if he even had a chance to win the Revel. The fire of the competitor burned in him, but he knew his position was weak. If he pushed himself hard and by dint of sheer will could catch the next runner, it would be Ally, who would probably cause them both to burn out because the race would become a nonstop sprint.

Since Ally was the only one he really preferred not to win, simply so it would not give her any new ideas about challenging for pack leader, he actually entertained this idea for a moment. But this Revel was not about winning, though Tuck was certain that even he would fall victim to the rage of the chase before the night was over and yearn only for a fleeting victory. The point was to renew the land. For the Garou to spread their presence across it.

So even when Tuck began to run he held back. He wanted to see what the Revel stirred in the country-side. He knew Oliver and Sarah were doing this, and that's why they were not participating in the Revel, but Tuck needed it as rationalization for why his heart might appear to not be in the Revel. Why he didn't froth nacreous spittle in a mad dash to win. He would honor Gaia in his own way, by delighting in the landscape he passed. Taking time to observe it, he made it more his own, for if he remained pack leader it would one day be his, and by becoming closer to it he came closer to Her.

And it would also give him his best chance of winning the Revel. From the rear he would not be as prone to be caught up in the madness of the run. He could strike a solid pace that would allow him to win.

He ran for an hour. A white knight in the darkness. Tuck's pure white fur was imposing proof of his lineage—Silver Fang, the tribe that once ruled, and claimed they still did, the Garou.

A path plain to his crinos sense was torn through the forest. Tuck suspected an adept human tracker could follow the course as well, although he or she would have no clue as to what had passed. Four werewolves.

Eventually, Tuck emerged from the forest on the south edge of the Daley farm. It was a dilapidated old place, but the farmer and his family still worked the field hard. When it became obvious that the path of the Revel carried by the farmhouse itself, Tuck smiled.

After that, regardless of attempts to slow himself, Tuck found that he was running harder. An instinct driving him to catch the others. He knew what it was, but had to heed it.

When he came upon Passer an hour later, Tuck was urged even more to bolt. Passer was on the ground, breathing hard and alternately whimpering and howling as he tore at the long grass of the ground with his good left hand. Tuck ran past the Garou and was a distance away before he realized Passer had risen after their crossing and was making chase again. Passer began to run hard, and Tuck warned him off with a yell, but the metis Garou kept coming. Refusing to forfeit his position, Tuck ran.

Three hours later, or one hour after Passer collapsed a final time for the night—he'd fallen and risen almost a dozen times in trying to keep pace with Tuck—Tuck dashed upon Tom and Verse. Both on the ground, completely, utterly exhausted, but still crawling to be or stay ahead of the other. Tuck examined them with a flicker of a thought as he tromped by. For that instant he could see their souls and they were refreshed, though they were both spiritually, mentally, and physically drained.

About fifty paces beyond them he crossed Waganta Brook, a wide, relatively fast-running stream that connected to the lake. Tuck felt that whichever of those Garou managed to cross it would claim victory in their now very personal contest.

Only Ally was ahead of him now.

By the time he caught the Ahroun, Tuck had been running for almost the entire night. The energy he'd expended was great, and surely he spent as much energy resisting the Revel so he could experience it by not being lost in it as he had spent in the run itself.

Ally was shuffling through the forest in the northwestern portion of the county. To Tuck it seemed she felt as bad as he, since it looked as though the entire weight of her body was carried by a few muscles—her calves, as opposed to his thighs—that refused to give out. That made his steps long and jerky and her short and sliding.

As soon as he saw her, her nose raised into the air and she breathed his scent in. So tired was she that she stopped moving forward during the time of this great inhalation. Her head turned and her eyes met

Tuck's. He could feel a great hatred wash through her as she saw him, whom she might mistake for a ghost, or demonic specter, or a foe, her most equal opponent she'd thought defeated. Tuck was ruefully glad for the chance to teach her again never to count an obstacle overcome.

She had no more fight left in her, though. Tuck saw that as she mounted an effort to draw on a last vestige of strength, to crush Tuck with one final dash. He would not have been capable of matching her effort, but the effort alone of trying to summon that strength tapped her.

She collapsed.

Her only movement as Tuck plodded nearer was that of one barely peeking eyeball. Ally's lid was slit open and she watched as Tuck prepared to pass her.

Strangely, though, he decided not to. She had run hard. She ran the Revel as it should be run. Tuck found he had to give her that credit. So when he neared her he dropped clumsily to the ground and rolled to her side.

Ally won by inches. Her eyelid drooped shut.


The beauty of the region was not lost on Sower of Thunder, but for him it was less an aesthetic joy than a perplexing riddle. He wondered how the region could seem so unscarred by the consumption of the Wyrm, yet harbor those so obviously consumed with the task of spreading its decay and disease.

Thunder was nearly finished with his reconnaissance of the wilderness around the county's only community and was nearly ready to begin his onslaught against the Wyrm-spawn themselves. The only remaining task was to enter the town itself and reconnoiter it too. As much as Thunder despised assuming any form other than the crinos, he recognized the necessity of completely charting the region. Since the Wyrm-spawn were likely to seek refuge within the city among the weak humans once Thunder overpowered them and forced them from the woods, he needed to gain familiarity with it for his inevitable assault.

The day had been a long one, though, and he needed to adjust to the human schedule of activity in the daylight hours that his enemy likely held, so it was at this time when he felt ready, physically and strategically, for sleep that he heard the howls.

A wolf howl could carry a great distance, and Thunder heard a number of mingled voices mocking the dead wolves he'd found so recently. Oh, yes, he could hear the mocking disregard in the reverberating tones. Perhaps the song they sang was even another celebration of the evil they'd committed.

Thunder was tempted to attack at that very moment, but he knew it was unwise. However, he began to move in the direction of the howls, to the southeast, just in case he eventually opted to attack anyway. Thunder would always rather err on the side of lack of caution. That is why he was such a great warrior. That is why he was called an elemental force. Ever unpredictable.

Moments later, when the Revel began—and Thunder knew that's what it was from the cries that rang out—he knew he was missing an excellent opportunity to attack the Wyrm-whelps while they were weak. And what a joy it would have been to destroy them in the midst of a ceremony in which they rededicated themselves to the worship of their god, the Wyrm!

But it was not to be. Thunder turned and hurried to the northwest, away from the Revel and deeper into the portion of the county he most recently explored. He dared not continue his approach lest he be caught in the storm of rage as well and inadvertently join the wild run and contribute his energies to those the other Garou were building.

There was no telling what the mad run and the insane song of those Garou might do to him. He needed to wait for a better time. He knew that time would come. That pack was young and inexperienced, so therefore careless.

# CONVERSATION

"What did the land tell you as the Revel was run?"

"It told me it was in pain."

"It did? Oh, Oliver, what is happening to it?"

"The same thing that is happening to the world—it is changing too quickly."

"But things are supposed to change. Isn't that part of the Triat that concerns the Wyld, the only whole and untainted member left?"

"Change is not the Wyld. The Wyld is purely creation. Options are good, but the Wyld too must be maintained. It's because the Wyrm has driven the Weaver mad that this change I speak of is bad. The Weaver is working so frantically that it's trying to include every bit of creation spawned by the Wyld. And that's not the only failing of the Triat, though alone it would cause harm. Whereas the Wyrm might ordinarily cleanse the Weaver by weeding out the creations ill-advisedly incorporated, it is degenerating the entire process further. It is hastening the collapse of this already overburdened system."

"And this is what we take to be the ignorance of a mankind that seems to create and utilize before he understands?"

"Precisely."

"Then what does that have to do with Little River and the threat here?"

"The poison that haunts the world is about to assault our sacred corner of the earth."

"The information in the book that Tuck mentioned?"

"Yes."

"Is this an attack against Alexander, or is it the natural . . . well, unnaturally natural course of things?"

"That's hard to say, but I suppose it is the result of the Wyrm driving its message home. Alexander must be kept off balance for the Wyrm to win this psychological battle. To confuse Alexander, and remove him from the Garou for a time, is not enough. By thoroughly destroying Alexander's faith in himself, the Wyrm is achieving the symbolic victory of all Garou doubting their mission. It may seem impossible, but such a victory, even if unnoticed, will have profound effects on the psyche of our people. Something will tug at the back of their minds. Not only will Alexander reveal no more truths, but by losing he will conceal ideals that give us all hope."

"I understand how the symbolic can be true. I understand how a simple gesture from me, though in itself meaning little, can convey a whole range of feelings and emotions to you. It's like body language, such a mystery to humans, so natural to wolves, but integral to the language of the Garou— much of the meaning communicated is not consciously noted by the observer."

"Exactly."

"So what will happen to Little River?"

"Just what the odd book Tuck discovered indicates."

"But how? It's so much. It would take a decade or more to implement so much. An amusement park?"

"By consuming. The signs are conspicuous, I saw them. In the Umbra the trees are already disappearing. The progress that has stunned the world over the last fifty years will hit Little River in the space of one, or perhaps even just months. And those last fifty years represent the same degree of so-called advancement made in centuries before it. If it wrecks such ruin when condensed to a handful of decades, how great the damage when it unravels in just one?"

"The world truly is spinning to the Apocalypse! You're right. So much change cannot be incorporated or understood within such a short period of time."

"Yes, and the worst of the Wyrm is that people, and I mention them because they are the root of the problem and the cure, begin to crave change. The present is bad because they don't understand it and cannot accommodate it, so they need something new, something different. What comes, of course, is understood just as poorly, but now the previous beliefs, which may be decipherable to them now because of historians and storytellers and the sorts of truth-sayers like Alexander who are so necessary in the Garou world as well, have been abandoned completely and cannot be reclaimed. So the mass-mind moves on, searching yet again."

"Closer and closer to ultimate doom."

"Yes."

"Why can't this be stopped? Reversed? Even slowed? Why can't humans hold against it?"

"I don't know. I think some among them can recognize it, but it has become a game to them. It is a hope dangled before the hopeful, but it's snatched away and forgotten when it comes time for action. The long view is forgotten. No one can be patient enough to allow a cure to come slowly."

"They give up."

"Yes."

"And Harano is what follows."

"Yes."

"That's why Alexander must be preserved. He's the long view."

"Yes."

# 5

# FLOOD

---

Verse awoke feeling sore all over but thoroughly refreshed. The babbling of the nearby brook, the light aroma of the morning dew, and the chill of the morning air all contributed by setting his senses buzzing with messages. He felt purged and clean. Completely attuned to Gaia once more.

He remained reclined on the ground in this sense of utter contentment for a time. When Verse finally lolled from his state of half-wakefulness, he saw that in the end it was Tom who managed to pull himself a few inches farther. It was natural, he decided. It was the Ahroun who always felt they needed to prove something.

Verse felt the Revel was successful for him because of the momentary sense of peace he felt upon awakening. That meant the Revel itself was likely a success as well, since that serenity would not be possible if the Gnostic connection with Gaia and the caern was not renewed.

Still in crinos form, Verse sat up and pulled his legs beneath him. He sure ached! He hugged his legs close to his body and then stretched his long arms high into the air. His spine arched and popped. The center of his chest seemed to pop too. It was a deliciously new sensation to stretch in this bipedal form. Verse regretted never lingering over it the mornings he awoke in the Steins' house. But then he had never awakened feeling so sore, or so in need of a good loosening of the muscles.

Tom was on the ground nearby. Still unconscious. Well, sleeping. If Verse was able to waken, then Tom, too, should have recovered from his exhaustion, but it was no surprise that Tom would wake later. He was always the last to breakfast, if he came downstairs to eat at all.

His stretching complete, Verse still shifted to the wolf form in which he felt more comfortable. The change took but a moment, but the crinkling of bones and muscles that accompanied it was more painful than usual. The Revel had taken a lot out of him.

That worried Verse a little, because everyone in the pack needed full strength and alertness in order to face the enemy, but he also supposed this lack was more than offset by repowering the caern.

Verse loped in a few strides over to the stream for a drink. The water smelled particularly inviting and refreshing, and clean. He lapped a few tonguefuls and then dropped to a prone position to continue drinking. He needed lots of fluids after the run, but he didn't want to guzzle the delicious water too quickly.

As Verse lay there watching and drinking the water, he caught the motion of several small eddies in the flow of the stream. A couple places where the water spun in tight circles and formed miniature whirlpools. They were beautiful.

The radiance of the sun, which was still not too far over the horizon, refracted on the curved lines of the water and created wondrous images of dancing, polychromatic lights. The display was stunning and added immeasurably to Verse's delighted enjoyment of the morning.

Lazily, Verse bent to lap from the stream again. Suddenly, one of the tiny eddies seemed to scoot across the surface of the water like a waterbug and created a flux in the water at the very point where Verse's tongue was working.

Verse paused in shock and confusion for just a second before he recognized the possible danger and attempted to withdraw from his contact with the water. But he couldn't. It was as if his tongue was attached to the water and would not peel or pry loose. The suction of the spinning water was so improbably immense that Verse was stuck.

Verse panicked. He couldn't move, but he also couldn't howl to gain the attention of any packmate, even Tom, who was sleeping soundly only ten meters away. So first he planted his feet as soundly as possible in the cold but still soft mud on the bank of the stream. He could at least resist being pulled in further, he hoped.

It was maddening. His body quivered and shivered from the shock of being held hostage in such a peculiar, invasive manner. It was like wrestling with the other wolves when he was younger and one or more of his mates wound up on top of him smashing the breath from his chest. What resulted was a frantic, desperate drive to gain a deep breath and shake the ruffians from him. This was desperate in the same way. He wasn't being harmed, though he had hurt his tongue when he instinctively pulled hard to release himself before he understood the nature of his predicament.

He tried to cock his head to the side a bit both to gain a better view of the stream and to manage a glance at Tom. The latter was still snoozing peacefully in the nature Verse only moments before had relished as well. The former distressed Verse when other, and more prolonged, looks verified what he feared—all of the other little whirlpools he could see were slowly sliding through the water toward the point where his tongue was trapped. Verse didn't think that could mean anything good.

He feared they might join with the one that held him prisoner to create a more powerful suction that would either hold him more securely or perhaps even drag him into the water. And Verse didn't know what awaited him there. Perhaps a repugnant, vicious Wyrm-creature. Perhaps this was where the Wyrm had made its home—in the waters of Lake Waganta and its tributaries.

And perhaps this was why the elementals of fire were destroyed two nights ago—because this Wyrm-creature possessed a natural affinity for water. It was trying to make the region safer for it and the entropic influence it exerted.

Verse worried then that the water he had imbibed moments before might be contaminated in some way. What foul concoction of corrupting chemicals had he ingested? Verse's imagination ran wild for a moment as he pictured the corroding effect a Wyrm brew might afflict on his insides. The choking reflex came strongly, and but for his distended tongue that stifled the motion, Verse might have vomited the water so pure to him moments before.

And if the water was contaminated, what of everyone in Little River who drank water that came partially from the spring that fed the lake? The people in the county might be spared, but surely only for a time. The effects of the blight would spread through the water table and affect their wells, and if not that, then the corn and other produce they grew.

All of this could happen if Verse could not free himself.

The other whirlpools were drawing near. They did not shoot across the currents like the one that trapped him. They seemed to paddle rather than scoot toward the first. The steady current of the stream worked against them as they appeared to adjust their motion to it.

Perhaps Verse was just imagining that part. However, the pain in his tongue wasn't imaginary. He pulled again, slowly building pressure this time, but there was no give, and he ceased before he caused himself greater harm.

A sudden worry for his packmates hastened him to action. Ally and Tuck both passed him during the night, and he was relatively certain Ally had led the revel through the stream. That meant whatever was in this water, be it Wyrm or otherwise, might have done something to one or both of them as well.

And if that was true, what risk had they all run the night before last at Lake Waganta?

Now frightened and worried, Verse clawed and racked at the ground with his paws and decided to growl as loud as he could. He knew he could manage quite a loud sound, but his mouth was directed at the water, which would mostly muffle any attempt he made. His neck was also distended, and that decreased the volume he could create.

But the panicked howl he managed was still quite loud. So loud that he surprised himself. It was a Howl of Summons. It said he, Verse, was in danger and needed his mates to attend him quickly. It echoed across the nearby fields.

He got the howl off just before a pair of additional little whirlpools joined the first. Verse immediately recognized a difference in the force holding him in place. It didn't pull him any harder, but it was more certain and secure. He could no longer turn his head even slightly to see if Tom was roused by his cry. In a moment Verse might be forced to decide whether his tongue was worth his life.

Without his tongue, Verse knew he would be crippled. His song would be damaged irreparably. Admittedly, it would only be for a short time. With Garou magick, and the help of the spirits, and the Garou's naturally amazing healing capabilities, the tongue could be coaxed to regrow in just a few days, but the pack, and the sept, might need his songs in the meantime to help defeat their enemies.

That in mind, maybe this was a very calculated attack by the Wyrm meant to strip him of the greatest personal asset he provided the pack. Verse was confused. His mind was buzzing, concocting fears and paranoia to overcome the shock of what was happening.

Better perhaps to risk whatever was going to happen to him than lose his tongue for certain just yet. Besides, maybe Tom heard his howl and would help at any moment. Better yet, maybe Passer, as well as Ally and Tuck if they were okay, would respond too.

Just then he did hear Tom shaking off his sleep. It apparently took something as desperate as a Howl of Summons to crack through the unconsciousness of

Tom's slumbering mind. Verse was going to give another cry, but just then he was jerked toward the water.

His feet slid through the sloppy mud and that kept him from the dunking, but Verse felt blood well into his mouth. His eyes watered from the numbing pain and his ears flattened against his head. There was another jerk, and Verse, hoping his decision was correct and submitting to the inexorable hold the underwater power had over him, changed the bracing on his feet so he no longer resisted the pull. Instead, he tucked his butt under and cannonballed wolf-style into the deep stream. He had no wish to enter the spinning vertical tunnel of water headfirst, so he went as a whole unit.

His last thought was to take a deep breath. He succeeded, but it was a difficult feat considering his hostage tongue.

His eyes shut, Verse had a hard time analyzing what was happening to him. His sense of balance was completely gone and a twisting vertigo overcame him. He did feel the hold on his tongue loosen and then release, but he couldn't tell when it might be safe to breathe again. His whole body, it seemed, was mercilessly tossing with the rotation of the waters in the whirlpool.

Verse could only assume the spout had grown larger with the conjoining of the others.

Then he heard snatches of a shouting voice. He thought it was Tom's voice. Thank Gaia someone could help him.

His breath was running low, but he still dared not breathe or he might swallow only water. A few gulps like that and he might begin to drown.

With his last strength, and seconds of oxygen, he

struggled to right himself. It was a precarious effort because he had no sense of direction and nothing to truly brace against. He squirmed regardless, trying to home in on Tom's voice. Verse hoped Tom would continue to shout, as it was the only steady source of perception he could tune in to with his addled senses.

So the wolf used his Garou gifts and delivered a mental picture to Tom's mind. There wasn't much time to hone the image, but he hoped the Ahroun would see a picture of himself crying loudly and Verse, blindfolded, homing in on the voice.

Whether successful in that effort or not, Verse continued to hear Tom without a break in the human's voice. Verse struggled some more, and when he heard slightly more than an instantaneous bit of Tom's voice, the Galliard knew he must have righted himself somewhat and somehow.

He gasped, spraying water from his mouth, and took a deep breath.

It was another moment, though, before he was able to make sense of his surroundings. The landscape was spinning in circles around him at a terrific speed. It was a long wash of grayish blue interrupted often and randomly by brown splotches.

He could at least clearly hear Tom, who shouted, "Verse, keep your head above water. Above the water, Verse!"

Verse tried to nod in human fashion so Tom would know he'd heard, and it was then that Verse's sense caught up with his predicament. He found that he was in a very large, perhaps six-feet-wide, whirlpool that spun hellishly fast in one, aquasyncronous spot in the center of Waganta Brook.

———

As Passer trudged through the forest back toward the house of the Steins, he thought maybe he was still sweating from last night. He was proud of his effort and performance. With some trickery, he'd managed to hold the lead until he was forced to turn the run northward.

It proved impossible to delay the inevitable any longer at that point. A sprint through an open field was not his choice of races.

He smiled, though, when he recalled again how he'd managed to push past Ally for another moment after that farmer's dog lunged for her.

He wondered if she'd won the race, and suspected it would be close between Tuck and her. Tuck had come along later, but he was moving at a good, steady pace and didn't seem too overwhelmed by the madness of the Revel. He suspected Tuck managed the strategy he had considered. Good minds think alike, Passer chuckled to himself.

This reminiscing and self-satisfaction instantly dispersed when Passer heard the call. One of the pack members was in trouble. It sounded a bit like Verse, but the voice was different. Not at all the full and clear howl he'd expect to hear from the Garou. That scared Passer more than the howl itself. The natural-born lupus might already be hurt if he was crying like that.

Passer could barely imagine running through the woods anymore, but as he accelerated he found that he wasn't as sore or tired as he thought. Passer wondered if there was magick in Verse's howl that aided his run.

When the howl was not repeated, Passer grew even more frightened. It was going to be difficult to home in on the source of the call if it wasn't repeated. The situation was obviously more urgent, though, in that case too. It was the sort of snake-eating-its-own-tail loop that frustrated Passer.

He continued to hurry in the direction he thought was right, but he began to doubt his course more and more. Fearfully, Passer decided to pause to investigate. He was afraid of what he might discover. He took a deep breath and concentrated. If agents of the Wyrm were near, then he would sense them as he had at the football field.

The sensation he gained was very slight. He closed his eyes to concentrate. They popped back open. Oh, dear God, he thought. He received a tickling of the stench of the Wyrm in the very direction he was traveling. He said a silent oath to the Phoenix totem of the pack, and then resumed his run. This time, however, he ran with certainty of direction. And also certainty of fear, for it was the Wyrm.

For assistance, Passer called again upon the gift taught him by the cheetah spirit when he had traversed Africa years before. That was during a time when he still traveled with a group of Garou of his own tribe, the Silent Striders. He had not yet discovered that even among the homeless of his tribe he did not have a home. Years before the Steins told him he had a home with them.

As he thought, Passer gained speed. Speed that would have surely helped him win the Revel had the use of such gifts been allowed. He ran faster than any mortal could dream possible. Faster even than a wolf at a dead run, though he held his birth form of crinos. He could have gone much faster yet if he used this gift as a healthy wolf, but transformation into that shape would also hinder him, because then his crippled right arm, which didn't affect his foot speed when he ran on only two feet, would become a crippled foreleg when running on four.

He whistled through the forest.

Nearing his destination he slowed. He'd traveled it in half the time it might have taken him. Because of the magick taught by the spirit, though, Passer was not extraordinarily tired. He breathed heavily from the long run, but not from any added exertion of speed.

He saw Tom, in homid form, standing on the bank on what Passer guessed to be the Waganta Brook. He was calling to Verse but taking no other action.

At an unaccelerated speed, but still in robust strides, Passer approached Tom. The Ahroun seemed startled to be set upon by such an imposing figure, but settled immediately.

"Verse is caught in some sort of whirlpool," he said, pointing to the water.

Passer asked simply, "Where is the Wyrm?"

Tom looked back, confused. "The Wyrm? I guess it's what's got Verse. Verse just got his head above water and I was shouting out loud because that's what Verse wanted me to do for some reason. I didn't know what to do next."

Passer saw that the situation was an odd one. He scanned the water but didn't see anything that could be causing the odd effect, so there wasn't something that could be rended with crinos claws. There didn't seem to be a ready way of pulling Verse out of the whirlpool either, especially because the Galliard was in lupus form.

Passer didn't know if Verse was too bewildered to effectively change to another form. He thought Verse might know he was here now too, because each time the current pulled Verse's face around to him and Tom, the wolf turned briefly against the current to track them before shifting the other way to prepare for another look.

The situation seemed intractable.

Passer asked, "Do you know if Ally or Tuck are nearby?"

"No. It's just the three of us."

"Wait," Passer said, suddenly excited. "I have an idea that may work."

He padded closer to the edge of the bank.

Again, it was a gift he'd learned long ago that he had used recently. It allowed him to create fire when he stood at the top of the bleachers. But now he could use it to create the kind of element associated with the elementals that taught him the gift—elementals of earth.

He glanced back at Tom, who was now also approaching closer to stand beside him, and said, "This may take some time, so don't interrupt me unless you feel you must."

"Okay," Tom said. "I'm just going to get ready." Almost instantly, hair began to sprout from Tom's face as he began to change form.

"Good," Passer muttered as he crouched, bending his legs at the knees.

He stretched out his hands and recalled the words of the elemental who writhed through the sands of the Sahara and finally poked its way to the surface to speak to him. It was the first gift Passer had learned, and the elemental told him he was chosen to learn it because he was a metis, and so more in touch with the ways of the Garou than the fools who'd looked down upon him and called him a mule.

Though they could not reach the bottom of the stream, Passer's outstretched hands felt for it. Searching, searching, he found it. The silky mud slipped through his fingers. The hard rocks, rattling around and rolling in circles because of the unnatural currents above, knocked against him.

Or so it felt.

With his hands still spiritually submerged in the spinning water, Simon took hold of that fine mud and imagined it as a mortar that would hold fast all the rocks drifting near. A small mound of earth began to form, and as the rocks caught and held, new layers formed atop the first. Soon, a column of stone and earth was taking shape below the center of the waterspout.

If he could just build it high enough!

Passer continued, absorbed in his work. There were no interruptions.

He continued to build the mound of earth, mud, and stones. It needed to push higher. It was now high enough that the force of the current washed away the top layers before they could fully form. Passer fought hard against this erosion by seeking to build more solid earth into the structure. The mud could no longer be used. It was pulled free too easily.

The pile surged up again, and suddenly Passer sensed contact. Contact with Verse's mind as well as contact between his pile of earth and Verse's foot.

In his mind's eye formed a picture of Verse spinning in place and something large, and unknown, pushing against his feet. It was obvious from this presentation from Verse's mind that the wolf did not know Passer's intention or even of the metis's involvement. Verse was trying to communicate more danger from below, and as the picture gained complexity, so too did it become clear that Verse thought he was about to be swallowed or attacked from the now murky—from the tumbling water and billowing particles of dirt—depths by some spawn of the Wyrm.

Thanks to the power of this gift Verse knew and

the wolf's ability to concentrate even under such circumstances, Passer was able to draw a picture back. He showed Verse what the scene looked like from the bank. How the wolf was spinning helplessly in the water out of Tom's reach. How the thing he sensed beneath him was not a threat at all but a perch from which the wolf could fly.

And fly Verse did. The connection Passer felt in his mind faded instantly, and the wolf called upon another gift Passer knew he possessed. The wolf's legs coiled, bracing against the pile of stone beneath him, and then uncoiled, and with a great splash the wolf vaulted as if propelled by the legs of a kangaroo above the surface of the water.

However, the direction of the leap was unfortunate. Undoubtedly very dizzy from his spinning, Verse misguided his jump. He would have fallen directly back into the water—not directly back into the whirlpool, but Passer had no doubt the effect would immediately track the Garou and snare him again—if not for Tom's preparedness.

The Ahroun was now in his powerful crinos form, and while he could not perform a leap like that demonstrated by Verse, he could still easily clear the width of the brook. Passer watched as Tom tensed and sprang, grabbing Verse in midair and alighting on the opposite bank with his wolf cargo safely stowed.

The whirlpool, empty now of its victim, swirled around desperately. As Passer watched Tom set Verse down, the metis also watched as the whirlpool began to fragment into several, perhaps a dozen or so, smaller versions of the same. They scooted around the surface of the brook in a frenzy.

It was only when, like at the football field, the cold shadow of the Wyrm drifted overhead that

Passer realized what was happening. Elementals of fire the first time. Now these funnels in the water. The Wyrm was going to destroy elementals of water. In their misguided way the elementals sought help from the Garou. Now everyone would pay for the lack of communication.

Passer shouted across the brook, "It's like before. The Wyrm is here to claim another element as its victim." Then he looked up to where he vaguely sensed the Wyrm. There was nothing there to strike against. Aware of it and what was going to happen, Passer could analyze the Wyrm. The force he sensed was more an ambition, a thought, than it was a force, though, so Passer had trouble identifying anything of use for future encounters.

"Where," Tom shouted, his razors glaringly sharp on huge fists waving in preparation to attack.

"Here. There. Everywhere," Passer said ineffectively. How to fight a impulse? A desire? Was this the evil of the Wyrm? The quality that rendered it undefeatable? Were there not legends of great duels between Garou champions and horrid beasts spawned by the Wyrm? How could such a battle be staged? Or waged?

Then the Wyrm coalesced. Still not into a form capable of dealing or receiving mortal blows, but it somehow became more tangible. In this moment, helpless to do anything else, Passer desperately attuned himself to the presence to gain more information.

There was nothing more.

This was an omnipresent enemy. Passer sensed it here, but it was everywhere.

All three Garou watched, incapable of assisting the elementals, as the madly spinning spouts wavered and then slowly, very slowly, whirled softly to a halt until they dissipated into the water of the brook and joined the current to be carried away.

Passer looked after a piece of wood floating in the water that he imagined traveling downstream with the water so recently rotating. The wood passed from view.

He looked across at Tom and Verse and managed to crack a grim smile. At least Verse was safe, Passer considered silently. The wolf, though, stood with its tongue draped uncomfortably out of its mouth.


Far to the northeast, where the Revel of the Phoenix Pack passed about halfway through the night, Sower of Thunder awoke. He had no memory of the last several hours of the night. He recalled resisting the Revel by rushing to stay ahead and away from it, but as he knew it would, the Revel overtook him.

Used to hard travel and hard living, though, the Red Talon ronin was not much affected by the lingering effects of the night's activity. What pains he felt were inconsequential. Unless an injury crippled him, and even then only if he was truly maimed, Thunder thought it best to overlook it. Countless sores and scores crisscrossed his body, and the exertions of the Revel tore open the worst of the battle scars—a long band across his back inflicted by a crazed Get of Fenris he'd once battled who thought to win by surprising Thunder from behind. Instead, the Get got death.

Thunder crouched, remaining silent. This was an excellent way to test his familiarity with the region, he decided. Tall hardwood trees, almost completely barren of their leafy cargo, towered around him, though if he stood at his full crinos-form height of over nine feet he would have skewed the perception of the trees and from a distance make them seem smaller than they were.

Thunder slowly swiveled around, still crouching low to the ground. These hardwoods! He could be almost anywhere in the county. The wintry sky was of no help at all. Gray and nearly overcast, the sky was uniform across the whole of the horizon. There was no sun to gauge the time of day or his position in the county, though he still rested with the instinct that he was somewhere in the northeast.

Of course, the fact that he left no scent when he traveled—thanks to the instruction he'd forced from a fox spirit not tricky enough to elude him—meant he couldn't detect anything about his former visit near this area. The fox claimed Thunder could forever after leave only the scent of running water, which was essentially no scent at all. Maybe a truly skilled tracker could mark some points he crossed, but he doubted anyone could long simply follow his trail.

He continued to scan. He assumed he would note a distinguishing feature of some kind to give away his location. If he couldn't complete this simple task, then he wasn't ready to tackle the Wyrm-spawned pack. If he could, then perhaps he would go hunting prior to even entering the town itself.

Thunder worked harder. The chances that he'd walked over this very plot of land on his tour of the region were minimal. So he stared off in one direction after another, trying to imagine how this piece of land must look from such perspectives. What shapes might the limbs form?

He stopped suddenly. He'd asked the right question first, a sure sign his unconscious mind was already on top of the situation. Now if his conscious mind would just catch up.

Then he knew. He'd walked about thirty meters to the south of this point. Looking northward he'd remarked to himself how the limbs of the trees seemed to spiral upward. Every trunk north from where he stood grew lowest limbs that were each higher than the one before it, and the angle had been such that they seemed a continuous line.

Thunder smiled. He was ready. His quiet and stillness broke as he leapt to his feet. Yes yes yes, he chanted in ragged puffs of breath. The time for the slaughter of his enemies was finally upon him. He relished with merciless glee the prospect of finding one of that fetid pack alone and tired after the night's Revel.

Divide and conquer. Thunder especially liked the idea of dividing his foe.

Into tiny, pulpy pieces.


What he'd intended as an honor to the effort she'd made turned out instead to be a snub, another reason for Ally to look to strip the mantle of leadership from him. But the same event also put Ally in a position that made a struggle between honor and pride. She had won the Revel, but she couldn't speak of it with pride because she knew Tuck could have staggered past her.

She was upset because the event seemed to have been staged. There was no pretense, but to Ally it must have seemed that Tuck planned this all along. Perhaps even from the very beginning when he proposed the Revel.

Tuck shook his head. These were the conclusions he was coming to on what he felt was going to be a long morning of conclusions and troubled thinking. How could she think this? How could he have chosen to act so incorrectly?

It made him wonder again at his position of pack leader. He thought a Revel would be a good idea because it would recharge the caern, but it was also a sacred activity to pull the pack together. Perhaps the mistake lay in the decision to make the Revel a race. But that couldn't be it. Revels were inherently competitive. If anything, the race idea brought that into the open and made the Revel more a game than a serious rivalrous affair. Once you'd fallen, you could still cheer the others on instead of being entirely consumed with your own failure to go faster or harder.

Tuck stamped his foot in frustration as he stalked farther away from where he and Ally had parted. They'd awakened at the same time. Tuck wore a smile and was about to introduce Ally to the very cold, wintry morning with an invitation to hurry home for some hot cocoa, but all he received was a glare. It was a look not of contempt, for Ally could hardly feel that for one to whom she was bound by duty and loyalty for life, but instead one of deep hurt. She didn't respond to his calls. She simply walked away. The lack of cursing or tromping left a frightening mood behind. An empty feeling that made Tuck question his right to be leader.

The woods were cold and Tuck could do with that hot liquid, but there were too many things to ponder. And there would be too little time. If he needed to execute changes, then that needed to be done immediately, and before the impending threat grew beyond ominous to apocalyptic.

He knew he was well suited to being the leader of the pack, but Tuck backtracked to find the basis of justification for that conclusion in his own mind. Eventually, sorrowfully, as he walked dragging his feet through dew-sogged leaves, Tuck admitted to himself that there were two reasons. First, because he was the leader of the football team. Second, because he was a Philodox.

The first simply could not apply. The magnitude of difference between the two was inconceivably vast. It was perhaps ethnocentric to adopt his new-found race so heartily and without question, but a Garou among men was certainly a leader. There was much that his presumably instinctual understanding of group dynamics led him to do. When to show dominance and pull rank on another. When to be magnanimous and let something go.

Among a group of other Garou, though, it naturally took more than that to set him apart. And the thing he felt did set him apart was his Auspice. He was born under the half-moon, a Philodox. He was the Keeper of Ways. Among Garou he was to be among those who mediated. He was to join the select group of Garou for whom leadership seemed natural. As he found balance and evenness within himself, so was he to do the same for a pack. Or sept. Or even tribe. The vicious full-moon Ahroun versus the lighthearted, sometimes comedic Ragabash. The rage that burned in the Garou and haunted their consciousness for release against the enemies of Gaia versus wisdom and the honor of the Garou that called upon them to be better than that which they sought to defeat.

Could the position and shape of the moon at the time of birth determine so much?

Tuck was skeptical, especially now. Humans made jokes about the zodiac. What sign are you? It was a tired line worn out even in old, bad jokes.

He continued to walk, letting this issue float unexamined in his mind for a time. All sorts of concepts, learned and overheard, flittered through his mind. Genetics. Nature versus nurture. Hormonal imbalances. Free will. So many things that claimed to govern how a person was and would be.

Tuck wished he could examine the issue more in terms of the cosmology of the Garou, but he didn't think he could translate such decidedly human concepts into those terms.

But he tried, and Tuck's mind swam. Structures and preconceptions slipped away like melting ice. Ways of acting. What is good. What is worthy. All these judgments were so grounded in Tuck the human that the world seemed vitalized and brilliant the moment he saw it through the eyes of the Garou.

Whether it was due to these Garou eyes, or whether the animal actually waited for him, Tuck spied a large wolf sitting in the forest ahead. It was long-haired and fluffy—a wolf with a confused environmental response or one far from its home in a much colder clime. Its fur was the spectrum of colors in the gray wolf—black, brown, and gray—mixed into a jumble. This coloration shifted and shimmered with each step Tuck took. The bright sunlight glared in different ways and drew out different colors.

It sat regarding Tuck.

In the back of his mind, his still human-thinking mind, Tuck knew this could be dangerous. This could be the animal responsible for decimating the campers. But while his human mind might be tricked, Tuck could not be. This was no killer, this was Tuck's thoughts personified—a vision.

It was a spirit.

Not a mirage, or a phantom. Those were make-believe. This was an important spirit among the Garou—the spirit of the wolf.

Odd, though, that it should be alone. A wolf was not a wolf if it was alone. Among the Garou loners were called ronin. They were outcasts from the pack or tribe shunned for a misdeed or mistake. Some insane Garou even left of their own volition.

His human mind thought it overly sentimental, but in an unweepy way Tuck realized the wolf was not alone—it was with Tuck. Or perhaps it was a part of him.

Tuck stopped to regard the majesty of the beast. It still watched Tuck, but without scrutinizing him. It seemed unself-consciously calm and beyond scrutiny itself. Tuck could imagine the wolf sitting like this in a woods all its own. It was how it was regardless of the circumstances.

When it slowly stood and walked away, Tuck could only watch. There was a strength in the simple being of the wolf, a strength Tuck knew he possessed as well. A strength that he relied on as part of him, but a strength he could never purposefully tap. Now he thought he could.

When after a lazy time the wolf disappeared beyond the furthest trees, the forest seemed to stand back from Tuck, leaving him with his thoughts only. The Philodox walked without regard for a destination or direction. And he wondered if maybe that wasn't a key to success, because whatever he tried to do, it was too late to change who he was and how he reacted to things.

Tuck knew he was naturally disposed to working issues through like this. Pounding them relentlessly with theories and conjectures. He accepted that. He did it naturally. It was only afterwards—except like now while thinking about how the things that worked happened without forethought—when he paused to examine what he'd done that it seemed right.

Tuck paused, surprised at how sincerely profound this idea was. To put it in perspective, he went back to his human grounding. It was like playing football, when everything falls away because you are so naturally being yourself that nothing else intrudes. The most important exclusion was the realization of the act itself. There was no voice of conscience making background remarks. No analyzing of what you were doing.

It was a dangerous answer to accept, though, because in a way it was really no answer at all. It was justifying your actions in part, or even mostly, because they were your actions. But in a way that reassured Tuck. He trusted himself. He knew his inclinations would not lead him to savagely murder a person. Or rob a store at gunpoint.

He was also reassured because he felt this acceptance demonstrated an underlying shift toward the Garou perception of the world. A view he needed to balance, like so much else, with other views, like his human thoughts, but still it was an acceptance of something countless generations of a people largely worthy of great respect accepted.

As a human it was foolish to give blind credence to something so foolish as moon signs and times of birth instead of looking at the kind of childhood he had and the genetic makeup of his parents, but the Garou worldview did not count such things as important. Whether that was the fact that therefore rendered them unimportant, or because that was a greater truth, Tuck didn't know.

What he did know was that he was confident again. The depression weighing on him for the last hour and a half lifted and his step became jauntier.

So he turned, to approach Little River to the east, and turned his mind toward happier things, which also consequently fit his new theory of trusting himself. A happier thought named Melissa.

He considered how his sudden kissing of Melissa earlier in the day was unlike other kisses in the past when he was so aware of the person he embraced. That kiss was natural. Instead of trying to create an intimate moment with someone as he'd done in the past, that moment with Melissa seemed to create itself. It blossomed wholly from Tuck just giving in to his instinct.

Tuck smiled, able to take his new philosophy with a grain of salt. Because he wondered how much easier such a philosophy must be for wolves to accept. Born wilder, without social conventions and demands to weight them down, they truly did act merely as impulse, or instinct, told them.

A romance with Melissa would be so much easier if they were both wolves. They could still mate for life, since wolves did so, but the impetus Tuck thought they both felt to be together would not have to dig out of such a pile of habitual bullshit.

Mate for life? Tuck shook his head; he was scaring himself.

Tuck wondered aloud just once more before settling into a steady stroll toward home. If it was actually the wolf that relied solely on instinct, and if the Garou, especially he as a Philodox, were to find a balance between the tendencies of human and wolf, then was he right as a Garou to trust his first impulse?

He realized he wasn't trusting it. Otherwise, he wouldn't catch himself questioning himself and his decisions so much. Maybe he was a true Philodox. A good leader of the Garou.

The Garou was even marked by the Wyrm.

It wandered carelessly through the forest, never suspecting that its doom was moments, and about forty meters, away.

Thunder decided to play with this first prey a bit before demolishing it. Aided by his familiarity with the terrain, Thunder knew he could manage to confuse the Wyrm-spawn, creating in its feeble mind the impression of landmarks that were nearby but not exactly here, and also by presenting such impressions out of order and out of time with how the landmarks occurred naturally.

It was another opportunity to test his knowledge of the vicinity.

Thunder concentrated on the basics of this other lesson taught by that same not-tricky-enough fox spirit. He created subtle alterations at first. The moss on the trees now seemed to grow on the wrong side of the trunk. This caused a slight adjustment of course by the Garou, who over time adapted unknowingly to the false stimulus. Each time his path was blocked by a tree and he was forced to round it, he came off at a slightly different angle. This happened as the woods-wise Garou unconsciously assessed the direction clues it received from the terrain.

This little bit would be enough to confuse the Garou, but when he came upon other landmarks of note, he would realize he'd made an error and adjust his path back to the original course. To do more damage to the Garou's directional-challenged sense, Thunder needed to wait for the Garou to be confused. Once the Garou consciously looked for new clues concerning his whereabouts, Thunder would then provide false clues.

It didn't take long. Certainly not as long as Thunder expected it might. That meant that as crippled and puny as the Garou seemed, it did possess gifts from the Wyrm that made it powerful. Thunder would have to be careful, though he laughed at himself for such apprehension.

The Garou slowly drew to a confused stop, looking at the tree in front of him. He then looked right and left. As the Wyrm-spawn turned hard left, Thunder was afforded a better view of its swollen and lumpy—and useless—right arm. When it came time to fight, Thunder confidently thought, this Garou will pose no threat at all.

With a shrug of his shoulders, the Garou turned a bit to the right and began to walk again.

A few moments later, careful not to act too soon, Thunder began to mislead the Garou again. Strategically placed impressions of rocks and trees, including a beautiful blue spruce that seemed to the affected Garou to be over a half mile from where it grew in reality, completely jumbled his mind, which Thunder now judged to indeed be that of a metis, the likely inbred offspring of the Stargazers.

The metis seemed frustrated and began to stamp off in a new direction. Thunder revealed himself to possible sight, though he walked behind the Stargazer pup. Thunder did maintain his silent stride, however, and now shadowed the soon-to-be-dead Garou rather than stalked him.

The metis soon realized its last error, though, for thanks to the misguided guidance of the Thunder's magick, the whelp walked into a corner. It was one of the rockier spots in the region's forests, and the Garou found himself confronted by a steep circlet of stones that might serve as great cover for campers because they so well protected the interior against wind and rain, but that did not serve as a possible means of passing through this portion of the forest.

So he turned around. Thunder smiled as he was recognized by his enemy for the first time. The pup almost fell down with fright. Thunder grinned, squinting his eyes predatorily. The first of the wolf-slayers would fall.

"I am an elemental force," he said to the fated Garou. "None may stop the power of nature. None may stop me."

Passer could not fathom why the gigantic and powerfully built crinos would want to slay him, but he knew he was dead. Passer did not doubt what the Garou said to him, though even in the face of death he could not help but wonder at the scene.

Oliver could fight this monster. Oliver was a master of Kailindo, a martial art that would probably handle even a brute like this. And Passer could imagine himself telling the story. The beauty of the art Oliver used to slay a horrible beast.

He stood still, the puzzle of his ailing directional sense somewhat solved. The ring of rocks behind him was a kind of security, though it was also the prison sentencing him to death. Without it there he might be able to outrun the other crinos, though that depended on the sorts of spirits it consorted with and the tricks they knew. Still, he would have to try.

Passer thought of crying out. Perhaps salvation would come as he had come for Verse so little time ago. He should have gone directly with them, but Verse looked fine, if tired, and besides, Tom was accompanying him, so why stay? He wanted to think about what he'd seen for a time. He wanted to provide Tuck with not just a good account but a good theory. The very elements this killer called his own were dying.

He didn't cry, though, because he knew that would only summon the others, one by one, to their deaths. Passer knew this thing was responsible for killing the campers, and if it wanted to slay one Garou, than it would not hesitate to kill three, or five.

Even if the others arrived in couples, Tom and Verse or Tuck and Ally, he doubted they would fare well in such a fight, especially when this enemy would have the advantage of surprise. So he kept his mouth closed.

The other did not. "I am Sower of Thunder," it claimed.

Passer noted that there was a hint of the Wyrm in Sower of Thunder. For a moment Passer felt pity for what must have been a great Garou warrior, one undoubtedly the subject of many heroic tales of his own. Perhaps he had even once told a tale of just this once-hero without realizing this eventual tragic fate.

And scarcely before the huge monster was gutting him, Passer realized the beast was moving. Its speed was stunning, and Passer quickly lost any hope of eluding it in a footrace.

Passer managed to duck the blow, but only by calling on his own cheetah-blessed speed. A rushing paw glazed the still air above him and Passer took the opening to sprint. His legs still tired from the Revel and his race to reach Verse, Passer nevertheless flew at a great speed.

Fear gripped Passer's heart and mind, but it subsided and he ran with great calm. Knowing that he was perhaps living his last moments on earth, he drank in his environment. Even the tiniest things did not escape his notice. A lone leaf hanging at the end of a limb. The abandoned chitin of a beetle attached to a trunk.

Passer wondered if these were the frozen moments that moved slowly by in the last moments of death. Moments in which some Garou, or people or wolves or whatever, realized the profundity of the world around and of existence itself. Passer felt relief, realizing that hopefully many who died touched this serenity for at least that moment.

It was a feeling or sense, though, that Passer often recognized. How glorious that his life could be filled with so many moments like this. So many moments of grasping hidden beauty and revealing it for himself. He appreciated this final reminder.

His legs still churning, Passer was looking upward when a spacious view of the sky opened. His spirit was still reveling in the heavens when he suddenly came to a sloppy halt. At first he simply lost his footing and stumbled across a slimy surface. Then the ground began to snag and grab his feet. The ground was mush. The solid, still, cold earth was now a heap of viscous, gooey turf that cloyed his feet and clogged his movement.

His feet would not move forward, but his body maintained its momentum and slung him face forward down into the sludge. Within moments he was helplessly stuck. Essentially one-armed, Passer knew he had little hope of pulling his way out of the muck, a kind of quicksand the Garou warrior must have created, for there was no explanation for it to be here.

The best Passer could manage was to roll over onto his back. From that position he could at least meet his killer. The mighty Sower of Thunder, minion of the Wyrm, was not long in coming. Within a moment, the beast was standing at the edge of the slop pit.

Passer caught a glimpse of an open wound on the creature's back. He prayed it had not been inflicted by one of his packmates, for his friend must be dead if this abomination still walked. Perhaps he too should fight the monster in hopes of harming it further so his brothers and sister might face a further weakened enemy, but he knew he could cause it no harm, and he refused to deny himself a last moment of peace.

"You run fast." It smiled.

Passer, holding on to his last realization of contentment, said nothing.

It spoke again, saying, "No final tricks, Wyrm-spawn?"

Passer had to smile. A chagrined smile. "You are so misled, warrior."

"Words are to be your trick, then? I knew there would be something. But your words will not affect me."

"I suspect no words could move you," Passer said sadly.

Then Sower of Thunder walked toward him. With each step the Wyrm-pawn took into the adhesive soil, the ground beneath his foot reverted instantly to hard soil once again. Passer simply reclined into a mass of the pasty stuff and accepted the earth into his soul as it grabbed him and held him firm.

"You are no sport." The Garou warrior sounded authentically disappointed.

"Gaia, take me," Passer mumbled, resisting the urge to howl his own dirge.

"Pathetic," said Sower of Thunder.

Passer kept his eyes shut tight, so he did not see the first blow coming. It hit him fully on the side of the head and pushed him into the mushy ground. Completely bewildered from the force of the blow, Passer could only think to heal the blight before him, even though it simultaneously sought his death.

Passer reached out toward the wound on Thunder's back. The enraged monster, probably finding this pitiful attempt pathetic, allowed Passer to touch him, briefly.

Passer said, "May the hand of Gaia shed your rotten flesh and heal the Wyrm within you." There was a glimmer of light where Passer's hand touched the wound on the back of Sower of Thunder. The wound there miraculously closed and healed instantly.

Thunder seemed enraged and struck again without pause.

The blow rended Passer and rendered him unto death.

Passer's consciousness faded as his flesh and blood merged with the wet earth. Sower of Thunder was not done, though, until he pounded and clawed the definition from every portion of Passer's body.

When the earth became solid again, as Sower of Thunder strode silently away, the matted fur and red puddles swirled with the reforming earth to create a delicate pattern in the soil.

# CONVERSATION

"It seems to me that there was much in common between them. Each born under the crescent moon. One a wolf, the other a metis, but neither human, and lacking of familiar human ways."

"And both were inspirational in their manner."

"Please at least don't speak of Alexander in the past tense."

"But the Garou we now call Alexander is not the Garou we hope to find, but the former one is truly dead. As dead as Passer."

"Passer gave his life for Alexander, though. Do not let the source of Passer's undoing be undone just yet."

"I have given up nothing. I still see success as possible. You are not questioning again?"

"No, though it's harder to balance one life against many when some of the many actually begin to perish."

"Yes."

"But in this we need to think more as Garou. Leave our human behind. Recall the symbolic. I believe Tuck is discovering this, which is a very good sign, and let us not forget."

"Passer's death at the hands of some monster does not concern me so much. I understand that event. I do not, though, know how much longer I can understand our decision to keep Alexander's identity, and even existence, secret from the Phoenix Pack."

"Because they must champion their own cause. If healing Alexander's spirit becomes the focus of their efforts, then they are bound to fail. Alexander, I think, does not so much doubt the ability of Garou to stand together as he doubts their ability to stand against. A battle for his hope will not win his hope. A victory over that which he fears will win his hope."

"I am beginning to find the entire effort hypocritical, though. How can we claim to wish to create hope when we deceive the ones who surely carry more optimism and exhilaration than any of us? Their faith in themselves and each other is paramount to success, for if they give up then we have failed too. What if they discover our secret and learn that it is not to make them whole and give them peace that we brought them here, but is instead to make another whole and return peace to him?"

"That is a risk we have assumed. We are pivotal to the success of the mission as more than technicians who examine the equation, find the constants, and let the unknowns vary until there is a success. We are scientists, using intuition and not completely trusting even the givens in our experiment. That is, we have obligations beyond setting the process in motion. Discovery would be disastrous for either party, so the truth must remain hidden."

"It's a weak case to choose a path simply because the only alternative is ill-advised."

"Perhaps, but remember, the Phoenix Pack has a very real mission. They must stop the Wyrm here for more reasons than just Alexander. They are defending us, our caern, and their future home. Those things, I believe, will be reward apparent enough for their efforts that they will not feel deceived even if they learn the truth."

"Maybe."

"Regardless of whether Alexander responds to their efforts, this battle must be fought. Perhaps new heroes will be found. Perhaps it will be Tuck, as Passer so diligently chronicled and believed, who ascends from this experience. He fights for himself as much as Alexander. Or at least he should, and that's why the masquerade must continue."

"Yes."

# 6

# BIG RIVER

It was only three days after Passer's death, but Tuck knew the storyteller wouldn't recognize either Little River or the kind of life the Garou of the Caern at Little Rock lived.

Despite countless hours of searching, always as a pack because Tuck insisted that no one wander alone now, the Phoenix Pack did not have any better idea who killed Passer or, earlier, those campers. The bloody remains found both times promised that the killer was vicious, and the odd way Passer's remains striated the ground suggested the killer was more than natural. He, she, or it possessed a familiarity with what Tuck used to think of as the supernatural.

Fortunately, the pack members and the Steins did not have to deal with repercussions of Passer's death beyond the death itself. Even as Simon, the metis was not enrolled in any of the Little River schools, and he was thought to be a lonely, troubled sort of child. Though they expected few questions, since most people preferred to ignore the handicapped child and thought little about him, the sept was prepared to tell a story of how Simon returned to the home from which he was adopted.

It was troubling to ponder such matters. That death could have such an earthly component was a shock to Tuck. Being among the Garou and their culture for over a year now, he had grown used to seeing everything more spiritually. His perceptions colored, and the world he saw was more delightful, by far, than the one he saw before.

Certainly, the revealed world of the Garou brought ugliness as well, and the sort that could obviously be deadly, but it was a heroic world. Where death meant sacrifice. Where failure meant trying in the face of overwhelming odds. Accepting that worldview made Tuck forget the elements of the world of his birth. Made him forget that humans did not know werewolves existed.

The spirit was gone from the world of man. That's why the town was being eaten alive. There was hustling activity everywhere. The pack, through many talks with Sarah and Oliver, began to piece the puzzle together.

The Wyrm was in Little River, and it was destroying the natural elements. The beauty of the region was being snuffed out. Half the elementals of the classic Garou worldview were now barred from the region. Attempts to call upon either elementals of fire or water proved fruitless, and they were sorely missed. The replacements the Wyrm brought degraded the wonderful land. Fires burned smokier and left food cooked over their flames tasting charred and tainted. The water tasted different too. The once spring-pure water that refreshed Tuck in the woods, at home, or during his hard, sweaty foot-ball practices now tasted metallic and didn't restore him as before.

There was also a killer wandering the woods. Surely allied with the Wyrm, the monster could not be found. That's why Tuck ruled that everyone must at least be in pairs. That made it difficult for Verse, already feeling ridiculously guilty about Passer's death because he'd been saved just a little earlier, who was forced to remain at the Steins the whole of the day when Tuck, Ally, and Tom were at school. A pattern had developed, though, that allowed him some time out. He stayed with Tuck during football practices after the end of the school day.

The football matter was difficult. Tuck gave a lot of consideration to quitting the team and using that practice time to widen the breadth and degree of the pack's search for answers to the many dilemmas of the town. But in the midst of some changes in the town, people, even those not usually excited by sports and those without children at the high school or in school at all, were excited by the prospect of a small-town state-champion football team. Beyond failing his teammates, Tuck decided it would be inexcusable to deny the inhabitants of the region this remaining small-town hope.

Tuck wondered if a possible solution to the prob-lem of the Wyrm might be not in battling it as Ally demanded, but instead through somehow drawing the town together. Exploration into this matter is what took Tuck and Verse to the small newspaper office in George Stipes's home after the last practice of the week on the Wednesday before Friday's game in far-off Headway.

Stipes was the publisher, editor, and staff writer

for the county's only publication of record. The middle-aged man worked out of his home about a half mile east of Little River's downtown along the county road. That made the walk one of about a mile from the high school, which was north of the downtown on Main Street.

The newspaperman had spoken with Tuck the night before. He asked him to come by the office for an interview to appear in a special edition of the paper he was preparing for release Friday morning before the game. Tuck was happy to oblige and accepted, making sure the Steins, Tom, and Ally knew he and Verse would be home a little later than normal.

Tuck slightly dreaded the walk through the town. So much seemed to be changing. There was certainly no amusement park under construction, but the face of the little downtown was altering. Changes that at first seemed so innocuous grew on each other as the days passed. Before Tuck realized the sweeping degree of the changes, he found the whole downtown was completely different.

Lenny's was gone. The previous home of the store was an empty shell that Tuck and Verse passed as they approached the downtown. The new owners of what was now the Little River Package Store were set up in a flimsy prefab building just north of the barber shop. They were two rowdy young white men from Chicago who claimed they had moved here to give up the big city, but they brought the big city with them in the music that blasted from the store and the new displays installed in the store. Cardboard displays they called dumps offering every possible kind of alcohol littered the floor. The dumps had pictures of fast cars, loose women, and beer bottles wearing football helmets.

Tuck's objection grew not from any sort of morality. Cars could be fast, women loose, and maybe a beer bottle could take his place in Friday's game in Headway for all he cared, but the character of the store was gone. Friendly Lenny, who knew the customers and what they liked to drink, and who displayed bottles and cans of his product in old glass cases that once lined the walls, was gone. Now those cases lined the back of the outside of the store from whence they would be hauled away as soon as the county trashman, Clifford, could figure out a way to load them onto his pickup truck. The two proprietors, besides remaining nameless, apparently refused to help Clifford lug them away after moving them once from the old Lenny's and apparently deciding they simply wouldn't work in the new store.

Tuck felt like calling Clifford and lending a hand, but Tuck had too much to do already. However, something needed to be done to remove the unsightly cases. They looked hurriedly removed, and that lack of care shattered most of the glass doors. Tuck could see the cases even now as he approached the intersection with the county road. Verse loped in wolf form a few feet to the side and ahead of Tuck.

Patty's too, though it kept a friendly if new name, was not a friendly place. With a little money in her hands already, the lady became purely profit-minded and edged prices higher seemingly every day. With no local alternative for food, residents unwilling or uninterested in making the forty-minute drive to the nearest chain grocery had to pay the higher prices.

Tuck did not see the completed project himself, but one day at school Melissa told him that the work Willford Stems did that Saturday was now the new Little River post office. The days of handing the mail to the barber were gone too. Now the mail was in the hands of a woman who frowned on giving you service for stamps and packages unless you bought some groceries.

Melissa, at least, seemed aware of these changes, and was discouraged by them too. So many people just accepted them. They didn't register Patty's greed or the arrogance of the Chicago brew boys. At first this made Tuck feel he was jumping to conclusions or showing a small-town nature that could not yield to change or the intrusion of technology.

So he talked about it with Melissa the day before when they both skipped biology class for some independent study. Tuck smiled, because they mostly did just talk. The studying was sublime, but very limited. He found that he could speak with her freely. Of course, he couldn't talk to her about the Garou, but he was concerned not just because he was Garou. The changes in Little River disheartened him because it was people getting ahead of themselves again, as Oliver often ranted.

People making plans without regard for the consequences.

Tuck, though, didn't know whether simply to blame the Wyrm or hold the people themselves at fault. Were they so easily swayed that any effort at manipulating them would bend the course of events to come? But then he was confronted by people like Melissa. People who saw the changes and wanted to resist but alone did not possess the volume to call the others another way.

Melissa was worth a fight in her own right, but Tuck knew there must be others like her. Others aware of how much was wrong with the world. It was for those people, and the kind of assistance they needed to see that the world could be a healthy place, that he needed to play in the football game. It sounded very odd to Tuck, but he knew it was true.

Tuck's thoughts were interrupted by a screeching of tires, and he quickly looked up to see a massive collision in the intersection of Main Street and the county road. A black-and-yellow bumblebee Vega from the mid-70s was met midway through the intersection by a pickup truck that apparently didn't even stop before barreling through.

Alerted in time to see the accident, Tuck watched as the northbound truck crushed the driver's side of the car. The Vega bounced northward as well and shuddered to a stop. A trail of metal and glass marked the path the now interlocking vehicles traveled.

Verse was the first to react. He dashed toward the accident, and Tuck quickly followed. Apparently relatively unharmed, the driver of the truck pulled himself slowly out of his seat and stood beside his mangled vehicle, rubbing his knees.

Tuck asked him quickly, "Are you okay?"

The man, a bit dazed, suffering from the shock of disbelief that always follows an incident like this, nodded.

The driver of the Vega didn't appear to be quite as fortunate. Verse was at the crushed door trying to paw it open when Tuck neared. Through the blown-out window Tuck saw that the driver was a classmate of his, Ralph Cleveland. Ralph was a bright, unatheletic boy, and Tuck knew him reasonably well because they had cooperated on a couple of papers for a literature class during Tuck's first quarter at Little River High.

Skinny and redheaded, as it seemed all Ralphs were, the boy wasn't moving. Fortunately, Ralph appeared to be wearing his seat belt. His body hung limply in it.

Verse was still working at the door. His large wolf paws were digging along the seam between the crumpled door and the crushed body of the car.

"Shit," said the man behind Tuck. Tuck glanced back and saw the man still dusting himself off.

Tuck hurried around to the other side of the car. It was badly damaged as well, but it seemed as though this door would open. Too bad it was locked.

"Is he hurt?" asked the man.

"Yes," Tuck clipped at the man. "Just pulling right through the intersection, were you?" he added with more than an edge of anger and frustration. He didn't recognize the man.

"Settle down, boy, I didn't do anything wrong. I'm sorry the boy is hurt, of course. How's he look?"

Tuck was amazed. The man was telling the truth! To Tuck's gifted senses, it wouldn't matter even if the man simply thought he was telling the truth. He stood stunned until Verse whined, frustrated at the stuck door.

"Over here, Verse," Tuck said as he took off his sweatshirt.

The man asked, "That a trained wolf?"

Tuck ignored him and wadded the sweatshirt around his left hand. It was silly to think about when someone was hurt inside the car, but Tuck would need his right hand and arm to be perfectly healthy on Friday, so he couldn't risk injury now.

His hand safely padded, Tuck put his weight into a jab at the passenger-side window. It cracked but did not shatter. A second hard blow completed the job. Tuck shook out his left hand, and the sweatshirt unspun and sprinkled glass shards as it fell to the ground. At the same time he used his right to pull the lock on the door. His left was ready then and pulled the car door open.

As soon as he crawled into the car he saw the pool of blood dripping from Ralph's face. Tuck saw that it might be dribbling from his mouth, which was bad because he knew that meant there could be internal damage. He called over his shoulder to Verse. "We need emergency help here. Call an ambulance or something."

"Me?" said the man, a little confused. His face shone big through the cracked driver-side window. "I'm over here."

Tuck smiled grimly. It wouldn't do to have Verse go make the call. "Yeah, please go into the barber shop over there and ask Frank to call for an ambulance."

Then Tuck reached back out of the car and retrieved his sweatshirt from the ground. He shook it out and then used it to brush fragments and slivers of glass from the passenger seat. He could not settle into the seat better, so he crawled back in for another look at Ralph. The boy still wasn't moving. Tuck saw he was still breathing, and steadily too, so that at least was a good sign.

He used his sweatshirt again, now to wipe the glass off Ralph's hands and face. Then he turned his attention to the blood.

"Ralph?" he whispered to the unconscious boy. "It's okay, buddy. This is Tuck Statton. You're going to be all right. Help's on the way. Just hold tight."

Sitting in the totaled Vega stanching the blood of his perhaps nearly dead friend, Tuck noticed the most recent change in Little River. Tuck sat staring at it dumbly. It was a traffic light.

The light was the kind suspended by wires in the middle of the intersection. It had four different facings in its shiny yellow casing that each directed the three signal lights toward a different approach.

He couldn't believe it. Where were the warning signs suggesting a change had been made to the intersection? Ralph must have stopped by habit at the intersection and then proceeded through it though his light was red. Seeing the oncoming truck, he must have assumed it was going to stop at what used to be a stop sign. Instead, the driver, not from the region and heeding the traffic light he noticed because he was not in the habit of doing otherwise, did not stop his vehicle.

"Verse," Tucked asked, "can you do something to help this boy?" Tuck knew the wolf had been taught some gifts of healing by the spirits. He hoped they would work on a human.

Verse yipped an affirmative, so Tuck crawled out of the car. "Then hurry before the man returns."

Verse hopped in and unleashed his long sticky tongue on Ralph's face. After a moment, the blood ceased to dribble from his mouth.

Meanwhile, Tuck wondered why no one came from their shops to investigate the collision they must have heard. Just then the man came huffing and puffing back from the barber shop. "He's calling," he said.

"Thanks," said Tuck, utterly discouraged. How could he live in a town where the people wouldn't even help each other?

"You know," Tuck added, "this intersection doesn't need a traffic light."


Sower of Thunder saw the Wyrm-spawn beckon the child to his death. Of course, Thunder felt no remorse for the pitiful human life, but the young Garou who walked with the wolf displayed a disregard for life that Thunder found repulsive. The same casual attitude was no doubt taken when he helped murder the wolves further upstate.

Thunder was also in homid form. It was a shape he found repugnant, but he was here to glean every last bit of information from the surroundings that he could. He wore clothes taken from a house in a sub-division a few miles from here. It had been a simple matter to walk in the front door as a crinos, and while the Delirium shed its blinding light on the poor humans' minds, Thunder took what he needed. The humans inside, a woman and three children, would likely suffer from years of nightmares and maybe even psychological problems, but they were all prob-lems that were not Thunder's. Besides, if these Wyrm-infected Garou were allowed to roam the streets much longer, then that woman and her fam-ily would have far greater worries than a troubled night of sleep now and again.

Thunder instinctively knew from the way the wolf acted around the other Garou in homid form that the homid was the pack leader. Not even an Ahroun. How pathetic. At least Thunder's pleasure would be drawn out through several kills. The Ahroun could be enjoyed separately. The pack leader would be a joy all its own. Especially now that Thunder knew him to be a Silver Fang, that tribe of blood-tainted, inbred weaklings. Thunder would fight that one in crinos or lupus form so he could watch the oh-so-white coat drip delicious red.

Thunder desired better fights than that sad metis offered several days ago. He almost regretted not let-ting the mongrel live so it could spread stories of Thunder's might. But he was not in this Gaia-for-saken place to earn a reputation. He was here to end a threat, so the creature had to die.

Thankfully he was done in town. He could return

to the wilderness and prepare for more slaughter. He considered waiting for these two Garou, but Thunder thought that might be too much of a rush. Better to return to the forest and shake off the doldrums this town instilled before asking too much of his senses and reflexes.

Besides, Thunder thought an attack next on the home of the Stargazers when all the pack was away was the best move to make. He smiled at the thought of taking the battle to the enemy stronghold.

Because Ally insisted on touring different parts of the county each day on their trips home from classes, Tom was forced to run the countryside as well. He didn't know what she expected to find, considering that a number of attempts to find a trail or even a scent of Simon's killer had already failed.

Today's run back was to be a longer one. They would circle north of downtown Little River and loop far to the northeast before clockwise circling back around the town proper to return to the Steins' farm.

Tom was careful to remain on his guard on all the trips because there was no telling when the Wyrm might attack again. He thought anything would be foolish to attack two Ahroun Garou on the hunt, but none of them knew the power they were up against. Only poor Simon knew.

The search was as fruitless as ever. There seemed to be nothing to find, which is why they all felt so helpless even three days after Simon had been killed. There was no way they could seek vengeance. It really upset Ally, and she took that frustration out on others, though not on him so much as she used to. Now it was Tuck, whom she blamed more and more for being a poor leader because nothing was being done. But nothing could be done.

There were perhaps some exceptional means of tracking the killer, but those would only be used as a last resort. For example, there had been talk of holding another moot and joining their voices in an irresistible Howl of Summoning, but Tuck struck that idea down. He claimed, and rightly in Tom's mind, that they should try to find out more about the enemy before forcing a confrontation. It might to their benefit as well to remain as secretive as possible, hopefully learn something of use, and then attack the enemy with surprise on their side.

Regardless, Tom enjoyed these runs with his sister. There was always a closeness between them, but all they had been through since the earliest moments they began to discover their Garou heritage brought them even closer. Tom was thankful they were twins, so that they both received the recessive gene that allowed them both to be full-fledged Garou. It would have been disappointing if one of them was only a Kinfolk.

As Kinfolk they could still be involved in Garou society, but it might have created a chasm between the two instead of bringing them together.

Tom and Ally both heard the men at the same time. Neither was particularly surprised. Several of the other kids at school were remarking about the construction crews wandering the fields around their houses. Sometimes, apparently, the men would first approach the house to announce that they were investigating the property, but usually, it seemed, they simply helped themselves.

No one was very worried about it. Some were actually happy, hoping that a new road was being planned that might better connect Little River to the outside world. Tom and Ally both tried to convince such fools that they should be happy for the lack of traffic through the town. Traffic only brought trouble.

The twin Ahroun slipped quietly through the forest and neared the edge of a clearing where there was indeed a group of men in utility jumpsuits. There were no heavy vehicles other than their trucks, which unfortunately and ominously bore no insignia. A machine was attached to the back of one of the trucks, a large borer of some kind, but other than that the men appeared to have only a standard variety of handheld power tools.

The two Ahroun watched for a while as men activated the borer at a couple of carefully marked and measured locations, but they talked little other than the occasional request to turn the machine on or off.

They seemed foreboding to Tom, but he supposed that could simply be because he didn't know what they were doing. They might be very ordinary men simply doing the job assigned them, or they might be servants of the Wyrm injecting foul substances into the ground. There was no cause to suspect the latter, though, so Tom held his emotions in check. No sense getting riled up about something that wasn't even happening.

Tom wished they could approach the men and ask questions, but they would be naked if they changed back to homid form, and since they had come from school they were not wearing the special robes charmed by Sarah and Oliver. Maybe they should consider wearing those during such trips in the future.

As he continued to watch the men, Tom also noted that Ally was becoming impatient. Maybe she wasn't doing as well controlling her emotions. So many horrible things were taking place lately that Tom couldn't fault her for giving in a bit to her inner rage. He dearly hoped that these men, if innocent, did not pay for her anger. Tom was certain Ally possessed more control than that.

Then again, he could be wrong. Still in the form of a wolf, Ally charged the workers.

Taken completely by surprise, Tom bolted after her, trying desperately to catch up. He wanted to be at hand to intervene if she was losing control. However, he needed to be wary of not interfering. Maybe she saw something that prompted her sudden rush. He suspected she would tell him if that was the case, but if she was near the breaking point with rage already, then maybe she was incapable of communicating a reason to him.

Barreling across the open field in north-central Illinois, Tom did feel a bit foolish. No wolves lived here anymore.

Ally's apparent onslaught was fierce. She growled and howled as she ran and immediately drew the attention of the half-dozen or so men. Tom had earlier counted six, but now saw there were seven. The man Tom supposed was the site manager rose from where he was seated out of view behind one of the trucks.

The men reacted by dropping their equipment and scrambling toward the trucks. They appeared frightened and seemed anything but diabolical servants of the Wyrm.

"Careful, Ally," Tom barked. "Don't do something foolish."

Whether she heard him or not, Ally veered sharply to the side. She did this though she could easily catch one straggler, a worker who had been kneeling and guiding the borer into the ground and so was the last to see the wolves. Instead, Ally completed a circle around the trucks, barking and baying the entire time. That she barked could have revealed to one of the men that she was not really a wolf, as only psychologically immature dogs (or humans new to being wolves) resort to such baby activity, but her size and obvious strength left no room for questions.

Tom slowed to a trot and settled back on his haunches to join his sister barking. He unleashed a furious stream of thunderous barks that caused the men to cover their ears despite the metal and glass that interposed.

Ally continued to run furious circles around the trucks.

As a final coup de grâce, Tom stood and ambled to some of the machinery the panicked men left behind. As the men stared wide-eyed at the wolves, Tom unloaded a steady stream of steaming piss on two shovels, a one-man hand rotor, and a spike-tipped jackhammer.

And that did it. The engines of the two vehicles fired to life and the trucks pulled away. Ally bounded briefly after one of the trucks but did not make lengthy pursuit.

When Ally returned to Tom, she wore a toothy grin. Both yipping with laughter, Tom and Ally began the jog home.


As had been the case for the past several days, Tuck woke Thursday morning and stared at the empty, unrustled bunk over Verse's bed instead of beginning his usual morning rituals. The bed was always empty when Tuck rose, but the blankets usually draped over the side and formed part of a canopy around the still-sleeping Verse, who usually arrived downstairs before Tuck anyway because the wolf didn't make use of the bathroom despite Sarah's imploring. He waited to take care of his morning business after breakfast when in wolf form again and in the woods.

Tuck felt lonely when he woke now. The coziness of being the middle person to rise was somehow reassuring. That sense was now lost. The family, the pack, was minus one member, and Tuck dwelled on that each morning.

Even after he pulled himself out of bed, he couldn't help thinking of Passer because the bathroom was so clean. Before, it was always in a bit of disarray because Passer was still unaccustomed to the finer points of its functioning. There were little, and sometimes large, messes later cleaned by Oliver, who continued to complete the unwanted job of cleaning all the bathrooms in the house even after the pack members took residence.

Tuck relieved his laden bladder (he didn't comprehend how Verse could wait until after breakfast!), and then set about the remainder of his ritual. For Tuck it truly was a ritual. He called it his Rite of Purification, and as no elder or spirit tutored him in it, he assumed it was one he created and developed by repetition. Regardless, it could have a very real effect.

By concentrating on the very mundane tasks of brushing his teeth, washing his hands and face, swabbing the wax out of his ears, and dressing in fresh clothing, Tuck created a breathless moment to begin his day. The calm and care he put into this task settled his mind and was a time he could recall later when hard-pressed. At that later instant, the clarity he'd experienced earlier in the day soothed his mind and allowed him to proceed with greater care, caution, and confidence.

There was no guilt in how he later recalled this moment. Whether it was in the heat of a pass rush to allow him to find his receiver and deliver a pass with greater assurance and accuracy, in the frenzied final seconds of a timed test in history class, or in the face of embarrassment and hesitation when he leaned to kiss Melissa in a grocery store, Tuck did not worry that the enchanted moment passed without proper use.

The ritual so encompassed his thinking, though, that it was not until he was completely awake and at the top of the stairs about to descend that he remembered there was no school today. Classes were called off today and tomorrow in celebration of the Huskies' place in the regional-final football game. He was supposed to rest for the big game, sleeping late and waking only in time for the two o'clock pep rally.

Another bonfire. Tuck shook his head remembering how well Passer performed that evening of the other bonfire only a week ago. What would the fire be tonight without the fire elementals Passer sought to warn and preserve?

Tuck stood motionless at the top of the flight of curved stairs as he considered this. He ran his hand slowly on the banister on the top of the handrail. He grinned when he recalled the first night the entire pack was in the house after they completed the Rite of Passage in the Umbra at the Caern at Little Rock.

Passer, shifting from his natural crinos form to the more manlike, so slightly lighter, glabro form, slid down the railing and smashed the banister at the bottom. It was a repair Oliver had not yet made, though he claimed he knew how, a point he became very defensive and argumentative about whenever it was broached, which was therefore often, of course.

The smile broke the spell over Tuck, and he wandered downstairs even though it was a day to sleep in. He wanted badly to take a walk alone in the woods, but he couldn't break his own rule. Verse was a good companion for such walks; he was quiet and walked in wolf form, so they did not converse much. But there were times when Tuck just wanted to be alone to think.

So Tuck entered the empty kitchen, poured himself some orange juice, and settled down to read more in the Severnson book. He would wait at least an hour before calling Melissa to see if she was going to the pep rally.


It wasn't like being the leader of a pack of wolves, but enough of the girls in the pep club were bitches, so it was almost the same. Ally chuckled to herself. Actually, these rural girls were as tough as nails, as tough as any she'd ever met, and they knew how to not take any shit from the hefty farmers' sons. Or the football players. That was their main activity during pep rallies, though they had to be especially vigilant when the players were so excited and the day was a holiday from school.

There was very little chaperoning for the day's pep rally, despite the more than one hundred students assembled around a bonfire burning on the same scorched earth and in the same practice field as before. Many of the teachers were treating this as a pre-Christmas holiday and were traveling to Chicago or Milwaukee. The teachers present were the ones most involved with the student body and the ones as proud of the football team as any of the students. But even they were attending in a largely unofficial capacity.

That meant more work for Ally and her glee club. And it meant more mischief from the rascally players.

Fortunately, Tuck was proving that he did have some leadership abilities, at least among humans. Ally watched as he tried to keep the players in line and remind them to rest for the big game tomorrow. She heard him whisper something to a particularly rowdy defensive back to the effect that there would be much more to celebrate if they came back this weekend with a regional championship.

Something in Tuck's attitude was odd to Ally, though. He was always very competitive when it came to playing this crazy game, but he seemed particularly earnest on this occasion. He was making the game seem like a very important thing, and the students were believing him.

Ally hoped he wasn't setting everyone up to be disappointed. Great quarterback or not, the Huskies were facing the defending state champs at Headway High. The Headway Hornets, as they were called, were a notoriously rough-playing, well-coached team. They were 29–0 over the last two seasons. Undefeated last year all the way through the state championship, they were unbeaten this year as well. That is what a school could do, Ally knew, when it operated in a rich county and commanded a huge budget. It meant better equipment, like elaborate weight machines instead of country muscle; and paid coaches, instead of volunteers, or maybe ones who split time with classroom instruction.

She supposed, though, that it was his job to fire up the players, and that meant in part the portion of the student body at the pep rally. Her pep rally.

Ally's Rally the other girls called it. She refused to think that Tuck was purposely grandstanding in order to take the credit for the rally, but after the way he'd humiliated her during the Revel, she wouldn't put anything past him.

Actually, she realized after a little thinking that he didn't let her win in order to hurt her, but even so, a leader who had that kind of judgment maybe shouldn't be leader.

There were no firemen here. Ally found it impossible to get any cooperation from them this time. Not that they were unwilling apparently, but within the past week the town passed by-laws setting up new series of procedures for holding a public gathering like this. So Ally just told everyone that the bonfire was okayed and the pep rally proceeded easily.

There was actually almost no danger of a repetition of last Friday's problems because fire elementals were unwilling or unable to enter the area. Sarah and Oliver both attempted summoning independently, and also in a joint effort, each of the last few days. Besides, Ally was just as happy not to have those ridiculous firemen here, though she would have enjoyed laughing in the face of the Duck-cousin Denim.

The girls in charge of stitching the fabric effigy of a hornet did a very good job. Their efforts were cheered by an appreciative crowd gathered around the same fire pit as last week. The hornet was a grand likeness of the one embroidered in the many flags and banners that flew over the Headway football field. A pair of bright blue wings lofted a bulbous, yellow body with several black legs and round, googly black eyes. The entire cloth-stuffed creature was attached to the end of a stick by a stout piece of rope.

The girls passed the hornet to a trio of cheerleaders, who each firmly took the stick and began to run in circles around the fire. The other two cheerleaders punched at the flying stuffed animal when it passed by them the first time. That prompted other students to join in, and when the hornet flew by the area where the football players were standing, Ally understood why it took three girls to carry the effigy. Some of the bigger boys connected with heavy punches that set the rope spinning and threatened to pull the stick from the hands of the cheerleaders.

One of the more athletic players, Greg Frederickson, a boy Ally liked quite well, jumped and managed to kick the hornet even though it was suspended at least six feet in the air. Ally knew it wasn't a tough test for a crinos werewolf, but it was a feat for an immature human.

All of a sudden, the bonfire begin to spit gouts of flame. An explosion knocked the three cheerleaders to the ground and the roar of the flame momentarily became deafening. Ally cursed under her breath. Her and her ideas about there being no danger! She'd never forgive herself.

She instantly hit the ground rolling, then squared back on her feet by the side of the downed cheerleaders. She helped them orient themselves so they could at least crawl to safety.

No sooner were they up and crawling than another explosion rocked the student body. Where surprised silence accompanied the first explosion, screams of alarm and panic greeted this second.

Ally struggled for an idea to protect the students and could only think of something from her Wendigo heritage. Motionless near the bonfire where the cheerleaders fell, Ally summoned a gentle wind. At first the breeze only played tricks with Ally's hair, but soon it was a steady beat that fanned and swirled the flames upward so they could not blast out.

She was concentrating so deeply on this that she was startled by a hand on her shoulder. She opened her eyes. It was brother Tom.

"Good job, but you should stop. Look." Tom put his hand under Ally's arm and helped her stand to see where he was pointing. A group of boys wearing sweatshirts of gold and blue sprinted away from the bonfire and toward the parking lot on the other side of the football field.

"Fireworks," Tom said.

"Fuckers!" Ally shook off Tom's helping hand and chased the boys.

A large group of football players were already pursuing, though they had little hope of catching the saboteurs considering their lengthy head start. Ally had an advantage, though. Tuck may refuse to do it in football games, but Ally had every reason right now to slightly transform her legs to thicken her already healthy and sleek thighs and calves.

With this added muscle power, Ally quickly overtook the slow linemen, who exchanged perplexed glances as a girl faster than any of the wide receivers raced by them. Even Ally, though, could not overtake the wide receivers who had the jump on her, and certainly there was no chance of reaching the offenders before they jumped in their BMW and sped away.

Ally was so intent on the chase and running so furiously that she barely avoided a collision with the handful of players and couple of students who pulled up short in the parking lot. She braced herself to a stop on the back of one, who turned out to be Greg, but she wormed her way through the small crowd without recognizing or caring about this fact.

She saw a splayed figure on the concrete pavement. A student near her vomited. The puddle of the chunks of food splashed over one paw of the dead animal. It was a beautiful dog, a husky. One that must have been young and healthy. Now it was mutilated and torn.

Ally didn't gaze long enough to record all the horrors committed on the poor animal. She dropped to her knees, mindlessly kneeling in the midst of puke and blood, and she clutched the husky's neck and raised its head to hers. It looked so much like a wolf!

Through the tangle of matted fur, Ally was just able to make out the words spray-painted in front of the dog in all caps: THE FUTURE LOOKS DUSKY FOR THE HUSKIES!!!!

Now it was more than a football game to Ally too.

# CONVERSATION

"Was it a foolish move?"

"She is an Ahroun."

"That doesn't answer my question."

"Doesn't it?"

"Obviously not."

"Or obviously so. She is an Ahroun, so it was not a foolish move. She was protecting her territory, and as an Ahroun she's disposed, and presumably capable against ordinary men, to do it in the way she chose."

"At least she didn't damage them with the Delirium because she remained lupus."

"That would have been too much. Ally is a good warrior, with a good sense of when to act and how to react. It's why there are bound to more problems between her and Tuck."

"Why?"

"Because they are both exceptional Garou, and both, I think I am right to suggest, have the makings of great champions."

"You don't think there's a bit of a cruel streak within her."

"There most certainly is, but that gives her an edge. While we obviously don't condone the more violent aspects of Garou nature, it is still a legitimate means of combating the Wyrm. A case could be made that it is Garou like her that we need first, ones not afraid to act in a way that's completely instinctual, in order for the more important ones, in our humble opinions, like Tuck, to develop. While he questions and pines and ponders, the Wyrm is moving."

"So you think Ally should assume the role of pack leader during this crisis?"

"No."

"But you said . . ."

"I said a case could be made, and it's one you've made extremely well in past debates, dear, which is why I admit to its potential plausibility, but it's not one I accept. I feel Tuck already trusts himself. I feel he's as capable of making an instinctual decision as Ally. He just needs to instinctually trust his instincts."

"That's something that's easier for a warrior to learn, I suppose."

"Yes."

"It's easy to fight, no matter your beliefs or culture, but it's more difficult to grapple with the implications of so much new knowledge. That, I imagine, is the problem Tuck is having."

"One we both experienced as well."

"Yes. But we haven't become Garou champions. Why will Tuck?"

"Will we not? Have we not? We came here because we didn't seek glory, but when Ragabash tell the tale of Guides-to-Truth—"

"Quiet!"

"—Guides-to-Truth, our role will be mentioned?"

"Certainly. And I suppose Tuck won't hide from this attention as we have done."

"Exactly. He's a quarterback, the center of the sports team. He's pack leader. It's in his nature to lead by example, not live by example."

# 7

# REAP AND SOW

The long wait finally paid off. The pack finally all left together. Just the two Stargazers remained inside the home. Sower of Thunder crouched in the woods in his smaller glabro form. He'd been waiting since a few hours after he slipped back to the countryside following his visit into Little River until now, more than an hour after the residents' brood had departed.

He felt entirely safe here. If the Wyrm-spawn did not respond to his presence immediately, then they were probably unaware of him. It meant they were not protecting themselves with spirit guardians or messengers of any kind. Foolish of them.

Sower of Thunder gazed at the house one last time. It was a big, two-story house. The front yard was short, and steep where it inclined up and away from the gravel road that passed in front of it. The side yards were large. Very wide, each was bisected by a line of trees running in line with the house.

Large but very climbable hickories, Thunder noted, reflexively recording any information that might impact the coming fight.

Fight? He chortled under his breath. He suspected there would be little trouble with a pair of Wyrm-degraded Stargazers.

Thunder was hiding in the woods behind the house. Standing, he crept silently to the back of the free-standing garage that was also behind the house. It was a two-car garage, and was in greater disrepair than the house, which meant it was in relatively poor condition. There was a door into the garage from the rear, so Thunder crept around it until he reached the front. Then he stepped backwards, away from the house, and melted into the shadows of the open garage.

He waited like that for several moments. He still received no sense of an alarm or received any indication that the Stargazers knew their death approached. He smiled at that thought. It would surely put the young pack off balance to lose their elders. Without them the youth would become easily dispatched, mindless morons.

When Thunder was again comfortable, he was again ready to move. He unfocused his eyes to spread his gaze to all the windows and door panes that stared from the back of the house. He watched them all for one moment to be certain no one was looking. He detected nothing.

Then he quickly made his move. He dashed to the back of the house, where he pressed himself against faded vinyl exterior protection. As he paused for a mere second, he shifted into his favorite, though definitely not birth, form—crinos. Almost instantly he became the ten-foot killer responsible for the destruction of countless enemies.

Poised to make his next move, Thunder cursed himself for a fool. He was so unused to fighting in any environment but a natural one that he forgot there were certain size restrictions indoors. In particular, doorways posed a problem. Oh well, he thought, here at least was something in the favor of those who would soon die. It just might allow them to evade him for a few moments longer. A few moments, of course, could be staggeringly crucial in a battle, but only in a battle so easily swayed by odd factors like that. This wasn't that kind of battle.

Thunder shrank back into his glabro form. Even so, he wasn't tiny. His physique was massive enough to make even the most powerful wrestlers or bodybuilders flinch, and the addition of slightly more than six inches of height helped add even more to his bulk. Even as a seven-foot, four-hundred-pound slab of muscle, though, Thunder was acutely aware of this form's shortcomings compared to the crinos.

From a fighting perspective, the only viewpoint important to Thunder, the most crucial difference was the lack of a tail. Though small, the crinos tail added balance and could be used to overcome inertia at critical moments in a fight.

At least his nails were still long. And as long as they were on his mind, he concentrated briefly and performed a miracle considered very minor among the Garou. His long nails now scintillated in the afternoon sunlight. They were honed to the sharpness of a razor.

Then he paused to see if he could locate his prey indoors. Left only with a feeling they were not in the first room, he tested the door. It was unlocked.

Thunder entered a large room he thought was the kitchen. Nothing seemed to be cooking on the four-eyed metal machine called a stove, so Thunder suspected he would not be met in here. He padded across the tiled floor to a doorway opposite. His stout fingers curled and uncurled as he got a sense of his footing. The floor, unlike what could be inside homes, was not slippery.

He noted with pleasure that the ceilings were relatively high inside. If in danger for some reason, he could assume crinos form and not be impeded too much.

Pressed to the almost nonexistent shadows at the doorway, Thunder saw a large room beyond and another doorway just beyond and to the left of the one he commanded. There were relatively few furnishings, which was all Thunder really comprehended of such things. He did not recognize, nor did he care about, anything concerning the quality of them or lack thereof.

He paused. Still not a sound. He preferred for the fight to begin immediately. Thunder found the insides of structures like this to be slightly unnerving. He wasn't always sure if he was looking for the right kinds of accesses. Did doors open to rooms or did they simply reveal closets?

He also missed crinos form.

But Thunder pressed forward. A glance to the left revealed a wood-paneled, windowless room. There appeared to be no egress other than the one Thunder controlled, so he moved on.

He tracked his position in the house largely by looking out the windows to his right. He traveled the entire depth of the house, which consisted of only this one large room plus the kitchen through which he'd entered.

The entire approach to the front of the house was

marked by Thunder watching his reflection in the large windows ahead of him. They permitted a view of the front yard. Watching himself like that allowed a 360-degree view, for he could see behind himself as well. He didn't trust these glabro senses enough for smelling and hearing only to do a complete job for him.

However, there was nothing. They must be upstairs, he thought. Hopefully in the heat of a ritual to the Wyrm that he could interrupt and desecrate.

At the front of the large room was a doorway to Thunder's left that opened to the foyer of the house. The floor here was wood-tiled. Thunder approached carefully. It appeared that the stairs were in there, and a few more steps confirmed that. Since that was the case his care was well-founded. The enemy would have the advantage of position over Thunder based on their superior height. Though he could assail tremendous heights by leaping, they might still use ranged weaponry to gain an early advantage.

When he entered the chamber he did so with a quick step and immediately looked above him. He was wise to do so.

The base of the stairs was to the right and behind Thunder. They swept up along the inside of the exterior wall of the house, curling slightly left until they reached a landing about twenty feet above floor level. This single landing then stretched to the left away from the wall, so its broad side faced Thunder and continued to burrow back into the unseen heart of the second floor of the house.

The two Stargazers were poised on that balcony.

Thunder's growl at them was almost a laugh. They stood with their arms at their sides as if conceding defeat already. Thunder hoped for at least some sport. There was one advantage—they had both assumed crinos form, though theirs was much smaller than the Ahroun's.

The female stood barely seven feet tall, Thunder's glabro height, and was much slimmer still than Thunder was currently. Her lustrous coat was pale with gray, almost vertical striping.

The male, whose head was bowed and eyes closed, stood in a very poised stance. He was perhaps a bit less than a foot taller than the female, but his coat was much darker. Almost entirely black, the fur seemed to absorb sunlight that shone into the tall room through the windows by the door as well as the two windows along the staircase wall.

Remaining poised himself, and unwilling to act until he could react, Thunder looked again to make certain the male's eyes were closed. They were, so he turned his attention to the female.

A mistake.

A trick.

She was staring directly at him. When their eyes locked, Thunder was unable to break the strange hold. Frozen in place, he was still able to think, though his thoughts became frenzied. They might pose no physical challenge, he supposed, but they might try to trick him.

Thunder hated to be tricked, but he couldn't break the eyelock. The female's eyes seemed glassy and frightful. Such was the intensity of the gaze that any being lesser than a Garou, perhaps lesser than himself, might flee before her. Thunder resisted that impulse, but he was unable to do anything else.

Though his eyes were glued to the female's, Thunder could tell that the male was moving. Not threateningly, but he was revealing something.

The male called down to him, "We recognize you now, ronin. You are He-Who-Serves-His-Master, an outcast among from the Red Talon allowed to roam as a ronin only because of your great rank among them. They disowned you but granted you the opportunity to break the hold the Wyrm has upon your spirit. They thought a champion so great might succeed. You have failed. We see the corruption of your soul, but I command that it be revealed to all. You will not be allowed to wear the hide of a Garou so long as your heart is sickened by the Wyrm."

Finally, the hold the bitch held over him slackened. She could not paralyze him for long. At the same time, though, Thunder felt his flesh begin to crawl. This caused a moment of panic until he realized there was nothing to fear.

After all, he was of the Wyrm. Nothing could harm him; so he knew in his soul. And his soul was revealed.

Free to move once more, Thunder turned to face the male, whose eyes were now open. The man's arms were extended over his head, though, and they held a long stick. The invisible fire from it rushed downward and streaked across Thunder's body in a great, searing gush.

The abundant hair across Thunder's naked, almost human frame flailed until it melted under the great heat and vanished to form great black welts on his Caucasian-pink flesh. When the great heat did not abate, the welts began to bubble and reddish buboes seemed to bob to the surface of the liquid black stains.

His vaguely Neanderthal glabro forehead flattened even more and seemed to crush the brain residing within. A thick green ichor dribbled out from all the orifices of Thunder's head—nose, ears, and even mouth.

While Thunder's body twisted and malformed under the steady attack of the fetish stick the Stargazer extended, the Garou felt no pain. Instead, he felt a welcome. As if the darkest secret he suspected, yet which remained unverified, had just been acknowledged. Thunder knew his power was partially that of the Wyrm and that he was but a piece in a great battle than could not be completely communicated to his limited brain. He also knew he had come to this house to kill the inhabitants.

The spirit of Sower of Thunder might have become perverted, but the conversion left all the strength, power, and courage of the great Garou he had once been. Thunder still intended for these Stargazers to die. But now it was because they did not accept the Wyrm.

When Thunder's transformation was complete, the stick the male held burst into flame. He dropped it and the burning dust scattered in the air over Thunder.

The man said, "Do your best, beast." Then he reassumed his odd, calculated stance. The female beside him took a step to create some distance between them, and then she assumed a more natural-seeming ready stance.

Thunder's answer was a ragged whisper, but the exact words didn't really matter.

Verse was sniffing at the corpse of the husky when a spirit threatened to pull him forcibly into the Umbra. He instinctively resisted, and even a moment later when he recognized that the spirit smelled like Oliver, he hesitated. He was within sight of too many humans.

So the wolf pulled himself away from Ally, who

released the dead husky. Tom and Tuck arrived at this time anyway, and Verse knew they would calm Ally.

Verse trotted behind the vacant concession stand and let himself go to the pull of the spirit. It was an elemental of the wind, the kind Oliver once told the pack was awakened when he entered a true Kailindo meditative state. That is, when he cleared his mind to use his martial powers to defend himself. Verse's mind jolted at the thought. Sarah and Oliver were facing some unknown threat. Perhaps whatever slew Passer was now attempting to crush the sept leaders as well.

Verse struggled at the hold of the wind spirit, who promptly released him back to the reality of matter. The wolf dashed back to the others. Frantic to get the attention of his packmates, Verse squirmed through legs of other humans and pounced at Tuck. The wolf stood on his hind legs and slapped Tuck's chest with his forepaws. He barked and in the minds of all three of his mates he formed a picture of Sarah and Oliver beset by a dark shadow who had the corpse of Passer slung on its back. It was a grotesque, shocking image to send, but Verse needed to communicate the dire nature of the need.

All three looked at the wolf, and Ally's anger cleared immediately to a look of dire purpose. Verse saw a fierce, baleful vengeance begin to shine in them. Stoking the fires of the eyes was an intense rage that Verse hoped Ally could contain until the pack arrived home.

The four scrambled toward the Steins' truck. Tuck shouted something to the students that Verse didn't catch. With Tom at the wheel and the other three in the back of the pickup, the Phoenix Pack flew home.

———

Sower of Thunder crouched in the foyer beneath the stairs in the house of the Stargazers. He watched them both carefully. Still completely confident in his greater strength and fulfilled by the admission that he was tainted by the Wyrm, Thunder readied himself for his onslaught.

Deftly, the male Stargazer (the Wyrm within Thunder now knew his name to be Oliver Nightsky) jumped atop the handrailing along the front edge of the balcony. At the same moment, Thunder felt a slight breeze gust, and gust again, though the windows in the foyer remained closed.

Oliver then initiated a series of impressive, nearly impossible, maneuvers. Thunder again felt helpless to react. Oliver's eyes were closed again, and the moment was perfect to leap and knock the weakling fool from his perch, but Thunder felt a need to watch. The Stargazer was displaying more than mere body artistry. When he moved with incredible speed, leapt and executed a series of complicated moves while seemingly floating, and rippled his body with a bizarre series of transformations that seemed to run full circle even from homid directly into lupus—though that was impossible—Oliver displayed a deadly art.

Thunder shuddered despite himself. Though Nightsky's claws were not even extended and his fangs not bared, Thunder felt suddenly ill at ease in the face of his enemy's calm, contemplative face. Thunder thought he was confident! This Garou possessed a disquieting air of self-assurance. It was as if he effortlessly accepted his indomitability.

Even so, Thunder howled. Windows unopened before now became lacerated with cracks, and the entire house seemed to shake as Thunder released his rage. From his crouch he vaulted upward, his razor-sharp claws glistening.

Oliver, still balancing with complete aplomb on the railing, spun to a stop—with his back facing the glabro.

Thunder smiled grimly as he hurtled to a collision with the Stargazer. Almost within reach, Thunder flexed his arm back and prepared for a mighty swing, though he worried that he wasn't outpacing either of his foes. Normally, his perceptions of combat flowed smoothly, quickly, and he was in complete control of the cadence of the moves and countermoves. When he leapt he usually seemed to be upon his enemy before the foe could even shriek in surprise. Such was not the case here. Thunder felt, if not slow, then at least sluggish.

He swung.

But Oliver wasn't there.

The Stargazer dropped to the floor of the balcony and quickly executed a backkick through the wooden struts of the railguard. Though the kick looked unimpressive because Oliver's leg lacked the huge muscles endowing Thunder, it was swift, and the tip of his toe generated a tremendous pressure cone at least six inches in diameter.

It was also accurate. It tore a gaping wound in Thunder's upper chest and sent the enormous glabro spinning backwards. Thunder blanked his mind and became a cat. The memories of a cat spirit filed his mind, and the Garou arched his body in tune with a cat's reflex. He struck the far wall, many feet above the front door, but even as he slid down the wallpapered surface, Thunder was obviously back in control of the motion of his body. He landed squarely on his feet and glanced at his chest.

The wound, though hideous, was trifling to Thunder. Not only did it not slow him for the moment, it would give him less pause after another moment. The tremendous healing capabilities of the Garou animated to seal the torn flesh. Had the wound been inflicted by a supernatural source, such as a spirit, or by silver, then the wound would heal painfully slowly, as slowly as it would take a human to recover from a similar sort of wound. The same would be true if the wound was caused by Garou fangs or claws.

It was the irony of intertribal warfare among the Garou, though such was not as prevalent as it was during some other times. Garou could withstand almost any foe except another Garou.

Oliver reversed his maneuver so that he again stood atop the railing. Then, in the tongue of the Garou, he said, "A warning, He-Who-Serves-His-Master, out of respect for what you once were. The Red Talons may have insanely granted you leave; I will grant you only another chance at redemption. Die with the Wyrm in your heart and you will die as the Wyrm."

As an afterthought, he added, "Feel grateful my Kailindo prowess is not as great as the one you seek. Yet the wind still beckons my body and soul and I shall ride it until you are redeemed or dead."

Thunder growled back also in the language of the Garou, "You should have used your claws when you had the chance, Nightsky."

Then Thunder spoke again in another voice. It was an echoing, unearthly promise of something to come that issued from Thunder's mouth but really seemed to emanate from a place far, far away. "You want wind, Windrider? Very well."

The experience felt at once invasive and comforting to Thunder. As only comfort remained when his new voice trailed off, Thunder ignored that instinct while giving in to another. He fought.

This time he charged up the stairs, his large feet overlapping two steps as he bounded up a half dozen every stride.

With a sudden gust of movement that was analogous to the wind, Oliver swept over to the top of the stairs and began to descend. In a series of pirouettes and dances, the Stargazer drifted down the stairs and met Thunder at about the halfway mark.

Razor claws streaking, Thunder launched a series of attacks at his slender opponent while still trying to move forward. Oliver, though, twisted forward and backward in opposition to the glabro's own changing momentum to avoid the blows. He spun forward as Thunder did, and when the Ahroun paused to strike a blow with a readied hand, the Stargazer just as quickly slid back out of range.

Oliver used every surface around him in his efforts. Thunder watched as the Garou bounded off the wall, the stairs, and the nearby banister and railing. Thunder found it difficult to get a bead on the whirling foe. The midnight black fur that shifted and swirled across Oliver's body as he quickly changed portions of the body from form to form hypnotized the Ahroun.

The same changes also provided the different kinds of footing and leverage required to generate the tornado of motion. A large crinos foot to check a motion. A human hand to grasp the railing. Lupus legs to generate speed.

The rapidity of these moves baffled Thunder, and despite his best efforts he was unable to lay a hand on the Garou. In all his battles he never fought an opponent who possessed more than an inkling of how to perform Kailindo, the only Garou martial art. The art combined forms of some human techniques, like tae kwon do, with the unique abilities of the Garou, such as the shape-shifting powers Oliver saw ably woven into his moves. Perhaps it was because he'd never faced a Stargazer or serene Wendigo, the two sorts most likely to possess even the temperament to master the art. Wendigo had a head start because they possessed an affinity for spirits of the wind, spirits crucial to the art.

Then the female, Sarah Rainsky, joined the fray. Thunder immediately saw that she was less adept at the martial art than her mate. She moved efficiently, but her moves displayed a conscious effort to incorporate the training she received, where Oliver's motion was flawless and flowing.

But Thunder couldn't scratch her either. Partly it was because he was so dizzy and addled. He might be unable to strike a foe hurtling directly at him at the moment. Partly it was due to Oliver, who took the offensive to distract Thunder from Sarah. The male Stargazer slashed shallow wounds in Thunder's arm, nipped at his back, and even raked Thunder's testicles once when he rolled between his legs. If these were the best attacks Oliver could offer, though, the battle would be a short one despite his obvious agility.

The Philodox and Galliard Stargazers spun in a dual orbit around the Ahroun Red Talon. Then, suddenly, they were gone.

Thunder stood alone at the top of the stairs. The slightest hint of a rustling whisper was the only sign from below that suggested where his enemies fled.

He raced after them. A rage was building in him. To know this rage and satisfy it was the only way to cleanse himself. Not of the Wyrm, for that was an immutable part of him now, but of the need the Wyrm planted within him.

Then he rushed through the doorway back to the huge room that spanned the distance from the front of the house to the kitchen. When he entered, Thunder immediately saw the pair at the other end, about forty feet from him. Oliver stood in front and Sarah to the left and behind him. She stood in the doorway to the kitchen. They both faced him.

The ceiling in this room was a good fifteen feet high, so Thunder decided to assume the crinos form. His rage made it a necessity. A Garou in crinos knew rage and bloodlust more than when in any other form, so by assuming it Thunder gave in to the rage he already knew.

Then he advanced. Oliver stepped out a few steps as well.

Also still in crinos, Oliver was eight feet tall, but perhaps only three hundred and fifty pounds. Thunder was in excess of nine feet in height and carried a bulky five hundred plus. Together they completely skewed the scale of even this large room. All the furnishings— a couch under the window, a long coffee table piled high with magazines like *National Geographic* and *Utne Reader,* several sitting chairs with side tables, and other pieces—seemed scaled down a couple factors.

Oliver stopped, but Thunder continued his approach. The little black mutt seemed determined to have a standing slugfest, which was fine by Thunder.

Keeping an even pace the entire time, Thunder looked to surprise Oliver once he was a few strides away with a sudden gallop to cover the remaining ground. One solid smash of his claws across the Stargazer's face, and the world of the Garou would be minus one Kailindo expert.

But Oliver seemed to anticipate the maneuver. Even as Thunder lunged, the other crinos stepped aside, his dark eyes glitteringly distinct from his black fur. Thunder rebounded from his attack. Reflexes simply couldn't be that fast.

He struck again, this time a looping left uppercut followed by a swipe with his right across the stomach. Oliver swayed like a quivering wire, first throwing his head back and then, even before Thunder's right began to move, his stomach as well. Both attacks connected only with air.

Thunder's rage percolated. He did not like being tricked and he did not like being made a fool.

Then the female unleashed a startling yipping howl. The obnoxious sound seemed in response to nothing that Thunder could see as he glanced at her.

Sharp claws lanced through his flesh.

When Thunder recovered from the spasm of pain, he saw, and felt, three long, parallel gashes along the length of this left arm. Oliver bobbed and weaved in front of him. Blood was dripping from his right paw.

Thunder howled his fury. He launched another flurry of attacks. A right-handed smash. A painful left jab. A short right swing. A sudden gnash with his fangs. All failed to connect with Oliver, though one of the attacks bludgeoned the end of the couch and sent it spinning through other tables and chairs.

Whether it was Kailindo or Garou gifts, the Stargazer seemed to anticipate every attack. Thunder remembered hearing tales of such. He heard a how master of the art might read your muscles' thoughts and attune his own reflexes so he could react to an attack with the audacity of an image in a mirror.

As Thunder was trying to gather his thoughts to prepare another offensive, the bitch began to bark and moan again. Reflexively, Thunder spun toward her again. And then cursed his foolishness. A longer, deeper triplet of gashes sluiced down his right arm. This time he responded immediately with an attack because he knew Oliver would be waiting.

Oliver ducked.

And Thunder went mad with frenzy.

He swung again immediately. And connected. It was an off-balance strike, and Thunder's claws did not rend the hated flesh of the Stargazer, but the enemy hurtled across the room and crashed through a window.

Thunder did not press his advantage on Oliver. Enraged, the Ahroun instead turned his attention to the female.

When he turned toward the doorway, Thunder found that Sarah had retreated into the kitchen. She still faced him, and her eyes twinkled ominously as she muttered something in a tongue the Ahroun did not understand.

Like a free man unshackled, the rage that moments before pounded through Thunder's veins was calmed. It was an unnatural release, though, and Thunder lacked the sense of euphoria that always accompanied a successful slaking of his rage.

He nearly wilted from fatigue and depression on the spot. He managed to upturn one eye and watch as Sarah completed working her magick upon him.

Then Oliver was on Thunder's back. The force of the landing staggered Thunder forward, and he smacked his head against the wall. An irritation that mostly just crowded him.

The Philodox's fangs dug deeply into the fur and flesh of Thunder's neck and gouged out huge hunks. It hurt. His survival and animal instincts were stilled dulled, but Thunder's warrior's instinct activated. He twisted his body around and prepared to drive the Garou into the wall.

Thunder lunged backwards, but his own back and shoulders struck the wall and drove into the plaster. Using superior grappling moves, the Stargazer shuffled down the back of the crinos, flipped between his legs, and rolled to his feet. Then he pounced again by leaping into the air and spinning quickly. A peculiar series of form shifts during this rotation brought more claws and fangs to bear on the Ahroun than should have been possible. The attacks unfurled the muscles from Thunder's breastbone and eventually scratched the bone itself.

Thunder roared his great pain and lashed out in his renewed rage to grab this annoying enemy. The rage clouded his thoughts and apparently rendered the Stargazer's Kailindo technique ineffective, because Thunder gained an armful of Garou.

The Ahroun squeezed the smaller crinos hard to his flayed chest. A choking noise erupted from the Stargazer, but then in an instant Oliver was gone again. A sudden shift to the smaller lupus form allowed him to slip free and scoot out of range.

Thunder lunged again and tagged Oliver's right flank. The Stargazer's legs spun from under him, so forceful was the blow, but he regained his balance and leapt two huge strides to create the distance he needed. Thunder charged after him.

Whirling and unexpectedly shooting upward into crinos form, Oliver seemed ready for the attack. But Thunder's instincts were blazing now. He reacted instantly to the new shape of his foe and shot a clawed paw at the offending head. The blow whistled by as a miss, shocking Thunder, who never missed such an easy shot.

When the shadow of his arm passed his line of sight, Thunder saw how Oliver managed it. Another instantaneous shift from crinos to homid reduced his height by over two feet. And now, his eyes blazing, Oliver drove a blow at Thunder's neck. His first two fingers seemed welded together as they moved like a mongoose taking a cobra and pounded the crinos.

Impossibly jarred and staggered by a strike involving no claws or fangs that caused no pain but nonetheless overpowered him, Thunder stumbled backwards. He felt his limbs seizing into paralysis.

The Stargazers did not hesitate. They showed no respite for a fallen foe. With demeanors of calm dedication to their task, they leapt upon him, the male at his torso and the female around his head, and began to dice him with their claws.

This paralysis did not mean loss of feeling, and the hurt of the wounds crackled through the fallen crinos. Then he dug deep. All the bile and hatred and corruption housed in his soul claimed his body and mind too. The taste of blood in his mouth was replaced by a cool, sinuous shape that soothed him even as it wormed through lips and shot forth in unbidden defense of the body that housed it.

And with a preternatural effort that threatened to crack the very bones refusing to move, Sower of Thunder's caged rage was loosed. His body shook with the vigor of a thousand earthquakes and tossed the tiny Garou from his awful frame.

When he stood, looming over the jumbled heap of Stargazers, with a thick cord of a sluglike tongue dripping from his mouth, He-Who-Serves-His-Master regarded the base creatures with disgust.

"I wonder why it spoke to Verse?" Ally shouted to everyone, including her brother, through the sliding window that opened from the cab of the truck. She seethed with rage, but wanted to know more about the enemy she was about to thrash.

"I know how to speak to the wind," Tom shouted proudly over his shoulder. Though he was also concerned, because he knew many spirits of the wind were active around the truck at this very moment.

No one answered for a moment as Tom drove the truck at breakneck speed and around turns so quickly that the passengers felt truly threatened. They were chasing the ominous warnings of the wind, but it seemed as though the wind was perhaps pursuing them as well.

As soon as they left the vicinity of Little River High, the Phoenix Pack hurtled into a maelstrom of winds. The trees on either side of the road bent and rocked. Some smaller ones were folded almost to the ground by the tremendous gusts that occurred every several moments.

"Maybe you can speak to them now," Tuck suggested. "They must be part of this." He waved his hand in an arc.

Tom said, "But I'm driving."

"No problem," said Ally in a flash, anxious to do something to feel useful and make the time until arrival home pass more quickly.

Though the whipping winds threatened to bowl her over, Ally stood hunched over and shuffled her way to the corner of the pickup bed behind the passenger door. She leaned forward and pulled the handle so the door popped open.

Tuck warned, "Careful . . ."

Ally kicked the door open and safely swung inside by bracing on the inside frame of the door and top of the wall around the pickup bed. The force of the wind blew the door shut behind her and actually made the maneuver less dangerous.

"Switch sides with me," Ally said with a smile possible only because of Tom's expression at her derring-do.

Ally grabbed the wheel and scootched forward so Tom could slide behind her to achieve the passenger seat. The speed of the truck slackened for that second, but then it jolted back again, and then rocketed even faster.

Tom grasped the rusted control and slowly cranked down the window. Torrents of wind pressed against his face and then did so even more forcefully when he extended his head out the window. He opened his mouth and breathed the spirits in. Then he communed with the wind spirits so familiar to the Wendigo.

Tuck was worried about the sept leaders. While Tuck knew they possessed powers he would not understand for some time, he wondered if they were capable of dealing with an assault by the kind of force responsible for killing the campers and Passer.

He prayed that the pack would arrive in time.

He watched as Tom spoke to the wind spirits. Opening his mouth to breath them in, then exhaling forcefully to add the fury of his breath to the windstorm around. Without realizing it, Tuck began to duplicate the effort.

The breaths he took were more replenishing than any he could recall. Even breaths greedily swallowed after running sprints or stadiums for hours didn't compare. The air was thick with oxygen or spiritual nutrients or something! Whatever it was he breathed, it shot him sky-high. Introduced to marijuana by the

Steins and now relatively experienced in its functioning, Tuck knew when he was high.

His senses became sharper in general, but they dulled at the edges, offering him the paradoxical view of a heightened, yet slightly dreamy world. Tuck didn't feel uncomfortable or threatened, though he realized in the back of his mind he should be. Why would wind make him high?

He didn't fear it was an attack of the Wyrm, though, so he continued to breathe slowly and deeply. His lids were drooping, but he insisted on keeping them open. And he was glad he did, for he gained some terrific insights. His packmates became somehow completely realized in his mind. He understood them and so understood the flaws in their characters, where they were weak and could be hurt. The areas that as a pack leader he must support or shore up.

The ferocious warrior Ally. The feeling of greatness and accomplishment she sought. But she did not see that the Wyrm was not a simple enemy to be bludgeoned to death in one or a thousand guises. It was a way of thought, a conspicuous consumption of wealth and attainment of status that was the same comforts she sought.

The spiritual warrior Tom. The glory he sought in the name of his Native American heritage. But Tuck saw how Tom succumbed to the glorified image of what his people were. Tom, too, saw them through the eyes of the white man in America too anxious to find or fabricate the sacred in these people so that as a race he might wipe away the horrors caused by his earlier ignorance.

The hopeful singer Verse. The peace and understanding he sought to bring to mankind, gleaned from his days as a wolf. But Tuck saw that Verse had no conception that mankind was also the Wyrm. That mankind was everywhere and too hurried and harried to much care for what one voice in a thousand might sing or say. Verse might send a signal, but mankind would hear only noise.

Tuck knew he could look upon himself as well, but that could be done at another time, for he felt the wind spirits had left him with something—a gift that could be used mundanely or magnificently, and would probably find use in both ways for many years to come.

The scene was horrific. All four members of the Phoenix Pack stared aghast first at the carnage, but then at the creature they saw.

Vaguely crinos in shape, it stood at least twenty feet tall. The flesh of its chest was ripped open to reveal the bone beneath. Mammoth legs the size of tree trunks rooted it to the ground. Enormous, flailing arms windmilled in mad motions. And the tongue. It whirled and lashed as if possessing a life of its own.

Around it were Sarah and Oliver. They danced like angry ants. Cartwheeling in and out of the monster's guard. Changing shape faster than any pack member could follow. Bleeding from dozens of wounds.

Oliver especially looked beaten. Though his claws found a mark in the monster at least three times in the split second it took for the pack members to register the scene, a huge arm connected with his whirling frame and sent him flying over twenty feet just as the truck pulled to a stop. The Stargazer landed on all fours in lupus form facing the monster, but he staggered momentarily before rushing and renewing the attack.

Meanwhile, Sarah, a small fire mysteriously burning on her back, seemed to be busy with just the foul tongue. Like a serpent that sprang from the beast's throat, the tongue struck at Sarah while deftly avoiding the raking attacks she made with her claws. It seemed to Ally and Tom, the ones most likely to instantly regard how the female Stargazer fought, that Sarah hesitated to bite the draping pillar of flesh. She couldn't be blamed.

The severe winds that surrounded the truck for the entire trip now ripped and churned across the whole of the Steins' property as well. The might of the wind spirits milling in mazy motions threatened to dwarf even the Wyrm-beast.

The wind tore at the ground, throwing chunks of earth skyward. It carved through the old house nearby, flinging siding and fragments of the broken and breaking windows into the air. It tore at the bodies of the three combatants.

Seven combatants. Ally, Tom, Tuck, and Verse leapt from the vehicle and joined the fray. Six against one.

The beast threw back its head and roared a maniacal laugh, though it was barely heard above the insane wind. Then it showed that it had been toying with its prey. In one swift motion, it raised a foot and struck, clubbing Oliver in the head. The blow sent him spinning and he collapsed too close to the beast. As the creature pounded down on the prone form of the Stargazer and then heaved him airborne with the kick of a clawed foot, the Phoenix Pack attacked.

A fast shifter, Verse towered upward as he ran. By the time he jumped, covering a great distance by means of the same gift that saved him from a watery grave, Verse was full crinos and he was in time to save Oliver from a terrific fall. Verse hit the ground still moving and raced Oliver to the side of a great hardwood the wind would not take down.

Meanwhile, Ally and Tom shifted to crinos too. With Tuck they were ready to harry their enemy with greater numbers and the strategy of a pack tackling greater prey, but the twin Ahroun were immediately in sync and barreled ahead of the slower-changing Philodox. Still acting in unison, the clawed hands and feet of the Garou lit with a brilliant flash and shone with the edge of the sharpest blade.

They charged side by side, and as they reached the edge melee range they suddenly split. Ally turned left and rolled. Tom shot right and sprung into the air. The beast was disoriented by the dividing foe and was caught reacting to neither attack.

Ally gained her feet near the right leg of the monster, where she dug her claws behind its kneecap. She screamed her rage, then screamed, "For the mule!"

Tom flipped and landed behind the creature's flailing left arm, where he saw the remnants of a previously inflicted wound. His wider, sharper claws dug deeper troughs along nearly the same lines. Great gobets of gore gushed from the gash.

The beast was not addled for long. Its tongue, dripping with a ruinous bile, lashed in a complete circle, traveling in an arc over its head from right to left where it clobbered the unsuspecting Tom. The noxious saliva on the tongue stuck to Tom and burst aflame. The ribbon of fire ran along Tom's entire right side and he instinctively threw himself to the ground and rolled to extinguish the hellish blaze.

The beast apparently foresaw this reaction and was prepared. Ignoring Ally, a charging Tuck, and the now foeless Sarah, the creature raised both arms, hands palm down, above its head. Its inches-long shiny black talons reflected a hoary light as they descended, like ten sleek stakes, to impale the coursing body of the fiery Ahroun. Almost all of the claws found the mark. With a syrupy glop, Tom slid from the gory fingers as the beast recoiled.

Tuck ached to hurry to Tom, but he couldn't let the opening pass. It was an opportunity created by the monster's attention to the Tom, so it had to be used. Tuck jumped and spread his arms wide like the wings of a bird. When he neared the Wyrm-beast he flexed his mighty chest and pulled his arms in a sweeping attack. The claws of each hand erased flesh as they ripped through the monster.

Ally, almost abandoning her position at the creature's leg in a defensive roll, stayed her ground to use the advantage of Tom's diversion as well. She splashed her razor claws into the fresh wells of the wounds she just inflicted. When she pulled her fists out, they didn't come empty. Fragments of muscle and cartilage oozed between her digits.

Sarah, exhausted from fending off the beast for so long, took a breath, so missed the opening for an attack.

Verse charged back toward the battle. He wanted to leap on the back of the monster and rend its hide, but he saw another mission of aid. Tom wasn't moving and lay in the path of the giant raging bodies. If Tom wasn't already dead, the lost bulk of the creature might finish that job.

Verse reached the side of the mutilated warrior and hefted him up. He saw that the Ahroun was indeed near death, so Verse dashed with his load back to Oliver's side. Hunkering down over the prone forms, Verse recalled a piece of the heritage of his tribe—the Children of Gaia. The most peaceful of all the tribes, the Children knew much of healing, and that was the knowledge Verse needed now.

It was almost impossible to concentrate in this

wind and tumult, but Gaia was everywhere, so with his eyes closed Verse found her and felt her warmth. He spread it down his arms to his outstretched fingers. One palm gently settled on the forehead of Oliver and the other on Tom. Oliver roused a bit at the touch, but Tom remained dormant. Verse thought the latter was saved, but only time would tell.

Behind Verse, at the site of the conflict, the Wyrm-spawned horror targeted attacks at both the foes within the range of its guard. It grappled at Tuck with its massive arms while its tongue swung back over its head like a glutinous pendulum toward Ally.

Tuck, though, was beyond the reach of the monster. After his attack he landed and darted forward between the legs of the beast. Nowhere, however, was out of reach of that tongue, and though Ally made a deft attempt to dodge it, she was not as skilled or practiced as Sarah, who had managed to evade it for so long. It grazed Ally on her left arm. The oily fluid left clinging to her arm afterward immediately sparked to flame.

Ally howled in pain, for this was a supernatural blaze and caused harm not easily repaired by the herculean healing abilities of the Garou. A deep chortle rumbled from the throat of the monster.

The rage burned deeply within Ally, though, and she acted with the instinct for causing pain that only an enraged Ahroun can possess. Instead of rolling to the side, she charged, and as she ran she reached inside to draw on her Wendigo heritage and blew outward in a breath that channeled the elemental spirits of the air over her crackling arm. The pain caused by the flames when fanned nearly blacked her out, but a week of hurt and anger kept her feet moving until she was near enough to the beast that the anxious flames lapped against its flesh too.

The flames seized on this new target and caught in a rush when Ally rubbed some of the sebaceous fluid onto the creature. The monster roared and a flurry of moves and countermoves between it and Ally initiated. Ally seemed completely in the rhythm of the fight and was able to match the beast. Each of their bodies blossomed fresh red wounds.

Then Sarah and Tuck waded back into the fray as well. The monster barely had to take its concentration off of Ally to dispense with Tuck's threat. It, too, was reacting perfectly, and a well-timed attack split a vicious gouge across Tuck's chest. Tuck went spinning.

Sarah was deft enough to avoid the miscellaneous strikes the beast made at her, but it also managed to evade her attacks. It and Ally simply fought on a completely different level. One of pure destructive desire.

Verse, too, entered the fray. He left Oliver and Tom at the tree safe from the worst of the wind and executed his attack at the monster's back. Verse's strong maw ripped a wound in its back while he dug handholds with his claws. When the tongue lashed over the monster's head to batter Verse off, Verse instead jumped, and the tongue narrowly missed spreading more fire on its host.

Verse rebounded for another attack, but the tongue kept him at bay even while the horror's attention was directed elsewhere. Finally it crushed Verse, and the Galliard became a fiery comet flashing over the windswept terrain.

Both Ally and the beast burned, but the blaze on Ally seared even higher when the tongue returned to renew its assault in tandem with the monster's claws and fangs. Eventually, the fiery python tongue succeeded in coiling around her. Soon feeling the last of her strength fade, Ally tried at least to buy her comrades a reprieve. Though the tongue tried to hold her firm, Ally made one last powerful lunge and instead of inflicting a wound she simply curled her middle finger and popped the creature in the abdomen.

The Wyrm-beast staggered backwards from the force of the gift-borne attack, its tongue trailing even further out of its dank orifice to maintain its hold on Ally. She tried to break out, but she was almost completely ablaze. After the tongue dashed her against the ground and flung her to the side, she rolled sprawling to a barely conscious stop.

Verse was at her side instantly, though she implored him to return to the fracas where Sarah and Tuck stood alone.

The Stargazer wearily retreated a few steps but took a ready stance once again.

Tuck found himself in a position just in line with the rising creature. As the Wyrm-spawned horror reassumed its footing, a sense of calm washed over Tuck. The Philodox returned the heavy stare of his enemy.

Then, a silvery blue nimbus of light flared around Tuck's body. The glare was so bright that Tuck's three dimensions seemed to melt into two as he became barely a silhouette against the wind-tossed darkness.

"I harness the will of Gaia," Tuck shouted to the beast. "You are a blight upon her, so you will now perish." His voice was confident because he suddenly saw how to kill the beast. Just as he saw the emotional and character flaws in his packmates during his recent vision, Tuck could see the breaking point in the thing that was once Garou. A spot just below the monster's abdomen stood out to Tuck as the architectural brace holding the seemingly indomitable yet wobbling beast on its feet.

When Tuck charged, the light around him flared as it must have eons ago for the greatest champions of the Silver Fangs. Momentarily blinded, the monster could not respond to the assault with anything more than random strikes. To Tuck, still in his zone of peace and single-minded attention, the attacks were easily evaded.

His taloned paw plunged into the tissue of the Wyrm-creature and shackled a giant cyst inside it that coursed like a radiated bomb. His eyes closed, Tuck withdrew the egg from within the shivering Garou. Behind it trailed the thick cord of the creature's tongue, which simultaneously sloppily retreated into the giant mouth.

When Tuck squeezed the cyst it burst, showering gelatinous fragments everywhere, and the tongue, then still writhing, fell limp.

"As Gaia guides my hand, so will I guide this pack," Tuck stated fiercely.

As if to add both an emphatic and inauspicious note to this solemn declaration, the wind reached a peak roar. The roof of the nearby house undulated from the strength of the shearing blast, but the Garou—Oliver and Tom in a bloody pile beneath the tree, Ally on her back still blazing with fire but head slightly up, Verse still crouched beside her, Sarah collapsing from exhaustion, and Tuck standing defiantly against the wind—all escaped the brutal pounding of the gale.

Then, accompanied by the popping of a vacuum that echoed in the skulls of the Garou, the wind disappeared. Completely.

A shadow fell across Tuck's face as the silent sky darkened, and the spirits of the air were banished too.

# CONVERSATION

"You're awake."

"Yes, barely."

"You would awaken the one moment I'm away from you."

"I know you sat with me."

"Yes?"

"The spirits who spoke with me in my dreams told me a beautiful changeling princess tended at my bedside."

"You dream of other women?"

"I knew they meant you. Spirits can be a romantic sort, you know."

"Yes, indeed."

"And what of our children? Are they okay as well?"

"They all survived, though Tom has yet to awaken. I just visited him and he seems somewhat improved, but he has not awakened, nor have his eyes fluttered with sleep. Verse has been tending to him as I watch you. And Ally speaks to him. She has

told him perhaps a dozen times how jealous she is of
the battle scars he earned."

"And Ally and Tuck?"

"Ally is scarred too—by fire. It will be some time
before she has a full coat of hair again, though fortunately no harm is apparent in her homid form. Tuck
has bruises and pains, but escaped as I did, largely
unharmed."

"And how am I?"

"Scarred as well, but you will live."

"I do not recall the conclusion of the battle.
Through my glazed eyes I saw the beast topple, but
that is all."

"Ally fought the creature face-to-face and created
time for Tuck to tear the ronin's Wyrm-heart from
its body. When that was crushed the creature died."

"Why did the wind howl at its death? I remember
feeling as if I would be lofted away."

"The wind howled for its own passing. Just as the
water and fire elementals have been razed from
Little River, so too have the spirits of the air gone
too. Already this morning the sky seems darker.
There is no industry, but a smoggy pollution has battled aside the freshness of the land and clogs the
lungs with but a few breaths."

"Was this the revenge of the Wyrm-beast? Its last
stroke?"

"No. It was dead already."

"Then it was but a servant. A horror to destroy
the safekeepers while the real enemy, the shadow of
the Wyrm itself, crawls deeper into Alexander's
soul."

"That's what I've concluded as well. A battle has
been won, but the war remains unfought, and
largely uncontested."

"No, we shall fight the Wyrm this very day."

"Today you're resting."

"But the pack will not."

"Why?"

"Tuck must participate in his sporting event."

"Oh, yes . . ."

"The others will journey with him to Headway."

"Tom is not going anywhere."

"Of course, but the others must go."

"Why?"

"To see in Headway an image of what they still fight to preserve here."

# 8

# GAMEDAY

Tuck almost interrupted his morning ritual to check on the others, including Verse, who he suspected had remained with Tom throughout the night, but he waited until he was dressed to check on the twins in their room. Verse had insisted that Tuck get a full night's sleep in preparation for the game. Tuck maintained that he was still going to play.

Tuck didn't want the success or failure of the team to rest completely on his shoulders because there were a lot of other very fine players, but realistically he knew that's the way it was. If he didn't play, then the Huskies would probably lose. Then everyone in the town would fall deeper into the depression already nagging at the back of their minds because of the rapid changes in the town. Humans in Harano . . . They needed to experience some small-town pride, and Tuck intended to deliver them a reason to feel what they had always felt without question before.

He turned out of his room and walked left down

the hallway toward the Kachinas' room. He caught a brief glimpse of blood and carnage on the balcony and staircase behind him, but he ignored it for now. The beat of the Wyrm-cyst was still palpable in his hands, and he shook them out to sling away more imagined vestiges of the blackened goo.

"You look pale," Verse told Tuck as Tuck entered the room. It was one of the few diagnoses Verse could make on humans, but this time it probably applied. Tuck did feel like he was swooning and perspiring a bit.

Verse sat in a chair next to Tom's bed, where Tom sprawled unconscious in homid form.

Tuck said, "I just can't get that monster out of my mind. I think I dreamed last night that it walked onto the field to play defensive back for the Headway Hornets. But it's the feel of its innards." Tuck shivered.

"Out, out damned spot," Ally whispered wearily.

"Yeah," Tuck said, still unconsciously rubbing hands as he stepped toward Ally's bed. "Are you okay?" She was in her natural homid form. Though blankets covered a lot of Ally's body, Tuck could see burns on her bare shoulders.

"I was fine last night, I'm fine now."

"Well, we didn't know what kind of poisons the tongue fed into you. Tom and Verse too."

Ally sat up in bed. "No. We're okay. Tom's still not awake, but his breathing is regular and strong. His eyes haven't moved, that's what Sarah was asking about a little earlier, but he did turn his head away from the light a little bit. At least Verse thinks so. It happened while he was moving the pillow."

"God, that's great!" Tuck exclaimed. "He's tough and healthy; he'll pull through."

Ally said flatly, "I understand you still plan on playing in that damn game tonight."

"Yeah," Tuck admitted, feeling a bit ashamed of the decision. "It's what has to be done. I think a win tonight might be the means of beating the Wyrm."

"What?" Ally's face was screwed with disgust. "What kind of rationalization is that?"

"Well," said Tuck, "I think it's true. The fight against that monster last night was just a battle against a physical manifestation of the Wyrm. The real battle is a spiritual one. The changes in Little River are already drying everyone out. They don't care about things like they used to. They are just rolling with the punches, trying to stay on their feet and not really caring where they're being led. They need a jolt, a reminder of what it is about this little town that made them happy."

"That's a bunch of rubbish," spat Ally.

"Oh? I think I have a feel for the enemy now, Ally. I knew where to strike that monster last night, and I know how to strike against the shadow that's been snuffing the spirits that would be our allies."

Ally nodded slowly. She was wrestling with the thought all morning. Trying to make herself accept Tuck as the leader the moment the beast was felled the night before by Tuck's blow, she knew that there were no grounds for her to challenge him for leadership. She was proud of how she fought, but in the end she felt more pride in how the pack fought. It was the pack's victory, that much Tuck had made clear immediately afterward last night, and she would honor it as such too.

"Well, then, you're not going alone," she said, trying to warm to the idea.

"I hoped I wouldn't," Tuck smiled.

Verse said, "If Sarah thinks she can handle the wounded, then I'll go too. We'll be a pack of three until Tom recovers."

Since Ally sometimes helped keep statistics during the games and because Verse was the team's unofficial mascot, the three members of the Phoenix Pack all rode the team bus to Headway together.

The trip was a relatively long one, especially for many of the players on the bus who may never been further from home than the county line more than a handful of times. Probably all of them had been to Chicago. If nothing else they went as part of field trips to the Museum of Science and Industry every other year when the teachers chaperoned all the fourth- and fifth-graders.

Tuck and his packmates arrived at Little River High at 1:00 P.M. for the 2:00 P.M. departure. The bus was the newest one of the county school system's fleet of eleven; a far cry better that the buses they received for most of the away games—whichever bus was handy. Volunteers had scrubbed it clean and painted slogans on the sides. They were the usual sorts of pithy sayings meant to inspire team spirit and echo bravado. Phrases like "Swarm the Hornets" and the like.

A great number of other very flattering efforts were made as well. The team's uniforms were all freshly cleaned by a number of cooperating households.

Healthy lunches were prepared and packed by the high school's lunchroom staff, and much to everyone's surprise, good food could come out of there.

A teacher from the English department at the

middle school handed a booklet to each player as he got on the bus. Inside were poems and essays written by the sixth-, seventh- and eighth-graders to inspire the varsity team.

Finally, a whole bunch of students and parents showed up to wish the team well. The small school band played the Husky fight song. The students threw confetti and streamers.

And Melissa kissed Tuck good luck.

That's what Tuck was thinking about as he sat alone in his bus seat. He reclined against the window with his legs stretched out across the green vinyl of the seat. His feet draped into the aisle, but the bus wasn't stopping to let anyone off this trip, so people could make themselves much more comfortable.

The window was warm behind his head, and Tuck imagined that his lips were still warm too. Each player was cheered as he boarded the bus, and the roar for Tuck was the loudest. With one foot on the first step up into the bus, Tuck grasped a bar on the door and swung around to wave to the crowd. His already beaming face blushed a deep indigo when Melissa strode out of the gathering and planted a huge kiss on his lips. She whispered, "For luck."

While Tuck struggled to maintain his composure, and his grip on the bar, Melissa disappeared back into the crowd.

He hadn't wiped his lips yet. He was savoring the thought they'd last been touched by her.

Ally sat in the seat behind Tuck. Verse also rode there when he wasn't pacing the aisle, where he slipped under all the dangling feet, Tuck's included.

Though it was relatively warm, Ally wore bulky clothing to hide the burns smeared across her body. Some of the players asked about the clothes, but she just explained that it would be cold tonight on the football field.

Verse also looked scarred and beaten. Brad Stems wondered if this was a bad omen, but Ally quickly countered. "It's actually a good sign. He rooted in a yellow-jacket nest yesterday but despite all the stings and the swelling and scarring that came from them, he lived. Seems pretty poetic to me."

That story occupied everyone aboard the bus for a good half hour as it briskly traveled around. It received some major alteration, but when Tuck took note of it through his puppy-love haze, he realized a legend was born. Assuming the Huskies won. Otherwise, while there might still be a story, it wouldn't be a heroic one. It wouldn't be the kind that Passer would have appreciated so well.

The countryside was beautiful, and it was the perfect day to be traveling it. There was a warm spell in the region; so while it could turn nasty and cold and snowy any day, today was glorious. The landscape was flat like most of the state, and that meant there wasn't much to see on the horizon—no mountains or forests—but that could be good too. The flatness made a land without boundaries, so it could also make a spirit soar as high as a mountain might. The thought, even if just an illusion, that everything was laid out before you was euphoric.

Something else that was euphoric was chocolate ice cream, and that's what Tuck's mind immediately shifted to when the bus pulled to a stop a bit over an hour into the drive at a roadside store. Everyone piled back out and chose a dessert for the fine lunch they'd already eaten. This was a treat from Coach Conroy, the kind and big man who was also a history teacher at the school.

It was called just The General Store, and it turned out that an older couple owned and maintained it by themselves. They used the extra income, in addition to some nice pensions from years of good work, to add more and more to the impressive acreage they already owned. A sign at the front of the store imparted this information along with the suggestion that the store would not survive them. All the land was to be granted to the Nature Conservancy when they both died.

It was good land too. With his ice cream in hand, Tuck walked into the woods with Ally and Verse. Ally declined to eat anything, and Verse, being a "dog," was treated by Coach Conroy with a rawhide chew that Verse now ridiculously carried in his mouth.

The land had the smell that Little River did up until about a week ago. Fresh. And it was teeming with life too.

There were no trails, but the three pushed on for the few moments they knew they had.

"Better breathe the good air while we can," Ally said. "Headway is going to stink."

They were almost ready to turn back, satisfied with a last romp on the good earth for a time, when Verse sniffed something amiss and encouraged Tuck and Ally to press forward with him. They entered a small clearing and all simultaneously shivered. There was a bad presence here. Something amiss. There was a hint of the same shadow that hung over Little River, but none of them could quite pin down what it was.

Tuck mindlessly crunched the last of his cone, thinking that perhaps every bastion of serenity was being harassed by the Wyrm. The ground cover in the clearing was gone. Some sort of cleanup effort had been made here. Maybe some hunters killed game or something, and the owners cleaned the mess. It was death they smelled.

A cry went up from the bus, so the packmates were forced to leave. They didn't speak about the clearing because they all sensed the Wyrm and they had all been too close to it the night before. They shuddered as one, but kept their thoughts to themselves.

The murmuring of the players and the excitement they bubbled for the coming game snapped the sour mood of the packmates a bit. So much so that once they were on the road, the strangeness of the glade fell aside, and Tuck fell asleep. The crisp, warm air, a belly full of ice cream, and pregame butterflies already kicking in combined to make him very drowsy.

Many others on the bus soon slept too.

The small-town team slept under the idyllic sunlight as they drove to Headway, the big city.


Tuck awoke and shook the remnants of sleep from his eyes. Though his head was below the level of the windows, he knew he was within a city because the hum of motors was all around. There was also a sense of compression. A feeling that limitless space had come to an end.

He sat up. Almost everyone else on the bus was still sleeping. In fact, he saw the heads of only three others, though others might be awake below the safety of their seats. He glanced over his seat back and saw that both Ally and Verse slept. Good, he thought, they needed it too.

Then he looked out at the city of Headway. The enthusiasm of a good sleep drained immediately from his face. The city was terribly disgusting. The bus traveled down a long, overdeveloped four-laned road. The frontage was lined with every kind of dilapidated, crime-ridden, and plain disgusting establishment that could possibly exist.

Sure, all of the businesses were legitimate, but the quick-stop food station the bus rolled past must have been in its fourth or fifth generation of use. That was okay; the blight was that it existed in the first place when there was another one on the other side of the street. The one Tuck examined was on its last legs again. There were at least a dozen abandoned gasoline pumps. One small set of three far to the side was so old that one of the pumps still read LEADED.

The building itself was so like the others on the strip. There was no maintenance. Weeds flourished in the cracked concrete that drowned the parched ground. Litter and junk of all sizes and ages were heaped in piles everywhere. Even the metal bars applied to the windows of the building were bent and sometimes broken.

This was a site full in the grip of the Wyrm. Tuck felt ashamed to see it. That building and the hundred like it on this road. And the fast-food joints—half of them closed and another portion once closed, like one operated by a local out of a shell of an old Hardee's that now served glazed fat to dull the bodies of men.

Tuck felt ashamed because this was what was happening to the world while he battled to save one lonely little spot. He laughed at his foolishness, though. He couldn't be expected to do so much. Not yet, at least. There were thousands of other Garou to help. But the world was so huge!

Change must begin within, Tuck recalled Oliver saying once. We must first change ourselves before we can expect the world to change. That meant leaving a clean home before looking to cleanse other locations. That meant Little River and its caern must be made pure again before Tuck could conscionably lead the Phoenix to renew other lands.

But he wondered what could be done for places like this. Almost nothing, was his sad conclusion. The Wyrm had so thoroughly corrupted the pattern of the Weaver that flaws were deeply ingrained. At the root of it was that there were too many people. How could change be effected when so many would have to be moved?

The people who lived here could be spiritually moved, but they possessed limited self-healing powers. Their spirits would never be renewed as long as they lived in such a hellhole, but the hellhole would never get better until the people raised their voices with ideas and courage.

How could both possibly occur at the same time?

They couldn't, and that meant healing would have to start with one or the other, and that meant the healing would take a long, long time to make a difference. Longer than Tuck would live. Was there a point if he couldn't make a difference?

But, of course, he could make a difference for Little River, and that's what snapped Tuck from his melancholy. He roused the other players on the bus and started stoking the competitive fires in them. No one forgot the dead dog left in the Little River parking lot.


Headway High was enormous. So big that it was difficult to find the football field, and that was so huge that once they found it they wondered how they could miss it. The school was the very best the

Weaver had to offer, but Tuck knew it was built at the expense of the way of life of the people who lived near that awful strip. It was also probably built despite an already standing building that could have been saved for far less money. A building that now stood as an empty hulk.

As the bus pulled through an expansive parking lot, all the players, and Ally and Verse too, looked for the car that carried away the twisted children who interrupted the pep rally the day before. There were so many very nice cars that ten different people swore they saw it, and they pointed at five different cars.

Coach Conroy, at a loss for where to drop the players, simply pulled up to the main gate. The players disembarked at 5:00 P.M., two hours before the game.

The long line of horn-hooting cars following the bus broke apart as everyone sought a parking space. Many of the cars drove around in circles, just as confused by the immensity of the structure as Coach Conroy.

A sizable number of Headway High students were already present. Tuck had the foul impression that they were assembling early to gawk at him and his teammates, gawk at the big school's edifice.

Tuck had to admit, though, that the stadium itself was impressive. The plaque on the amazing white marble archway at the main entrance indicated that the field had been inaugurated last year, the year the Hornets won the state championship. Another plaque made sure that title wasn't forgotten by anyone who entered. They obviously thought they were building a dynasty here.

Well, Tuck knew he had a dynasty to maintain. That of a sovereign earth. One that predated this place by, oh, only several billion years. But an over-whelming number of signs made it clear that the Huskies would not challenge these championship dreams.

Tuck took the point and walked boldly through the open gates. The field was just visible beyond, behind an odd array of fences and barriers. Tuck assumed they were to keep people from getting a free peak at the action. A permanently painted sign at the entrance indicated the admission was eight dollars per person! No pay no stay. Or, no pay no stadium. Tuck doubted the city would make back even a fraction of the gargantuan construction cost anytime soon, even charging that exorbitant price.

Tuck slowed. He wasn't really sure where to go. He looked back for Coach Conroy, but saw that he was shaking hands and exchanging words with a sharply dressed man in his mid-thirties. Maybe it was the Hornets' coach. At least he had enough tact to meet the guests.

"The dressing room is this way." The voice carried from around a corner. Tuck saw a younger boy, probably a freshmen. He was sharply dressed, too, in slacks and a sweater over a button-down shirt.

Tuck followed the boy and the other players followed him.

The locker room, or "dressing room" as the boy called it and the sign on the door proclaimed it, was sumptuous. It was spotless. It also prominently featured the colors of the Hornets. Blue and gold tiles formed repeating patterns in the white-tiled floors. The same was true in the shower room, where more than a·dozen showerheads with power stream selectors lined the walls.

It took the visitors only a second to find the

whirlpool at the rear of the locker room. As soon as
Tuck realized what the sound was, he shut the
machine off and implored his teammates, "Let's
keep our minds on the game, not gadgets. Let's
make Little River proud and show these big-city fops
that it takes more than money to build a championship football team!"

There was no dissent. Everyone here had more
than a couple of family members or friends anxious
for something to cheer about.

It was one of those days when the offense couldn't
be stopped. A kind of game they referred to as a
shoot-out. It meant that every time Tuck went onto
the field he was expected to score; he had to score.

The Huskies held a 36–34 lead at the end of three
quarters. Five touchdowns for each team and a field
goal for the Huskies, but the Hornets had the ball, and
if they scored as they had on all their possessions
since the end of the first quarter, the Huskies would
be down 40 or 41 to 36. It depended on whether their
kicker missed another extra point of not. It didn't
much matter, because it would mean being at least
four points down, so a field goal wouldn't even tie it.
Not that they really had the option of trying for a field
goal now anyway. The options just never got brighter.

The Huskies opened the game with an excellent
kickoff return, so even when Tuck, a jittery bundle of
nerves at the time, managed to move the ball for
only one first down, they were able to kick for the
three points on fourth-and-two.

But the kicker was injured on the play. A severe
roughing-the-kicker penalty was called against the
Hornets, but that didn't make Matt Thurman any

healthier. And the Huskies simply didn't have another player who could kick very well. The replacement was Harold Grotter, but he'd missed two of the five extra points attempted. The last two. Therefore, slowly, though they held the lead now, the Huskies were falling behind.

Tuck went to Coach Conroy with an idea. It was one the coach didn't like, but it was Tuck, so he was willing to trust it. The coach sent the lone ball boy, Chuck Pearson, to the other sidelines, where he delivered a message to the Hornets' coach.

The answer came back about fifteen minutes later. Two minutes after the Hornets made the score 41–36 with only about six minutes to go in the fourth quarter. The Hornet coach had no problem with Coach Conroy suiting a statistician to kick for the Huskies.

While the Huskies lined up to receive the kick-off—a play usually involving Tuck but not in this game because Coach Conroy wanted to limit Tuck's exposure to injury—Tuck delivered the news.

"Ally?" Tuck smiled. "Will you kick for us?"

"Are you silly?" Ally was incredulous.

"It's been okayed by both sides, and with a moment's practice I'm sure you can convert your soccer skills to a differently shaped ball."

"You're crazy, Tuck, but if you want me I'll try."

Tuck was delighted. He was pleased because he thought Ally really might be able to kick pretty well with some practice and tips from Matt, but also because he was able to go to her in a time of need. He needed her. The pack needed her.

Tuck saw Chuck and Ally running toward the locker room for a uniform as he walked onto the field. The kickoff had been a touchback, so there was a long way to go.

Tuck called the huddle and said, "Okay, guys, the pressure's on again. We must score. We must go eighty yards." Then he glanced at the defense. "Looks like they want to see if we can run the ball. They're going with six defensive backs to blanket the coverage." Tuck called a left sweep and broke the huddle.

The sweep was stopped for a loss.

The next run at least made it back to the line of scrimmage.

Forced to throw on third-and-twelve, Tuck dropped back and lofted a perfect spiral to a spot where only Marty Weathers, the tight end, could reach it. Marty broke one ankle tackle and managed a fourteen-yard gain.

The drive was alive on the Husky thirty-four yard line.

Hoping the Hornets would still think the Huskies would look to try to take advantage of an under-manned defensive line by establishing the running game, Tuck called another pass play.

He hit Greg Frederickson on a slant pattern for a thirty-five-yard gain that took the Huskies across midfield and to the Hornets' thirty-one.

In the huddle, excitement was high. Their offense could still move the ball too! Another score would put them back on top.

But the drive ground to a halt. It picked up a few more yards, but faced with a fourth-and-seven at the twenty-eight yard line, Tuck called time-out and walked to the sideline to convince Coach Conroy the best hope was a field-goal attempt. If they scored, then they could try an onside kick, and if the Huskies got it they wouldn't have to go far for another field goal that would tie the game.

If they failed, then they still had to get the ball back and would need a touchdown, but they might be able to sustain a drive better than gambling on a fourth-and-seven.

Tuck could see that Coach Conroy wondered which was a greater gamble—a walk-on girl kicking a field goal or a fourth-and-seven attempt. Tuck wasn't sure if he should breathe a sigh of relief or not when he got his way and Ally, barely into her instruction with Matt, marched onto the field after Matt showed her once more how to take about two steps back and one step to the side of where she would meet the ball.

As the teams lined up and Ally took her place behind the holder, Tuck saw that there was as much confusion on the Hornets' side of the ball as on the Huskies'. The opponents, Tuck was sure, were laughing at the country bumpkins from Little River who found a tomboy to kick for them. The Huskies, on the other hand, were simply confused.

Tuck shouted out to them, "Line up, guys. She can kick it!"

Time was running out anyway, and the Huskies hurried to beat the delay-of-game penalty. The Huskies still glanced over their shoulders as they assumed their stances.

"Remember to block," Tuck shouted again, laughing this time. But he was extremely nervous. This could mean the game. A success didn't mean a win, but a miss probably meant a loss because the Hornets would only need a field goal to stay ahead of what even a touchdown could do for the Huskies.

Tuck was so single-mindedly flashing through different scenarios for how the game could end that he almost missed the play. He shook his head and refocused on the action as the ball was snapped. Several of the Hornets just jumped and yelled to distract the novice kicker, but a few others made a good charge into the distracted Huskies' line.

It was a good snap. The holder, Tim Matheson, grabbed and placed the ball in one practiced movement. Therefore, he was ready far before Ally, who apparently wasn't told she should start moving as soon as the ball was snapped. She didn't move until the ball was in place.

She moved fluidly to the ball and hit it well. And in time too. The Huskies' line held long enough.

Sailing end over end, the ball floated toward the goal posts. It was in slow motion to Tuck, who choked when he saw that the ball was going to sail just wide right. The color drained from his face as his ploy to create another story, another legend to be told in Little River for years to come, failed.

But then the ball curved in the air as it was swept slightly by a wind that gusted through the stadium. The ball impossibly made it through the uprights.

Tuck stood dumbfounded. The rest of the team cheered madly.

Then Tuck chuckled to himself and looked back at Ally. She was standing smugly with her hands on her hips. Her body and neck were bent to the left as if she moved her body to try to help the ball move in that direction.

And Tuck suspected she had helped the ball move in that direction. Tuck didn't know what to think. That was cheating!

The players on the field swarmed her with congratulations, but finally she walked off the field.

Tuck was waiting with his mouth open to say something to her. She looked sassily at him and flipped her hair. She said, "We're fighting the Wyrm, Tuck. Be a Garou." Then she walked away.

Tuck still had his mouth open. He closed it. Because she was right. He couldn't do anything to threaten exposing the people here to the Delirium, which would mean they wouldn't remember the play he made anyway, and he couldn't chance doing something that would look fishy, like run faster than an Olympic sprinter, but he could—no, he should—remember that this game was a war against the Wyrm.

Besides, he wondered, maybe he was "cheating" this way all along. The morning ritual that gave him peace of mind was surely a part of his Garou nature not available to other players. Or wasn't it? And maybe here was a key to how things in Headway, in any ruined city, could be changed. Maybe revolutionizing the spirit and helping people just stop and think was a first step that could generate immediate results.

Or maybe it was good even if there were no discernible results. It was egocentric of him to wish for such in his lifetime anyway. What allowed him to be demanding in a centuries- or eons-long struggle for the human spirit? To shape the spirit of some people was good enough. And with what Oliver taught him, he had started in good form with himself.

The next events in the game were as good as could be hoped. It didn't look like the Huskies could hold the Hornets scoreless, but at least they didn't give up a touchdown.

The Huskies' onside kick failed, but after grudgingly giving up two first downs that ate much of the remaining time in the game despite two second-half Husky time-outs, the defense tightened. They sacked the quarterback on third-and-five, so the Hornets attempted a forty-one-yard field goal.

When the Hornets' kicker connected with the ball, it was evident on his face that he knew immediately it was perfect. He began to celebrate, but then stopped.

It sailed wide because of another gust of wind.

Tuck, on the edge of despair again, completely overlooked the possibility of affecting their attempts too. Ally smiled gaily when Tuck, his face again colorless, looked over at her.

The kicker dropped to his knees. His helmet was off and loose in his hands as he stared in disbelief at what happened. Tuck felt a twinge of pity for the player, but then he recognized him as one of the pep-rally interlopers. Tuck almost charged onto the field to exact a little more revenge, but instead he walked over to Ally, partly to keep her from doing the same.

When Tuck reached her, he knew she either didn't see the boy or didn't recognize him, so he let it go and just said, "You're amazing. I just knew they were going to make that one."

"Well," said Ally, "they almost did anyway. I can only create small gusts of wind. Tom can do a bit better. That kick was so on line that I was only able to puff it to the side because it traveled so far."

"Get ready," Tuck warned. "We may need you to win the game." Then he donned his helmet and ran onto the field.

In the huddle he told the others, "We need to at least make it within range for Ally to give us another one. A touchdown will win it outright, though, so let's just get one. Remember, these are the sorry assholes who killed that dog and interrupted our pep rally."

The huddle broke, and in the one play before the two-minute warning, Tuck scrambled wide right with the ball after a broken play. He didn't skip out of bounds, though, before a defensive player hit him. Every yard counted and Tuck gained three more with the player clinging to his waist.

The Huskies rested for a moment, and Tuck talked to Coach Conroy during the automatic time-out. The ball was on the Huskies' forty-eight—two yards from midfield. The good run gave them first-and-ten there.

The final calm before the storm, Tuck thought, and he suddenly thanked goodness this wasn't being played in Little River, because the earth elementals were the only ones remaining, and the packed earth of a football field might tempt them as a spot for their final exit.

There wasn't much Tuck or Coach Conroy had to say, other than agree that the Huskies would rely on the pass for the march downfield. Dropped passes stopped the clock, and receivers who caught the ball could get out of bounds quickly to stop the clock.

With 1:57 to play, the endgame began.

Tuck's first attempt was incomplete, and he was forced on the second play following the time-out to go the middle of the field to get any yardage. The Hornets were indeed swarming the receivers near the out-of-bounds lines. Tuck shovel-passed the ball to Marty Weathers, who shambled forward for seven yards. However, the play cost precious time.

It was third-and-three with 1:26 and counting to go, though the ball was now in Hornet territory. That was a psychological boost the Huskies needed.

On the next play, Tuck tried to force the ball to the outside. There was no sense playing it safe, except to avoid interceptions, of course. There were two more plays, since the Huskies would obviously go for it on fourth if necessary.

Greg Frederickson made a great play for the ball and almost caught it one-handed, but it slipped out.

The game was already one the line. They were well out of field-goal range, so it was another pass attempt on fourth-and-three. After he audibled to change the play at the line of scrimmage while calling signals before the hike, Tuck looked for Frederickson again, who broke off a post pattern to cut to the open middle. Tuck dropped the pass in perfectly, but Greg was pounded when two defenders sandwiched him before he even touched the ground again.

He just had the breath knocked out of him, though, so was soon on his feet again. Tuck was able to hold a quick huddle while the linesmen moved the first-down markers. He told the players the situation. "We still have some time and it's first down on their thirty-three. Let's punch it in!"

The clock was reset and began to count and the Huskies executed a play mere seconds afterwards. The Hornets played excellent defense, though, and Tuck had nowhere to go with the ball. He felt the time ticking away as he struggled to remain in the passing pocket long enough for a receiver to break open.

Big linemen swirled around him in muscled embraces, and Tuck was finally forced to run for it when a linebacker broke free of his blocker and threatened Tuck. Tuck dodged forward to avoid being sacked and bought time for one more look downfield. Still no one was open. So he ran, angling for the sideline.

However, two defenders cut him off on his way and tackled him while he was still inbounds. So the clock, now under one minute, kept ticking. The defenders were slow getting off Tuck, so the start of the next play would be delayed even further, but Tuck finally struggled to his feet.

There were less than forty seconds to go by the time Tuck took the next snap. He looked to complete a play designed for such a situation and passed across field to his left, where Greg ran a short hook pattern near the sideline. The defender reached him and shoved him out of bounds.

The clock was stopped for a moment, and Tuck tried to take everything in again. It was third-and-two on the Hornets' twenty-five. Thirty-three seconds remained. If they couldn't convert this third down, then at least they would be close enough to give Ally a chance to tie the game.

On the play Tuck found his second backup receiver, but it was in the center of the field, so the clock kept ticking with the Huskies on the Hornets' twenty.

Instead of looking for a short pass to stop the clock on the next play, though, Tuck quickly audibled Greg downfield. Tuck wanted to strike for the end zone. Tuck dropped back, arm itching to throw, ready to round out in the memorized motion it knew so well. The pass felt sweet when Tuck released it and looked to be on target. But the defender managed to bat it down at the last moment.

The incomplete pass still stopped the clock. It was second-and-ten with thirteen seconds remaining. There was time for one, maybe two more plays before they would have to settle for a field-goal attempt. That assumed, though, that the clock stopped each time. "You must get out of bounds with the ball," Tuck stressed in the huddle. "Any botch means there won't be time to set up for a field goal."

On the next play Tuck struck for the end zone again. At the last second he was forced to overthrow the ball because he saw another defender moving on the pass so that he might have intercepted it.

On third down, Tuck threw one of the best passes of his life. It was a perfectly tight spiral strike that hit wide receiver Nathan Faulker in the numbers on the four yard line and knocked him out of bounds before either of the nearby two defenders could.

With three seconds left the Huskies had the ball on the four. Tuck looked at Coach Conroy, who shrugged and sent the field-goal unit onto the field. Better to go for the win with another field goal than risk the clock running out after one more failed play.

Tuck agreed. However, he was slow leaving the field. He stood on the green grass and stared through the uprights of the goalposts. It needed to sail through there, he thought. Too much was at stake. Too much depended on a silly football game. Too much in the world, Tuck realized, depended on too little.

"Kick a good one, Ally," he said as they crossed paths when Tuck finally walked off.

But despite her natural abilities, Ally simply hadn't had enough practice, and the miss was so bad that a gust of wind wouldn't have helped at all. The snap was okay, but Ally hit the ball near the top instead of underneath it to loft it up. It was too low anyway, but a tall defender in the middle of the Hornets' line blocked it as well.

Tuck gasped and choked for breath. Goose bumps raced across his flesh, and he considered the magnitude of the loss. Then he realized that the Hornets weren't cheering.

Because the big gorilla who blocked the doomed kick had jumped offsides. There would be another attempt.

It wouldn't be a field goal, Tuck decided.

Overtime guaranteed nothing, but whoever won the coin toss would win because the offenses were moving the ball so well. But he was guided again as much by the story, the romance of the effort, as anything.

It was perfect, so in Tuck's mind it had to succeed.

He rushed to Coach Conroy. He hated that it might appear to Ally that he had no faith in her, but he had to try this. "She's kept us in the game, Coach, but there's no saying she won't miskick the ball again. Let's go for it."

Conroy nodded and sent the offense back in to go for the win.

"You did great, Ally," Tuck said as they crossed paths again. "It's too risky, though."

She nodded. "I know. I'm too nervous to try again anyway. Good luck." She hugged him.

In potentially the last huddle of the season, Tuck promised just one thing. "People in Little River will long remember what's about to happen."

Then the team lined up.

Standing ready to receive the hike, Tuck remembered his vision. The wolf that beckoned him and made him trust himself. He felt a surge of strength wash through him and he knew he couldn't be tackled.

Tuck faked a handoff up the middle that fooled no one and immediately rolled out to his right, pretending to look for a receiver. He might even have thrown it if there had been one open, but there wasn't, so facing three defenders, Tuck charged for the goal line.

The first one pounded him at the waist and wrapped his open arms around Tuck in what was taught as the most effective tackling method. The hold was too high, though, and Tuck spun out. Then the other two hit him. One could only snag his jersey, but the other got ahold of Tuck's knee as he drove forward.

He drove hard. Every ounce of grit and determination Tuck possessed went into the push, and he found that inner strength the wolf made him trust.

By the time he fell across the goal line, Tuck was dragging four defenders.

# CONVERSATION

"Oliver, Oliver! He's gone!"

"Yes."

"Do you hear me? He's gone! Alexander is not in the back room."

"Yes, I hear you."

"Has the Wyrm sent another foul agent to capture him? Do you think it gave up on crushing his spirit and instead spirited him away?"

"No."

"Then what's happened."

"He left."

"You mean he moved?"

"Not only moved—he left."

"He slipped into the Umbra? Opened a moon-bridge?"

"No, he simply walked out."

"When?"

"Perhaps a half hour ago."

"A half hour ago? You didn't say anything to me?"

"Say anything? I was dumbfounded!"

"You? Dumbfounded?"

"Yes."

"But why didn't you say something just now, when I walked through our room to the back room to check on him."

"I thought to surprise you."

"Surprise? You scared me, that's what you did."

"I'm sorry. I was scared when he walked out."

"Scared?"

"Yes. Our mission has been completed and I worry about what the future holds for us. The Wyrm is still here. I can sense it."

"Then why did Alexander leave?"

"I don't know, and that scares me too."

"Did he say anything?"

"No."

"Then how can you say we succeeded?"

"Because his face was no longer drawn. It was animated. His eyes were no longer sullen and dark. There was life in them; they were animated. His breath was no longer long and infrequent. He breathed deeply, as if the taste of the air intoxicated him again."

"But he said nothing?"

"No, he did say something."

"What?! What did he say?"

"He said thank you for the pen."

"What?!"

"Thank you for the pen."

"What does that mean?"

"It means that as he walked through the room he picked up a felt-tip pen from your dresser and thanked me/us for it."

"Did he write something with it? A note? A letter perhaps."

"No. He merely tucked it over his ear and walked out of the room."

"That's insane."

"Insanity? Perhaps, but we are all too quick to judge others insane. Is another insane simply because they subscribe to a different set of rules, a different worldview? Isn't—"

"Be quiet, weasel. For once I was having a normal conversation of question and answer with you. But I can see you were only waiting for the proper moment to begin revealing the mysteries of the inner mind and spirit to me."

"Many of the things I say came from you first."

"I know . . . but now we need to impart information, not ideas."

"The practice of that very thing may be at the heart of the problems in this modern world."

"Oliver!"

"Sorry. No, he just walked out with it. He needed something, perhaps, to remind him of the time spent in trouble here."

"So you think we succeeded?"

"Obviously. He left untroubled."

"How could he? Passer died to save him. Little River is being perverted to save him. You and Tom are bedridden and could have died saving him. How could he be untroubled?"

"I'm sure the terrors he escaped in his own soul are far worse than the casualties in this world of our war against the Wyrm."

"Then I hope he is truly healed, for there are many that need his guidance. But I have news of my own. A surprise for you too."

"Yes?"

"Tuck called. The team beat the champions of Headway."

"Ah . . ."

"Ahhh?"

"Yes, it's why Alexander left. I'm no longer frightened, because the Wyrm will leave Little River."

"Explain."

"I have. The spirit of Little River will be renewed. Good has triumphed over evil in the most simple of ways."

"But you said the Wyrm is still here."

"And I suspect it will always be here now. Its seed has been planted and though the weed is pulled, it will rise again. We must be vigilant. The Phoenix Pack has truly risen from the ashes. Perhaps now the Phoenix spirit will not punish them, or us, for presuming so much. Only the Garou he chooses may call upon him as their totem. Those Garou run with the Silver Pack."

"It was a risk, wasn't it? But only one of many and the metaphor was too powerful to ignore. The pack could have been dedicated to Chimera, but the Phoenix will lend the legend more power in the tellings of the Galliards. And I shall tell the story first. Would you like to hear it?"

"Of course."

# 9

# ENDGAME

It was a heroes' welcome.

It was just what Tuck hoped. It was what Tuck knew the town needed.

Already, Tuck heard the stories spreading. Just the victory wasn't enough. That was the main thing, of course, the pivotal event without which any of the other would be nearly meaningless. Or worse, instead of wondered awe, the people might hold the other events in disrespect.

What, a girl kicking field goals?

What, Tuck returned to the field when a field goal could have won it?

Such scenarios were never even considered in the euphoria of the victory. Instead, the stories of Ally and how a girl came to the rescue of the Huskies was probably already stretched beyond repair. And lessons of never giving up and giving everything you had were already circulating with the force of Tuck's bold move.

Tuck didn't want to correct any mistakes. He wanted to see the stories blown hugely out of proportion. Exaggerated beyond recognition.

That was, ironically, part of the truth of stories. The facts were often the least important part and got in the way of why the story was told in the first place. Often, it seemed to Tuck when he recalled the stories Passer told, the truth of the matter was in what the story became. The real message became clearer through the telling.

Or maybe the truth was in how the story changed. The difference between the beginning and end. But that was harder. Tuck wanted simple. Besides, he had a limited capacity to think with so much noise around him.

The bus had been abandoned further down the country road. An advance driver from the town waved the bus to a stop and informed Coach Conroy that the whole town was out and waiting for the team. So the players piled into the beds of several of the pickup trucks in the caravan of parents and friends returning home too.

Tuck was in the last pickup truck in the line. The others Coach Conroy and the players deemed most valuable and instrumental in the victory were with him. Ally, Greg Frederickson, and Gerald Jones, a defensive back key in stopping the Hornets in their final drive and whose father drove the pickup, were at Tuck's side. So was Verse. The mascot should be with them.

Tuck smiled. The mascot who survived a hundred bee stings the day before.

There were perhaps almost two dozen vehicles in front of the pickup he rode, so Tuck could hear the crowd before he could see them. A great cheer went up when the first players drove by. Tuck heard drums and trumpets, songs and whistles, noisemakers and firecrackers. The imaginations of the people of Little River were truly on fire.

The procession was slow, but the cheers went unabated. However, it gave Tuck time to look at the town he hoped the Phoenix pack saved. He knew they had won, that the Wyrm had been fought back, when he saw the traffic signal. He watched it intently as he drew nearer. The roar of the crowd became deafening as he passed beneath it. They cheered the heroes of the game, and Tuck swelled with pride.

As they passed through the intersection and turned left to go behind the shops and circle to return north through the intersection again, Tuck sighed. The Wyrm had been frozen. Its yellow eye was still malevolent, and it blinked steadily with a reminder of caution and warning, but it was beaten.

The light had been disconnected in favor of the parade.

Then Tuck could turn his attention to his surroundings. As Mr. Jones turned left, Tuck looked and waved at the people. Specific people. He knew them all by name. As they disappeared when the truck pulled behind Lenny's, Tuck saw that the old glass cases were finally gone.

When the truck turned left twice more and was going north along Main Street once again, Tuck remained concentrated on the people. Sam Harper was in front of his store, Mr. Italy's, where he was selling pieces of pizza for dirt cheap and recording the sales in a paper sales book.

He was working hard when Tuck caught his eye, and Sam rushed forward to the truck. "Take a slice, Tuck. All of you. Congratulations."

Tuck gratefully took a piece, and oddly the crowd cheered louder for a moment when he swallowed a big bite of the melted cheese and mushrooms. Tuck laughed and waved to them all.

The town was changed, but it was also restored. It, like the pack, was a phoenix. It had been dying in its own ashes, but it was renewed stronger than before. There was change, sure, but some change was good and healthy. It was part of rebirth.

As Tuck reached the intersection for the second and last time, he spotted Melissa. He smiled to her. She waved as if she were another part of the crowd. Maybe she didn't trust that Tuck would have time for her right now because he couldn't find her when the bus stopped and the players were piling into the trucks. Everyone was so excited and hustling that it had been impossible to insist on finding her.

Here she was, though, and Tuck wanted to repay her scene earlier in the day. He motioned to her, waving her toward the truck. She stopped waving, surprised, but seemed embarrassed to move. So Tuck leapt from the slow-moving truck and grabbed her behind her back and her knees and swung her into his arms like he was holding a baby.

She was laughing and making a show of struggling to get loose, but Tuck wouldn't have let her go even if she was really trying. He loped after the truck and dropped her inside. She rolled and sat upright. Then Tuck was in and by her side and extending a hand down to help her up.

She accepted and Tuck pulled her to her feet. And then he pulled her higher. And the whole town saw them kiss. She was so embarrassed and laughing so hard that her lips wouldn't pucker, but Tuck kissed her anyway.

———

Tom was among them once again. The pack would never have its fifth member back, but they were four again. When the parade through the town was nearly over, Ally suddenly knew Tom was awake again. Tuck made apologies to Melissa but promised to return for her at midnight, and he, Ally, and Verse rushed home to gather their wounded brother and come here: Little Rock.

Its bare surface was unchanged, and Tuck hoped it would weather all times as well as these recent ones. They walked about it thrice and entered the caern where they had all been born again during the Rite of Passage such a short time ago.

The waving tentacles of the vines that greeted their return to this other world swayed with a new energy, and the pack settled to begin the rite.

It would end for them as it began a week ago to this very night. It should be a simple matter for fire to return. The Wyrm was subdued and would not strike at the elementals again. So while Oliver taught Tuck and the others only the rudiments of summoning elementals of fire, it would really only be a matter of alerting them and hoping they would return of their own volition.

From Little Rock, the Umbra seemed safer tonight. No dark shadows loomed when Tuck began the ritual. He struck a match and lit the small pile of wood in the small pit they'd dug. It caught immediately and the fire burned pure and strong.

Tuck spoke solemnly, earnestly. "Just as Little River has been reborn through a test of fire, so too is it time for the fire which burnt us all to burn again."

Then louder and urgently, he said, "Call, friends, call the fire!" And Verse howled. The others joined him immediately and sang a song that danced and swayed like the flames before them. Ally and Tom and Tuck could mimic the voice of the fire, but Verse, the background to them all in song as ever, gave inflection to every flickering tongue of flame.

Soon, as the voices of the humans were fraying and the wolf's showing some wear, the fire flared and burned hot. The small amount of wood, almost gone because the fire had burned so hot and long already, disappeared no longer. The fire could sustain itself without fuel, so it meant the elementals had joined the blaze.

They flared brightly, seeking recognition and perhaps giving thanks.

Then, unimaginably, they cowered as they had done before. The eyes of every Garou present widened in horror as they anticipated the return of the Wyrm. Perhaps its final retribution was to be made. Tuck tried to throw his spirit over the burning elementals. He was unwilling to lure them to their deaths.

A fiery hot beyond the pittance the meager elementals could harness and control scorched Tuck's soul. Steam poured from his every pore, and in the tiny bit of recognition he could manage he felt the heat of a hundred suns stoking inside his body. Then it was over and he lay prostrate, still steaming, beside the small fire pit. His packmates were assembled around him.

Atop the fire pit, looming over them all, was a great bird of fire. Intricate patterns of blazing inferno formed the spirit that could only be Phoenix itself.

"Great Phoenix," Tuck muttered as he struggled to right himself, but another intense heat flared inside his soul and he breathlessly collapsed.

Then the great flaming bird spoke. Its voice whooshed like a flame out of control. "You dared to call yourselves my children."

The Phoenix Pack looked very small in the shadows the fiery spirit sent shivering over the ground. Even the huge boulder called Little Rock looked small, forever after earning its name in the minds of the Garou.

The spirit flapped her great wings, and arcs of purest, hottest flames seared the ground. She spoke again, her voice again a rush of heat with air. "I choose my own children."

"They dared to call you their own and they succeeded," shouted a new voice from behind the Phoenix Pack. "Surely that is due some accord."

Tuck, Ally, Tom, and Verse whirled in confusion to see who would speak on their behalf, for it was not the voice of either Oliver of Sarah. Even the great spirit seemed for an instant flustered at the interruption, but that passed in the briefest time.

The Garou who stood in the Umbra of the Caern at Little Rock was in crinos form. His fur was dark and lustrous, and it was that reflection from the light of Phoenix that gave away its true color, midnight blue. Spotted throughout were tiny points of white. Tuck felt as if looking at this Garou was to see through him and discern the night sky.

"Your children are the proudest among the Garou, and the Silver Pack justly receives accolades from all the tribes, but what of the daring these youths had to proclaim themselves yours? If they failed, then surely the hottest burning hell you sent them to would not be enough for the affront, but they have succeeded beyond all reason, beyond all hope. Beyond my hope. They understand where the Wyrm lies and how its perversion works. They have achieved a profound and proud victory." The Garou spoke smoothly.

The heat pouring from the bird made the features of everything nearby blur and become indistinct. But then it was gone, leaving only a trace of smoke, a sudden freezing cold, and a final warning. "Fly high, then, my children, but if you call upon me then you must fly ever higher."

All of the Garou of the pack were stunned. Tuck's pain passed completely away and he stood quickly. "Who are you that you enter our caern and save us so?" he challenged.

"I am a guide who wandered astray but who walks the right path once more."

"Wh—" Tuck began, but he was waved off.

"I have no time for such now. There is so much to discover again. Thank you, too, for you have reminded me that the best leader is the one who can follow first."

The young Garou were too confused and still too scared to react.

"Come here," said the impressive Garou.

It was finally dawning on them all that they regarded a Garou of tremendous rank within the society. They did not recognize him, but just as wolves, and humans too, can sense their place in a social order, the young Garou knew that the one before them was of highest standing.

They all approached him without question, but not without trembling.

"Show your hands to me," he said.

Tentatively, they all stuck their hands forward. As they did so, the fur on one hand each seemed to melt away, and the paws of crinos transformed into the hands of a human. The dark-furred crinos grasped their pinkish left index fingers and in deft, quick motions drew little faces on the fingertips with a felt-tip pen.

Tuck tried again. "Wh—" But he was silenced with another wave of the Garou's hand. His was an authority you did not question.

"Always questioning," said the Garou, looking into Tuck's eyes as he drew the last of the four simple faces on Tuck's finger. The pen strokes rendered a face wide-eyed and staring and a mouth that was open as if speaking and intently expressing some thought.

Verse's finger showed a wide-mouthed, close-eyed face of one lost completely in putting out, not drawing in. Ally's had eyes that squinted as if into a great light and a stern mouth that was a simple straight line. Tom's seemed to have sad eyes, but with a mouth slightly open and untouched by fear or tears.

The pen somehow gone from his paws, the crinos flashed his hands, which were also instantly adorned by homid digits. They displayed ten little faces in a variety of expressions.

"My counselors," said the Garou, smiling. "They have told me that your troubles are over but have only begun. Time builds up just as well as tears down. Build as much and as quickly as possible, but build well, not with haste. It's when done without forethought or meaning that the architecture of the future becomes the sort you saw in the guidebook. Take that as the symbol of what you fight."

Still overawed by the Garou, Tuck nonetheless couldn't resist. "The book? How did it come to be?"

"Who can say when it is of the Wyrm? I suspect it came from a pollination of the Wyrm and Weaver. As the former pushed the latter to greater lengths and unnatural speeds of progress, the book might have occurred as a by-product. The Wyrm went to great lengths to tear your Little River to little pieces by building it wrong, but you rekindled the spirit of the people living closest to the land, and the Wyrm was overwhelmed."

Tuck pressed, "How do w—" but he was cut short by yet another wave of the crinos's hand.

"We shall speak again," said the Garou, wiggling his illustrated fingers at the young Garou.

And then, when all the members of the Phoenix Pack blinked at once, he was gone.


Tuck would rely purely on instinct.

If he'd learned nothing else in the last week it was that this was appropriate, at least for him. In the years before the recent days he honored the human part of his nature. He was still full of ideologies and hopes that were purely human, and he might always interact with the world from a human perspective, but his ultimate decisions and actions would speak of his Garou heritage.

Tonight, though, he was being reminded of just how human he was. He was giving in to his instinct. Doing so was probably the right response for most people, but they get trained out of it. The right way to act is a matter of what's inside a person, not how society teaches them to act, though certain allowances must, of course, be made for the society. But just as a society can become dysfunctional when it is too fractured, so too can it become misguided and degenerative when no one can act from the heart. So, the difference between people is to what extent they either trust their instincts or refuse to give in to them even when they think they're right.

A powerful Garou, one that Tuck knew in his heart would guide him again in the days and years ahead, had disappeared. He left only a simple finger etching behind—but one that Tuck knew was more than what it appeared. It was the beginning of a new mystery.

It was that mystery that Tuck pondered to the very moment he threw a handful of tiny pebbles at the second-story window. When Melissa threw open the windows, thoughts of the mysterious Garou soared from his mind. If it was the wolf within him that he honored by obeying his instincts, then Tuck should howl at the moon.

She waved down at him and then slipped back inside. It was several moments before she emerged. "Be quiet," she whispered. "My father's still working."

Tuck greedily took her offered hand but was puzzled. "How? He's a farmer?"

Melissa tugged Tuck in the direction of the fields her father worked. Skipping to a jog, she said, "Oh, he just got a computer to help him manage the farm's finances. He's drowning in it, though, so he probably didn't hear me leave."

"Great," Tuck said a bit hesitantly.

"Is something wrong?"

"No," Tuck said still hesitating. Then he looked at Melissa, a worried look creasing her mouth. Instantly, everything of the last many days faded from Tuck's mind as he and Melissa wandered to the fields at the back of her father's farm. There was a spot, an oasis of two trees and a stone just large enough for sitting, in the center of one of the fields that Melissa led him to.

"I often come here to look at the sky," she said.

"I watch the sky too."

"For what?" she asked.

"The same as you. Stars. Signs of the future."

She laughed at that. "What do you see tonight?"

He looked at her, grinning, and then looked up to survey the heavens. "I see a cloudless sky."

"So what does that tell you?"

"That the storms are passed." Then he added, "For now."

"At least until the state semifinals next week, huh?"

"Yes," said Tuck, and he knew that the building would continue.

They both looked again at the sky and then slid together off the rock to the soft ground. So it was there under the clear, wintry sky, beside the impassive stone, that Tuck and Melissa moved the earth.

Out of the corner of his eye, Tuck swore he could see the vines waving on the face of this rock too.